The Morning After John Lennon Was Shot

LARRY DURSTIN

Copyright © 2012 by Larry Durstin
All rights reserved

I would like to thank Richard Messer, Tom Lorenz, Marcie Heidish and Steve Hesske for their creative assistance in the development of this work. Also, special thanks to Peter Taylor for providing me the opportunity to enhance my writing career.

Cover Art: John Beukemann
Book Layout: Jeff Greene

This book is a work of fiction.
Any resemblance to actual events of locales or persons – living or dead – is entirely coincidental.

Published by Current Publishing
2095 Bunts Road
Lakewood, OH 44107
216-227-0505
current@ldmedia1.com

ISBN: 978-0615553214
Library of Congress Number: 2011918415

Printed in USA

*"In memory of my sister Barb,
the finest person I've ever known"*

Part One Separation

We do not see things as they are.
We see them as we are.
— *The Talmud*

The Men's Group

"How did you feel when you got the call?"

"I was surprised his mother was able to locate me," I said, easing back into my chair as the group relaxed into its silently attentive mode. "I haven't spoken to him in over 10 years and we only hung out together a lot for a year or so."

In deference, I suppose, to the tragic circumstances I had just told them about, none of the group members took me to task for the indirectness of my response – the evasion of what I really felt. Cardinal sins of this magnitude are about as easy to slip by my Friday night men's group as it would be to sneak the sun past a circle of roosters.

"His mom said he hadn't been out of his apartment in months. That he wouldn't answer the phone. That he wouldn't even let her in when she came over. She asked me how he got that way. I didn't know what to say."

What I didn't tell her about was the strange feeling that rolled over me when I read a story in the Cleveland Plain Dealer earlier in the week. Under the headline, "Man Shoots Himself Rather Than Open Door," the brief item described how a man, who lived alone, had refused to answer the door to his one-room apartment for a routine utility check and, instead, chose to end his life. No name was given but the account stated that the individual had once told a neighbor that he just couldn't stand anyone looking at him.

"What was he like, Ray?"

"It's hard to say. I guess he was a lot like us."

"I think we should keep the focus on Ray," Gary, the group's self-appointed non-leader, interrupted in a firm but sensitive voice. Everyone nodded.

We all knew the procedure and the need to never lose sight of one's self. We were all veterans of the so-called Recovery Movement – exdruggies and alcoholics, adult children, sex and food and gambling addicts, codependents – and we knew full well the corrosiveness of focusing on the external, even when dealing with traumas like the death of a friend.

"Maybe this happened to help me finally get to my primal story," I said quietly. "Everyone else has told his. I've been struggling with it since I joined."

"You've been struggling with it a lot longer than that," said Gary. "It's all a part of your mythology."

The title of our group was "Male Myths – A Journey," and it was centered around the re-telling and re-experiencing of a significant time period–ranging in duration from a few weeks to a few years – in each man's life. These "primal stories" all began with the trauma of loss or separation, which was followed by a journey into alien terrain or wilderness (oftentimes away from the world of women, as in the initiation rites among primitive men) and finally resulted in a return with new knowledge, reconciliation and re-integration back into his world.

The reasoning behind the importance of mythologizing and re-experiencing one significant story was that by truly re-living a specific struggle (not merely re-interpreting it with hindsight) and "re-discovering" it on a feeling level as part of the eternal, inexorable journey towards rebirth, a man would have revealed to him all the great truths about himself. Truths that would help move him to the next level of spiritual enlightenment.

"Out of the darkness comes light," Gary intoned, silencing the group's idle chatter. "Maybe if your friend had had a chance to tell and re-live his primal story, he'd still be around. What he did means that your time has arrived."

Gary's own primal story centered around a week at the Telluride Film Festival in Colorado. After his wife of 15 years left him for a young male hairdresser, Gary—then the balding owner of an adult video store near downtown Cleveland – impulsively signed up for what he mistakenly thought was an X-rated seven days in an anything-goes resort town.

Initially disappointed that he was faced with dozens of serious films and hundreds of sophisticated, fully-clothed movie buffs, he first struggled defiantly with his displacement, then gradually immersed himself in the flickering, sometimes confusingly-subtitled images – and finally found catharsis and redemption in the several-times-a-day emergence from the darkened theaters to the blinding light of the mountain sky. Upon his re-entry and subsequent reconciliation with himself, he sold his video store, gave up his plans for a hair weave, began a career as a one-man wedding disc jockey (his first gig was for his ex-wife's marriage) and embraced the men's movement.

"If I hadn't re-lived that week, especially the chaos and pain of those English-dubbed Dutch films," Gary would often say, "I'd probably be wearing a toupee at a singles' dance in Beachwood right this minute, and never knowing why."

Gary was right, it was time for my story. And, because of the recent tragic event, I finally knew what it was, when it took place and who the cast of characters were. It began right after I left Crystal City and Lana left me. That's when I started hanging around with my three single buddies – including my recently deceased friend – and that's when I met Judy. In just a few months my whole world turned upside down.

"Looking back, I guess I was really lost." I began as the group tightened the circle around me.

"Don't look back, go back. Wherever you were, be there," Gary said. "And remember, the true seeker always becomes lost."

"Maybe I'll understand what happened to him, why he couldn't live anymore."

Gary didn't want to hear anything about anybody else. "Maybe you'll finally experience what's still happening to you."

The Morning After John Lennon Was Shot

December 9, 1980

Lana was on my mind as I drove to school that morning and heard the news about Lennon. I had been trying to call her for days. It looked like she was finally going to be free, and we had to talk.

Lana, you see, was the love of my life. She was one of those misty-eyed, Gypsy-bandana-wearing women who had learned all about leather and peace and love in the Colorado Rocky Mountains of the late '60s. She was laid back and cosmic and wore either flowing dresses or extra tight jeans. She had love in her eyes and flowers in her hair and sensed what I was going to say before I said it. In bed, she knew exactly what I wanted. But, most importantly, she taught me everything I knew about the moon and life's layers and the transcendent power of love. Always she would gently encourage me to never stop believing in magic, because everything else was just an illusion.

Unfortunately, during much of the time I was seeing her she was also involved with another guy. He was quite a bit older than she was, was out of town for months at a time, and Lana always swore there was really nothing between them. She claimed that he provided good old-fashioned financial security and the freedom to do what she wanted – plus she didn't feel like bouncing around any more, especially because of her twins. I was absolutely convinced that I provided the breathless promise of untapped mystic potential and the profound stimulation of a non-stop analytical mind, qualities I had tirelessly honed while living for more than a decade in the leisurely atmosphere of a small college town.

I was lingering in the background, waiting in the wings, and blissfully hoping for the best. This went on for nearly four years before I finally decided that if things were ever going to change, it was up to me to take action. So at the end of the summer, 1980, I moved out of the academic womb of Crystal City to nearby Toledo. A change, even a tiny one, seemed long past due – and astonishingly appeared to produce the desired effect. In early November I got a call from her.

"I'm leaving Galen," she said excitedly. "I made my decision right during the harvest moon. I thought about you. It's all so magical."

She said she would temporarily move in with her friend Sandy before permanently moving into a house, located between Crystal City and Toledo, that her mother owned. It was being rented by students but would become available in mid-December. She had already told the twins and they were ready to go. She added that there might be room in the house for one more person.

Unbelievable. We had been barreling downhill for the past year. Shouting matches, crazed phone calls, wild night-time drives. It all had seemed achingly, chokingly doomed. Then, Zen-koan like, she beckoned – just as I was turning away – to let me know there was room in her house. She'd done it again. Once more my life brimmed with the romantic possibilities that I first witnessed as a child watching "South Pacific."

"It will be a chance for us to move on to another level," she said over the phone one enchanted morning right before Thanksgiving. "Please keep in touch. I don't want to lose you."

***

"Lennon probably got it in the back while he was running away," one of my fellow teachers said after I arrived in the teachers' lounge that morning.

"What kind of idiotic thing is that to say?" I yelled and stomped out of the room. My head was spinning. I was sick and tired of listening to my co-workers' lack of any semblance of consciousness, upset over Lennon's murder and vaguely suspicious that something fishy might be up with Lana.

After spending the first couple classes talking to the kids about the

Beatles and the '60s, I tried to reach Lana. I called Sandy's place from a vacant counselor's office.

"Hi Sandy, this is Ray. Is Lana there?"

"No, she hasn't been here for days."

"Where is she?"

"She's at Steve's."

"Steve. Who's he?"

"He's the guy she's leaving town with."

While simultaneously trying to regain my balance and descending into numbness, I got the grim details. Lana had known Steve for quite a while. He had been around town off and on for years. Sandy wasn't sure what his last name was. The whole thing had happened suddenly. Sandy thought that I knew about it. Steve didn't have a phone but Lana was probably at his place now, or maybe at the lagoon packing.

"Where's Steve's house?" I collected myself enough to ask. She didn't know the address but described the location. It sounded like a place I had stayed at four years earlier – but it couldn't be. It was at that place, in August of '76, that Lana and I had hugged and kissed for the first time. It couldn't be the same place, I thought, then thanked Sandy and hung up. What struck me most was something in her voice – a casualness – when she said, "Oh, I thought she told you," and, "Yeah, just stop over there," that seemed to indicate that this wasn't a big deal. I couldn't fathom that Lana hadn't told her everything about us and concluded that the obvious magnitude of our relationship had simply slipped Sandy's mind.

I told the principal I had stomach cramps, drove home and called Lana's place on the lagoon, but there was no answer. I called again, still no answer. Thinking she might be out for a walk, I decided to drive the 30 miles there. I had no other choice, did I?

On the way, the radio was filled with Beatles' music and the reaction to the death of a hero. President Carter issued a moving statement. "Strawberry Fields" was played. Paul McCartney was in shock and seclusion. George was crushed. Ringo clung to his Barbara. "We Can Work It Out" played.

As I drove to her house I kept rehashing our last meeting, which was back in mid-October and really hadn't gone very well, searching for any indication that there may have been serious misconnection problems. I had been trying to call her for days but couldn't get anything more than a few minutes of hurried conversation, so I decided to stop by after work. Once again, we just had to talk.

I knocked on the door. No answer. I pushed it open and called her. Still no answer. I called again. "I'll be right down," she yelled. Fifteen minutes later she came down the stairs wearing tight, Levi-Strauss white-patch jeans and a black short top. Her belly button was showing. She gave me a perfunctory hug and headed towards the kitchen, but stopped to bend over and pick up a toy. She got on all fours to scrape something off the floor and remained there for a few minutes. I flashed on the day I came there and saw her in a similar position and, without saying a word, peeled down her jeans. I eased my way in while she groaned, then begged, then acted like she was going to pass out. But that was a simpler, more spontaneous time. It was the '80s now and things were starting to get incredibly complicated. So I just stood there, and she just got up and walked into the kitchen.

"How come you didn't call me back yesterday?"

"I didn't get a hold of Sandy."

"I tried to call back but the line was busy for an hour-and-a-half, then no one answered."

"I needed a nap so I took the phone off the hook," she snapped. "Then I had to take the twins to Brownies. You know it was their day to go."

Of course I knew, but that wasn't the point. "I call you, want to see you, you take the phone off the hook, then you leave. I drive down to see you and you give me a hug like I just joined a club, and you wonder why I'm upset, and you think I'm acting like a jerk so you don't want to spend time with me, and you don't understand what part your own behavior is playing in this whole mess." I you-you-youed my way into the kitchen.

"My aren't we testy." She was facing the stove, leaning against it, tasting some soup.

Deftly retreating from agitation I suctioned up against her ass, the way I had done so many times before. She used to grind away for awhile, turn for a passionate kiss, then undo my zipper. She turned but this time the soup spoon was between us. She licked it.

"I don't think that would be such a good idea," she said, continuing to lick at the spoon for a few tantalizing seconds.

She put on some water for tea and we went into the living room to talk. The phone rang. It was her sculpture teacher. They yakked for 20 minutes and made a date to go shopping for boots and jeans in Ann Arbor the next day. Lana could easily get a babysitter. They could stay the whole day. "No problem. Bye."

"Want some tea?" she asked.

I shrugged off her offer and told her the reason I wanted to talk to her was that I had developed some theories about what was happening to relationships over the past few years.

"I'm sure you have." She got up and walked over to a pile of firewood that was stacked in the corner of her living room.

"It was the late '70s that did it," I said as she cradled a load of wood in her arms and headed towards her pot-bellied stove.

As she pitched logs through the door of the wood-burner, I blamed disco, CB radios, a creeping Moral Majority conservatism and a hopeless kind of panic/surrender – which inevitably occurred in transitional times such as these when societal transformation was underway – that had insidiously supplanted the great magical/spiritual experiment we true believers from the '60s dreamed was going to burn bright forever.

Flames leapt from the stove as Lana stoked with determination.

"Aside from the socio-political factors," I went on, pacing the portion of the room that Lana reserved for her private "cosmic" possessions, "the whole phantom weak vs. strong set-up between men and women doesn't help things either. Because while the two parties seem to be moving towards the center, one is being sapped of the illusion of strength while the other is discovering a growing absence of imagined weakness. I've come to the conclusion that the friction of the movement towards so-called equality in relationship – which on the most essential level has always existed anyway – is what we've been all dealing with these past few years."

"Speaking of friction I've been getting a lot of shocks touching things around here lately." Lana slammed the stove's hatch.

I noticed a six-inch unicorn horn displayed on her special little table in the prominent spot formerly occupied by the crystal ball I had given her. I looked around the room for it and noticed it had been relegated to a musty corner near an antique shoe rack. When I had presented her with the mystical sphere I told her I wasn't looking for a piece of ass, I wanted someone who could tell my fortune. At the time she had growled a "right on," caressed it lovingly and promised it would stay on her table forever.

"Still speaking of friction," I said, pointing disdainfully at the slender curved phallic symbol, "what the hell is this all about?"

"It's a unicorn horn made out of ivory. I've always loved unicorns. This guy made it for me. He also printed a real neat little poem on it."

"Well, you don't have to be Sigmund Freud to figure out what this guy is driving at. Have you used it on yourself yet?"

"You've got a one track mind." Her eyes flared. "No, I haven't. Anyway, the ink would come off."

Painfully aware that verbal sexual gaming with Lana was the mismatch of a lifetime, I changed the subject to the near future and told her that if I were her I'd circle October 20, the harvest moon, on her calendar.

"It will be reaping what you've sown time."

"You also told me I'd fall in love with a young guy," she mused.

So I had, so what. I told her I had a lot more to say to her, too.

"You must have had your Wheaties today," she laughed and gathered her long black hair into a bun and rolled up her sleeves. "Go right ahead and talk all you want. I've got some cleaning to do but I'll be listening."

I cleared my throat and began my carefully prepared text. "Communication gaps result from the breakage of the sync of human interactions."

"That's a good place to start," she said, heading towards the sink.

While Lana began running the water, I rambled about past experiences and faulty assumptions and inner-dynamics and plain old bad vibes – along with the need for people to maintain their emotional equilibrium. She finished the sink and wobbled into the bathroom.

I stood in the hall outside and talked about how even the purest of motives are sabotaged by mutual self-deception. And how even in relationships where people talk about things often their "talk" consists of strictly structured gamesmanship or formulas for discussion where each person stimulies and responses his or her way to an interspaced and juxtaposed monologue which gives the illusion of communication.

"Will you please hand me the Windex?" she yelled.

I did so, then returned to the hallway and talked, while she squirted and rubbed, specifically about us. That the emotional intensity of our union would inevitably produce seismic jolts of both ecstasy and pain. That I really didn't know what would happen down the road, but all I really wanted was to look at her more, laugh with her more and feel the magic more. I candidly admitted to some expectation and control problems, but remained optimistic that everything just might work out for the best.

"We both do and don't have forever," I said, mentally noting how the word "forever" echoed around the bathroom.

"I don't know about forever, but I don't have all day," she laughed. "Just trying to lighten things up a little.

I acknowledged that levity was critical for maintaining perspective but that it could also be used as a technique of avoidance, something we had both learned a great deal about growing up in emotionally distant families. And because of our backgrounds there was no getting around the fact that we would always have some difficulty with intimate relationships. But, approaching it another way, we needed to understand that much of the darkness we were experiencing was nothing more than childhood skeletons rattling around in our memories' bleak closets.

Lana emerged from the bathroom looking hypnotized. "You mentioned closets," she said stone-faced. "I hear they have some herbal moth balls in Ann Arbor. I'll have to pick some up."

This was starting to feel like a runaway train. I could hardly remember a word I had said, let alone what my original point was. We sat at the kitchen table holding hands in silence before I got up to go. Lana walked over to the back door and stared out at the lagoon. There were tears in her eyes.

"What's wrong?"

"Maybe it really is impossible," she answered in a soft, sad voice.

On the way out the door, she hugged my waist real hard and nestled her head against my chin. "Next time we talk, you'll be doing better."

***

Information was coming in about Lennon's assassin, Mark Chapman, as I arrived at Lana's house. No cars. The house looked vacant. Rufus, her St. Bernard, was moping on the porch. I peered into the windows. No signs of life, only boxes. On the way back down the long winding driveway, I noticed that the makeshift clubhouse that her twins had waited in for the school bus was gone and I felt sad and sorry for them because the special haven they loved so much had vanished. Should I go to Crystal City and look her up? What kind of insane scene would ensue at Steve's pad? What would be waiting for me there? Would it be more of that feeling that had lingered with me since I was ten and heard my mom on the phone using all kinds of "honeys" and "sweeties" that she never used for my dad and carrying on in such a way that forced me to push the door of my bedroom – never again a secure haven, but a hideout – shut and keep it shut until. . .

I came to the fork on Sugar Ridge Road, turned my car towards Crystal City and drove the four miles past row after row of frozen corn stubble with Lennon primal screaming "Mother" all the way.

Arriving in town, I followed Sandy's directions with a kind of mechanical dread and spotted Lana's car parked next to a huge white house.

It was the same house where we had first embraced.

The only question was whether she was upstairs or down. Four years earlier I had stayed upstairs, so I opted to try downstairs first and glanced tentatively through the windows. There were no lights on. I rang the bell. A pale, dark-haired woman answered.

"Does Steve live here? I'm looking for Lana."

"He lives upstairs," she said and quickly retreated into the late morning shadows.

I went around back and looked at the creaky stairs in disbelief. The last time I had been here was that day she had come to see me. I had been staying here only for a couple of weeks, having been unceremoniously booted out of my residence on Church Street. Rob, an artist friend of mine, happened to be leaving for California and let me crash here while he was gone. I had immediately called Lana and asked her to stop by. She was dropping the twins off at The Child is the Father of the Man Nursery a couple doors down, and it would be convenient for her to visit me. I waited for her each day, but she never showed. Finally Rob came back and I was sleeping on the couch, ready to leave that day for a place in the country, when Lana knocked on the door. Like a patchouli-scented Buddhist truth, she always stopped by when I least expected or had given up hope. When she came that day, since Rob was asleep inside, we just stood on the porch/balcony and hugged. Romeo and Juliet then.

Now, going up the stairs I felt like I was walking through a minefield. I knocked on the storm door. She answered laughing, looking over her shoulder. She seemed thin and had on a tight red sweater that had seen better days. Her hair was a mess. When she looked at me she gulped and her eyes widened – like a little girl who had been caught with her hand in the cookie jar.

"Do you remember the last time we were here?"

"Of course," she said.

We both sighed, locked eyes and shook our heads. Then I began-with a certain dramatic detachment dictated by this all-too-perfect setting –

mouthing the script for this, our famous final scene.

"I talked to Sandy. She said you're leaving town with some guy."

"Well, for right now, that's the plan." She stressed the right now. Things with her were always subject to change. Draw your own conclusions but keep in mind the universe is filled with surprises.

"Why didn't you tell me about this?"

"I told you I would meet with you before the holidays. I was going to mention it then."

She invited me in but cautioned that a couple of the girls were inside. I decided to remain outside. The positions of a few years ago were reversed Then, she arrived and I was at the door, now it was just the opposite. Both times we never got past the balcony.

"I mean, do you love this guy or what?"

She gave me her sort-of look.

I started to feel a little faint and distant, like a cartoon step-out person, just about to disappear.

"I thought maybe you and I would be together. I'd have gone away with you. We even talked about it."

"I wouldn't go away with you." Dangerous when cornered, she spat the words out as if I were offering her a lifetime of leprosy.

"What about love?"

"What about it?" More devastating when detached, she assumed the demeanor of the lady-of-the-house, filing her fingernails while a suspicious-looking Fuller Brush man was making a pitch to her, the woman who had everything.

"Was it an illusion?"

"Yes it was, I guess." She sighed deeply and seemed to shrink a little. I had let her down.

"Last summer you said I was the only person you'd ever want to have a relationship with."

"Last summer, last lifetime."

"But you said you'd like to spend some time and go away with me."

"For a couple of weeks maybe, yes." Her face tightened, this path having become far too worn.

Suddenly a pizza delivery car pulled up in the driveway. "Crazy George's Special" was written on the side. An angular guy in an army jacket popped out, glanced up at the balcony, paused, and then started loping up the stairs.

I had seen him a million times before. He was in his early 20s, easily seven or eight years younger than Lana, and had been driving a pizza car around town for a few years. Rumor had it that he was due for a big promotion.

"Is this the guy?"

"Yes, that's Steffin," Lana said bravely, jutting her jaw out.

At this point, despite the pain, I managed a sneer. Steve, or Steffin as he was now known, was one of the young "happy hippie" guys in town who were always sniffing around the women. I had known his older brother, who taught reincarnation in the university's continuing education department, but had only really talked to Steffin once. He was wearing a cowboy hat then and seemed proud of it. He asked me if I wanted to try it on. I hated cowboy hats and said, "No thanks, I don't need a penis extension on my head." Perhaps I was a bit harsh- and I certainly didn't mean it personally – but Steffin gulped, shrunk in his chair and during the rest of the conversation his Texas twang disappeared. Before his cowboy stage he used to deliver pizzas with a pyramid hat on. He would make change and say, "Thank you," with a guru-like gesture and inflection. I looked at his pizza car. There was a unicorn sticker on the back window.

My sneer almost doubled me up. Steffin was bouncing up the stairs. The look on Lana's face said, "You better not try anything." I was satisfied that I had the presence of mind to sneer. What else did I have in this humiliating position on the porch with a couple of the girls inside, and the number one pizza driver in sales, a fact that had appeared in the Crystal City News under Steffin's high school photo, briskly bounding up the stairs two at a time?

"We'll talk later in the week," I said, my composure surprising me. "How does Friday sound?"

Lana nodded.

"You really don't have the slightest idea what in the hell you're doing, do you?"

Her face was as red as her sweater. I turned away and Steffin "How-died" me. I felt like we were tag-team partners as I nodded a pained smile.

"Instant Karma" was on the radio when I headed back to Toledo for an afternoon and evening of mourning.

***

I was sitting in my apartment the next night watching "Marty," the classic movie about bachelors of the '50s, when the phone rang. It was Scott. I told him what had happened with Lana.

"You ought to get down on your hands and knees and thank your lucky stars," he said. "You were ready to follow her anywhere, but now she's really gone and you're free." In Scott's eyes Lana was a killer and he had certainly had his share of experiences with killer women. "Maybe now you'll be able to find a woman with a good heart. I know you're hurting but in the long run it's the best thing that could have happened. Otherwise you would have trailed her to your grave."

"You're probably right," I said, "but I really thought she was the one."

"Well, just keep busy for awhile. What are you doing tonight?"

"Bert's stopping over. I don't know what he'll want to do." Bert and Scott and I had become friends during the past year. We had a lot in common. We were all about 30. Bachelors. Never married. Still looking.

"I've got a lot of work to do on my thesis or I'd join you," he said.

Scott was a professional student of nearly two decades and his thesis combined computers with the Transcendental Meditation teachings of the Maharishi. The project, he claimed, had global implications.

"I must take a nap, then meditate. Relax and have a good time tonight. Remember, you got a break."

Bert arrived just as "Marty" was concluding. He had seen the movie several times.

"I could really sympathize with those guys," he said, checking out his profile in the darkened window and attempting to smooth down his stomach. "I guess as far as these women go things really haven't changed too much in 25 years."

A portly fellow with short brown hair, Bert had returned to Crystal City University in the summer after an eight-year absence. He had graduated with a degree in drama, then spent four years in the Navy Reserve and traveling around Europe before returning to Cleveland and taking the position of assistant director of the Lakewood Little Theater. He heard about the three-to-one ratio of women to men at CCU and decided to take a sabbatical and return to the college scene, hoping for a change in his lady luck. It wasn't working out quite the way he had planned.

"Don't feel too bad," he said after I told him about Lana. "I haven't been laid in almost six years. What do you wanna do tonight?"

I shrugged.

"I'll tell you what Ray." He rubbed his hands together. "I'll treat you to a massage at the Oriental Sauna. Jenny is working tonight."

Bert spent a lot of time at massage parlors. He was constantly trying to get me to go along but I always resisted. From a strictly financial standpoint it just didn't appeal to me and – though I was certainly no prude and appreciated a well-turned ankle as much as the next man – it offended my feminist-leaning political sensibilities. All in all it just didn't seem like a positive step along the path towards enlightenment. Still, I agreed to go because I had to get out of the house and away from my non-stop ruminations about Lana. Plus, it would be nice to see Jenny again. Bert had introduced me to her in the early summer. She even had accompanied me to the TM Summer Solstice picnic given by Scott's friends and had helped me find an apartment in Toledo.

"You think you've got it bad," Bert groaned as we drove to the sauna. "I thought I'd have it made this year, what with the three-to-one ratio." He figured he was urbane, continental and had credentials.

"Those credentials of yours are a little shaky."

"Maybe so" he admitted, "but I still have six degrees. I am a certified golf pro, a licensed pilot, and I've got a brown belt in karate and speak four languages – and all it has gotten me is stood up 10 times this year. And that doesn't even count cancellations."

We pulled into the Farmer Jack Shopping Center, drove past the China Gate Restaurant, the Open Closet Lounge and the Golden Cherry Burlesque before parking in front of a sign that said, "Oriental Sauna. Open 24 Hours."

"Let me handle it from now on." Bert was all business, ushering me into his domain.

The woman behind the desk only had one hand. She greeted Bert warmly.

"Debbie," he said, cordially handling the intros. "This is my friend Ray. I'd like you to set him up with Jenny."

A sign above the window stated that any new customer born in even-numbered years could get a massage at half price. I produced my driver's license.

"You sure don't look like you're 30." Debbie batted her lashes demurely.

"Jenny's giving a massage right now, but she'll be free in about 45 minutes. What about you Bertsie?"

Bert wanted Jenny in the worst way. She was his dream girl. He had even asked her out for a pizza once during a massage and she had accepted, but when he came on her purple leotards ten minutes after making the date, he mumbled, "I was aiming at the ceiling," and forgot about the pizza. Kathy was the other woman working that night. Bert had characterized her as a chatterbox with four kids, who was always talking about her problems. He was a man who liked to relax on the table and have a certain amount of quiet, but he was also aware that Kathy quickly took the towel off and that his hand would be working overtime. Plus, he didn't want to hurt her feelings. "Set me up with Kathy," he said with a gallant sweep of his hand.

"I don't have to show you the way, do I?" Debbie laughed. Bert beamed with pride at the red carpet treatment.

Although the place billed itself as the Oriental Sauna, it had a distinctly Civil War South look. Bert explained that the establishment was constantly undergoing changes in management, and it was currently in the hands of a former truck driver from Georgia who also owned the Golden Cherry strip joint next door. This guy was always on the local news talking about the First Amendment. Bert had been to the Cherry a couple of times.

"The girls seemed to like me, and one of them even looked like Julie on 'The Love Boat'," he explained as we stripped to our towels in the locker room. "That part was great, but they were always hustling Cokes." No alcohol was served. Bert didn't have the heart to say no to the working women and a couple of times he'd gone through at least 20 bucks on Cokes while watching the dancers. This was after he had dropped 50 at the sauna and during a time when he had no income.

While we were changing, Kathy and Debbie walked in and out of the back room going to the john or brushing their hair. This was part of the place's appeal. Bert took off his towel as Debbie approached and was caught stark naked. He loved to stand there towel-less, hands on his hips, casually chatting to one of the women about the weather. He was just a simple, good-hearted guy who liked to take his pants off. He couldn't understand why women complicated things so much.

"Bert," cooed Kathy, a chunky, short blond in a brown leotard, "I was really upset that I was going just as you were coming the other night."

Apparently Bert had miscalculated the shift change, and Kathy saw him arrive just as she was pulling out of the lot. He didn't want to upset her – she thought of him as one of her and Jenny's regulars – but he had wanted to check out the graveyard crew.

Kathy playfully tugged at his towel and emitted a "naughty, naughty." Bert shrugged his shoulders innocently then smiled broadly as he led me into the dry sauna. He loved it in there. He could look at the women through the window, and it supposedly helped him pare off a few pounds.

"Is this where you got caught warming up by the cleaning lady and yelled 'Duck'?"

"Sh!" Bert looked around. "Don't joke like that, these girls are really sensitive about lewd comments. Remember, this is kind of a legitimate place," he pointed out with a combination of protective pride and utter despair. "Let's go out to the lounge."

Bert loved the lounge because he could lie around in his towel and talk to the women, get to know them and tell them stories about the theater. His towel would sometimes become unhinged; the women didn't even flinch. They didn't give a shit. "That's Incredible" was on the tube. Host Fran Tarkenton had the frozen, wide-eyed look of a man who had just accepted Jesus for the fifth time that week. We lounged on zebra pillows. Several pictures of General Lee were on a wall, above where "Shiloh" had been handwritten. Two other guys were sitting on the couch. I recognized them as Toledo television personalities. They did the sports and weather.

"How's it hanging?" I said. I had never used that phrase before in my life.

"Real good," they replied in unison, emphasizing the real.

Suddenly the Confederate Flag curtain opened.

"Hi Ray, Bert." It was Jenny. I hadn't seen her in a couple of months. She looked great. Tall and lean – possessing an outdoorsy-girl's sexual subtlety that belied her profession – with long brown hair sleeked back into a single braid that she would frequently finger and sometimes stroke.

Kathy arrived and she and Bert quickly departed.

"We'll get started in 15 minutes, if you don't mind. I need a little break." Jenny went over to her purple blazer and pulled out a leather bullet bag. She lit a cigarette, took a real long first puff, turned and tugged at her leotard.

We talked about Lennon and how he was our favorite Beatle.

"It was my birthday yesterday," she said sadly, "and I was ready for a party, but everyone was bummed out." She had just turned 22 but had a brother my age who had told her about the '60s. She had been smoking pot since she was 12, hung out in head shops while in junior high and even dated a teacher when she was in the tenth grade.

"I went out with Stephen Stills when I was 17." She flicked a lengthy ash from her cigarette. "He had a knife in his boot and a big vial of coke. He just scooped it out. That was the only rock star I ever met, but I would have loved to meet Lennon. I can't believe somebody just shot him." She maneuvered the filtered butt between her thumb and second finger and shot it into a South Carolina Gamecocks wastebasket. "Touchdown," she giggled and motioned for me to follow her.

She escorted me to a small, private massage room. The lights were dim. As I climbed onto the cot she set the timer. About five minutes into the massage I mentioned what had happened with Lana.

"Is that the chick you told me about this summer?" she asked while leaning her taut crotch against me. "How long were you seeing her?"

"Just over four years," I said, squirming a little.

"Relax. I don't bite, though some of the guys want me to." She laughed and squeezed my shoulders. "Do you want to talk about it?"

Lying on my stomach, getting rubbed down, I told her about Lana. How I had known her for about 10 years; how she had been married for the first time at 17; how her second husband deserted her and the twins; how she bounced around in the early '70s before meeting this Galen guy in Texas; how he was 15 years older than she and used to be gone a lot tending to his construction business in Corpus Christi; how I approached her while umpiring a women's softball game in '76 and told her she had been the object of my romantic fantasies and she had answered "How long do you want to keep them fantasies?"; and how I told her I loved her that fall while back-grounded by brown and gold trees reflecting in the lagoon next to her house at the end of Sugar Ridge Road just outside of Crystal City.

Jenny choked playfully at my neck. "An umpire gave me a ride home one time after a junior high softball game." She brought her mouth close to my ear. "As my mother would say he had Roman hands and Russian fingers, but his son was real cute."

With sounds from the adjoining room hinting that someone's south had risen again, I told Jenny how magical it was with Lana those first few years; how she wiped away laughter/tears at my stories, melted at my touch and sighed at my profundities; how the sex was steamy yet soulfully satisfying – after her softball games with her loose-fitting shorts still on, in the bathroom while the twins swung outside, in the daylight parking lot in front of Jo Ann Fabrics; over and under and sideways and through during the blizzard of '78; and how we just seemed to fit together without trying, until the summer of '79.

"What happened then?" Jenny nudged me to turn over and I continued the tale on my back.

"She went into the hospital to have her tubes tied. She had some complications and when she came out it was like she was broke in two or something. Galen gave up his Texas business and was around all the time. We hardly saw each other. She took up with a lesbian later that year. She started ignoring me when I'd run into her, hanging up on me, not returning my letters. Every now and then we tried to get it back together, but it was never the same. In spite of all the warning signs, I kept hoping. Right up until yesterday."

"I can understand that," Jenny said, massaging my upper thigh. "I still kind of hold a torch for my ex-husband." She had married a junkie when she was 18. The ceremony took place at the Lucas County Jail. As part of his parole, the groom was required to go to Synanon in California and Jenny accompanied him. They escaped after three days and honeymooned at the live sex shows in North Beach. Their marriage was over in six months.

"We saw a lot of each other over the past few years, though. In fact, I just finally kicked him out of my place last April. He was sleeping with a couple of the girls who used to work here. Hanging around. Throwing it in my face. I know he's nothing but bad news, but I'll never stop thinking about him."

"Deep down I guess I'd always feared there'd be trouble," I said as Jenny lathered her hands with more lotion. "She had those two brutal marriages while I was dateless until college and had only two brief relationships before I fell for her. I always told her it was like we met at the city limits of Las Vegas, me coming into the bright lights from the desert, her stumbling and broke from a too long stay in the neon's glare." The strains of "Shenandoah" filtered into the room. "Experience wise it was a mismatch from the start. But early on and against all odds it flourished, and not just because of the hot and nasty sex. It was communion, confluence, immersion – all that dreamy '60s stuff is what really made up the texture of our love."

"Wow, that's so neat." Jenny stroked gently at my hair. "Most of the guys who come in here try to get me to give them a hand job, but you're really romantic. I think I'm blushing."

"A lot of it was my fault," I confessed as the timer ticked to the tune of "Camptown Races." "I probably should have asserted myself more, especially during those first couple years when things were going good, but I always assumed that if I let things flow everything would work out by itself, like it was destiny. I didn't know you had to actually do anything."

The gong went off and I got up, making sure my towel was fastened. "Before I met her I had spent my whole life sitting alone and watching passion in Technicolor on the big screen. Letting go of her was out of the question. So I'd wait for her to call or stop by and when she did we'd give it one more try, each time a little more tentative and a lot less blended."

Jenny squeezed my shoulder as she opened the door. We moved into the hallway and I lowered my voice. "I guess what bothers me as much as anything is that, looking back on this past year or so, I realize that 90 percent of my involvement with her was nothing more than me talking to myself and imagining answers – just like it had been all my life before her. That's kinda scary."

"Are you going to see her again?"

"We're supposed to get together Friday. I don't know how that's going to go. It could be pretty rough."

"Just make sure you don't say anything you'll regret. I did with my ex-husband and I feel bad about it. I still really owe him a lot." She stroked her braid. "What I learned at those live sex shows comes in handy. Keep that in mind, big guy, and give me a call sometime." Her next customer, sporting a 4-Wheelers Eat More Bush t-shirt, scurried by us while hastily undoing his belt. Jenny rolled her eyes playfully, pecked me on the cheek and headed back into the massage room.

Bert was waiting for me in the lounge. He had taken the 20-minute special and was listening while Kathy talked about her varicose veins. I headed for the shower.

As Bert and I were about to leave, the truck driver owner came in brandishing free tickets to the Golden Cherry. He looked like Oil Can Harry itching to foreclose a mortgage and spoke with a thick southern drawl. He had on a green knit shirt and checkered pants, and grandly gave Bert and me a couple passes saying, "Pussy, that's the name of the game." Debbie punched him with her only hand.

"It was good to see Jenny," I said to Bert as we walked towards my car. I may give her a buzz and get together. How did it go with Kathy?"

"Pretty good, but," Bert sighed and stuffed his hands into his pockets, "I think she wants me to tutor one of her kids. She invited me to a cookout Friday."

"That's great. Are you gonna go?"

"Nah, but I might catch her Saturday night in here. Boy, she took that towel right off."

"Bert," I slowly began after we had driven into the night a while and were stopped at a light. "This was kind of fun and I won't rule out coming back again sometime, but do you ever think that going twice a week is a little. . ."

"Sick," he interjected.

"Yeah," I continued. "You know, distorting the concept of sexuality and moving you further and further away from a normal relationship."

"Nah," he shrugged, squinting at a solitary blond standing near a night-time bus stop. "I just wish it wasn't so expensive, but it's only money."

***

The next night Frank dropped by to visit me. Scott had told him what had happened concerning Lana, so he borrowed a car and drove up from Crystal City to Toledo. Frank was about the only married guy

I ever hung around with. In fact, he had been married three times – though his third marriage had ended in '77, when he was 26, neither he nor his ex/current had been able to get the money together to file for divorce. He had even had a couple near engagements in the past few years and had moved away from his most recent fiancee earlier in the year. He was currently living in a rooming house, collecting welfare, working on his poetry, and obsessively studying the historical, mythic roles of the sexes. Frank was also proud to announce that he was presently in his sixth month of official celibacy.

As I filled in some of the details about Lana, he nodded his head vigorously. "She always struck me as a heavy-duty seductress. You're lucky she's gone."

Because of his decade of intense involvement with wives, fiancees and girlfriends, Frank was particularly focused in on the seduction aspect of relationships and often would tirade at length about women and the whole messy business of sexual gamesmanship. I felt that many of his observations were unfairly severe, but I always found them pungently humorous and at times startlingly insightful. Most of his recent poetry was concerned with the dangers of becoming too involved in what he referred to as "the infernal vaginal death spiral." Since his celibacy had freed him of all that now, he was seeing everything more clearly than ever.

"I knew you were in a lot of trouble when I saw Lana hanging out with those Women Now people." He sat down rigidly in my easy chair.

Frank was constantly warring with this group, which was the feminist political organization on campus. In fact, he explained he had just had another run-in with them at the Take Back the Night March over the weekend. The march was organized to protest the most recent surge of violence towards women on campus. Frank was supportive of the cause but extremely skeptical of the motives of some of the leaders, most of whom he'd romantically pursued at one time or another.

"I was walking about 10 feet from the main crowd, just puffing on a joint and basically minding my own business," Frank said, steadfastly maintaining the stiffness of his seated position.

One of the leaders, who was dressed as Mussolini and who had had several run-ins with Frank over the years, told him to "Put that thing away."

"I politely told her I could handle it," he said.

Soon the group started to chant, "Take the toys away from the boys." Most of the men present at the march were characterized by Frank as castratoes of the boy's choir who always hung around the hard-core women, whiffing the air. They were chanting. Frank wasn't. Suddenly his arch-enemy, the Mussolini woman, shouted, "Some of the men don't have the guts to chant," looked right at Frank and added loudly, "Maybe their mothers didn't toilet train them right."

"I turned to her and said, 'Look, I'll leave your vagina alone as long as you leave my soul alone. Otherwise I'll charge you with rape'."

"What was her reaction to that?"

"Well, everyone got real quiet and I left." Frank got up, walked over to the window and snuck a look outside. "I've been laying low for these last couple days. I think I'm probably being crucified around town – they might even have some envoys follow me up here – but I'll be damned if I'm going to let these hostile women bully me."

Frank signaled me that the coast was clear so we headed out and went to Tiffinanny's, a wine and cheese place known for its bohemian atmosphere. I commented that it reminded me of places in New York or New Orleans and seemed a million miles away from provincial Crystal City.

Frank nodded absently, then returned to railing about the Women Now group. "As far as I'm concerned they're all a bunch of hexographers. They're just casting spells and dealing in a lot of dark, murky fears. Getting involved with them is like tumbling into a pit of vipers. Thank God I'm celibate."

The waitress arrived at our table. Her name was Cara. She was wearing a black leotard top and a long, purple and black old-fashioned skirt. She crouched down at our table to talk – bunching her skirt between her legs and tight against her crotch – and informed us that she was a "dahncer" and the Toledo University student leader of the

Committee Against Registration for the Draft. She grabbed our hands and squeezed them and talked more about dancing. After she walked away I mentioned to Frank that I thought she was nice.

"I'm suspicious of how she moves her body. I think she's trying to suck us in." Frank scraped at his hand as if trying to remove the Stigmata. "I do appreciate the way she's attempting to get away from the mucousy, discoey, late '70s sleazy look into more of an Earth Mother motif, but I'm still suspicious of the way she's working her skirt. It's just a sophisticated form of peeing on your bone, no matter how you look at it. All this sexual innuendo and flirting nonsense makes me want to throw up." Frank scratched his knee and peered down to examine it carefully, before looking up just in time to catch Cara making a ballet-like twirl. "And as far as this dancing business, I want it known that from now on I'm keeping my dancing leg in my pants."

Sensing Frank's obvious discomfort – he was clutching both chair-arms and sitting stiff and upright as if he were awaiting electrocution-I suggested we try somewhere else but Frank said he was through for the evening. As we left Cara winked at us and told Frank she liked his "dark, Kerouac-like good looks."

"Even if you're not directly involved in the conflict," he muttered, quickening his pace to the street, "you're always fighting some inane border skirmish somewhere."

When he dropped me off in front of my apartment, I told him that I would be meeting with Lana the next day.

"Just don't get sucked in," he warned and pulled the door shut hard, testing it several times before cautiously driving away.

***

Friday after work I was sitting in my apartment watching a CNN commentator speculating that the death of Lennon marked the official end of the '60s. I was wondering how to get in touch with Lana. I already knew what I would say. I was simmering. The phone rang.

"Ray." It was Lana. "I don't think it would be a good idea to get together."

"I agree," I said, surprising myself. "I think we should just leave it at that final scene." She agreed and I continued. "But we can say a few things over the phone." I had an arsenal ready.

"I don't think that would be a good idea."

"I've got a few things to tell you about your karma."

"I've got a few things to say about yours, too, but I don't think we should."

Her hang-up beat mine by a heartbeat.

Winter Solstice

"It will be a good chance to meet some new people, " I said to Scott over the phone. "You really ought to come along with me."

"Why don't you stop over. I might be able to fit it into my schedule, besides I want to show you something."

I had heard about a Winter Solstice Party to be given by the Safe Energy Alliance of Northwest Ohio. It was to be the party of the holiday season for the hipper folks of Toledo, and I figured it would be a good opportunity for Scott and me to make some connections. We had both moved out of Crystal City at about the same time, and neither one of us had really met anyone. Lana had occupied my mind most of the fall, while Scott had been, as always, deeply immersed in his work.

Scott's residence in the heart of a black neighborhood was the unlikely location of the TM headquarters of Northwest Ohio. People purportedly levitated there in the modest white house where Scott lived with Harriet, the mother of one of his friends. Surrounding the house were the Skyrocket Lounge; the Pit Stop – Astrological Reading and Advising; the We-Up Body Shop; and a small lot with broken bottles and an angularly-parked '67 Buick – sans license plates – with a Capricorn sticker on the back window. This fly-by-night neighborhood was where the advanced TMers came to rise each evening.

Scott shushed me with his index finger to his mouth, pointed downstairs and mouthed that the flyers were down there and gingerly led me into the dining room, where his thesis was sprawled over a huge table. There were several books on cybernetics, a volume of Hegel and the Bhagavad Ghita Quarterly, a TM publication, stacked near the edge of the table.

"It's all here," he whispered reverently, surveying the table. "I'd like to go over it with you when we have more time, but here's what I really want to show you." He reached into his briefcase, plucked out a letter and handed it to me, saying it was from Army Intelligence inquiring about the nature of his work.

I glanced at the official epistle, but could make no sense of it since Scott had blackened out just about every word.

"How do you feel about whatever this says?"

"I have mixed feelings," he sighed, a speck of a smile showing. "I love the way they use the word clandestine, and sometimes I want to be part of an international spy network using decision support systems so bad I can taste it, but I know that's not part of the Maharishi's plan. My primary goal is to get back in his good graces, and I know I have to be careful with these army people."

Earlier in the year Scott had a falling out with Kimberly Vishnu, one of the Maharishi's top assistants, over a risque mantra he had whispered in her ear and found himself summarily relegated to the state of transcendental exile. Scott suspected that Kimberly was using any method she could to sabotage him because she feared he would leapfrog over her in the TM hierarchy, and also because he had withdrawn his support for her as Queen of Rebirth when they were students at Maharishi International University in Iowa. Scott knew Kimberly was a powerhouse, which is why almost all of his attention these days was devoted to finding his own way out of the great man's doghouse.

He carefully placed the letter back in his briefcase and wedged out a thick book entitled "Technical Control Over History." "I just got this one yesterday," he said, his hand trembling. "I get the chills reading it. God, it excites me."

I pointed to a dog-eared copy of "Eros and Civilization" at the center of the table. Scott blushed and smiled sheepishly, intertwining the fingers of both hands together. "Well, it's all interrelated."

I had arrived early and Scott hadn't quite made up his mind whether or not he was going with me. He went upstairs to meditate hoping for a sign from the Maharishi about the wisdom of attending this particular party. I flicked on the television for "Kung Fu." A cable station from Detroit broadcast re-runs of the show three times a week. During my alcohol/depression years of '74-'75, I used to catch it every Thursday night for glimpses of spiritual insight. It was my all-time favorite show, and I had been watching the re-runs religiously over the past few months.

With my recent separation from Lana, I found myself identifying more and more with Caine, the main character of the show. He was half-Chinese, half-American, was trained in a Buddhist temple and unfairly exiled from China for a crime he did not commit. He roamed the wild American West alone spouting Eastern wisdom, teaching by humble example that the journey is the destination and truth can be found only in a deeper relationship with one's self. I felt I was ready to do the same thing around the Toledo area, but – despite intellectually knowing better – hadn't sufficiently evolved past the decidedly Western notion that finding another woman would help grease my skids.

The episode showing while I waited for Scott seemed appropriate for my dilemma. Entitled "The Elixir," it concerned a beautiful woman traveling with a devoted hunchback, selling bottled medicine. Caine helps them flee a hostile town, and the woman asks him to travel with them. She confides to him that she wants to be free, then attempts to seduce him, but he catches her in a lie.

"Can you be free without the truth?" he asks.

"A woman who wants to be free in this world has to use anything she can," she answers. "Don't understand me, just love me."

In a flashback, the "Grasshopper" – Caine as a child in the temple – asks his master, "I saw a girl in the market, she sought my friendship and when she had it she didn't want it. Why can't females be open and honest?"

"Is it not enough that she acts like a female?" the master answers. "Male and female are like coal and flame. If the coal does not seek the flame, can either fulfill its destiny?"

The simple wisdom of this episode readily reinforced my view that the upcoming party, for starters, just might be a step on the road to destiny fulfillment. I hoped Scott would feel the same and agree to join me.

"Two can play at that game!" Scott roared from the hallway on the second floor.

He rumbled down the stairs, muttering that the Maharishi needed him just as much as he needed the Maharishi and maybe what the Maharishi really needed was one less female assistant obsessed with blocking any meditative messages from him – Scott – to the Maharishi and that maybe it was about time for him – Scott – to stop worrying and go out and have some fun.

"If we're going to go we better get going," I said.

Scott held up one finger, stood in the middle of the room, debated whether or not to take his briefcase with him, settled on a small notebook and did one last check of the table to make sure his notes were all in their proper places. As he revolved around the table I talked about how the winter solstice symbolized a new beginning. He couldn't agree more and added that the day on which there was so little light provided an opportunity to learn from the darkness. Then I made the mistake of mentioning the Summer Solstice Party that we had attended six months earlier. Scott sank in the nearest chair as if he had been shot with a stun gun. His face paled and his brow wrinkled.

"I've been trying to forget that day," he whimpered, fetally clutching his briefcase. "That's when it all started. That's when I realized she was sabotaging me."

The summer party actually had been a picnic given by Scott's TM friends and turned out to be important for me since it set in motion the events that led to my leaving Crystal City, which in turn hastened my ultimate separation from Lana. Jenny was there that day, as was Frank. At the time Scott was nearly broke – Honeywell and IBM were not returning his calls – and was desperately awaiting career guidance from the Maharishi. Actually both Frank and Scott were getting desperate for work, so much so that they had decided, despite a deep mutual distrust of each other stemming from various female-related skirmishes, to team up in search of employment.

Scott was adamant in his insistence that he needed the right kind of job in order to continue work on his thesis, while Frank knew his ability to live off welfare checks and change from food stamps couldn't last forever. Feeling that Frank would make an excellent salesman because of his verbal skills and analytical mind and that the two of them would represent an irresistible package to employers, Scott had arranged an interview on the morning of the solstice party for him and Frank at a computer store in Toledo. Eager to find out the results of this landmark undertaking, I had picked up Jenny around noon that day and drove to the picnic site.

It was baking hot that afternoon when we pulled into the parking lot at Swan Creek. Frank came running to the car as if he were being pursued by evil spirits.

"How's the big day going?" I asked.

"Pretty much a disaster," he whispered, white as a ghost. "Scott was swooning the entire morning. The only time he strung an entire sentence together was when he was talking about Rousseau." Frank seemed parched and drained following his first job interview in over a year. "The Arab hardly understood a word either one of us said until I used the term pussy." He looked at Jenny. "Oh, I'm sorry."

I handled the intros, then asked Frank if he wanted to smoke some pot. "Hallelujah," he said.

Jenny excused herself to use the port-o-john.

As we toked away, Frank described that morning's scene. Following a brief tour of the store, Frank, Scott and Ahmeche, the Arab owner, breakfasted at Bob Evans. Scott spent most of the breakfast discussing his need for flexible hours and his dread of ending up like Rousseau's whipping boy. Ahmeche, who was having trouble selling computers because of language problems, just smiled when Scott mentioned Rousseau or made reference to Aristotle's teoreas. As Scott rambled, Ahmeche kept looking quizzically at Frank, who had hardly said a word all morning. Finally the beefy foreigner's gaze rested on a leggy teenage waitress and he rolled his eyes while biting into a sweet roll, licking his lips as she bent over.

"I sensed a bond with him at that point." Frank took a hit and held it in for a few seconds before bursting into a choking cough. Finally, he got his breath back. "I told him that a year ago last February I stopped by to visit this woman I was seeing after delivering pizzas one night. Believe it or not she had spent the entire day baking sugar cookies and still had my Valentine's Day candy on her kitchen table. We sat around drinking Pepsis and eating all that sweet stuff. Pretty soon my mouth was right there on her pussy. I told Ahmeche it was all a conspiracy no matter how you looked at it."

"What did he do?"

"He picked up the tab and drove us over here."

Jenny returned and the three of us walked to the picnic area, too late for the organized games but just in time to strap on the feedbag. The women were quite plain-looking and the men seemed to be a little on the swishy side. The children appeared bewildered. A quote from the Maharishi, delivered by a pregnant woman in terri-cloth, graced the meal.

Jenny was getting a lot of attention from the group, what with her see-through top and painted-on cutoffs.

"Do you meditate?" a birdlike woman asked her.

"No, but I space out a lot," she answered, twirling her braid. A how quaint look adorned several meditators' countenances.

Scott was not looking well at all. The job interview had been a total failure. He had not been offered anything, flexible hours or otherwise. He had produced his thesis at Bob Evans but to no avail. He even had an apologia ready but had forgotten to put it in his briefcase that morning. And to top it off, Robin Hirz had not shown up at the picnic. Scott was certain she would be bringing him a message from the Maharishi exonerating him from his naughty mantra faux pas. If anyone could put this unfortunate misunderstanding into its proper perspective it was Robin, the woman he had thrown his support to, instead of Kimberly, in the Rebirth Queen sweepstakes.

Aside from serving as the great man's emissary she was, in Scott's words, a ball-busting Jewess who talked so dirty it embarrassed even him – but she was also the one who helped him fully understand the universal truth that the brain is the sexiest organ, which is why he had stumped for her in college. Sensing she had been blocked from coming to the picnic by Kimberly, Scott was drinking Cokes and looked like he was going to pass out. Along with protecting himself from killer women, he had to watch his sugar.

"You have pretty hair," Jenny brightly offered.

Scott turned slowly and looked at her as if measuring her soul. "If that's so, why are women so brutal to me, why are they out to get me?" he asked weakly, wrinkling his brow and turning his fragile gaze back into space.

The mid-day sun was beating down and Scott appeared to be conversationally finished for the day, so Jenny and I moved to another table where Frank was intently conversing with a bespectacled, pasty-faced young woman with short, drab brown hair and neatly clipped bangs. Her face looked like it belonged on a jar of old-fashioned apple butter.

"I studied at Maharishi International University before coming back to Toledo," she chirped. "I'm going to try to get to Switzerland to study with the Maharishi next year. Anyone can meditate. It's sort of like physics."

"I meditate too," Frank said, "but pot helps me bring the whole thing into focus."

"My brother used drugs," she countered expressionlessly. "He thought he was the Zodiac Sniper for awhile, and now he's in the state hospital. The Maharishi says, 'Drugs are for the thugs.' He's a big fan of the gangster movies. I think he's very effective when he uses the idiom to get his point across."

At the other end of the table I sat down across from Clarisse, a wafer-thin school supervisor from nearby Monroe, Michigan – the birthplace of General Custer. She studied me intently and asked what I did for a living.

"I'm a high school special education teacher."

"I knew it," she said, bowing her head reverently. "The Maharishi wouldn't allow me to come here for no reason."

She explained that there was an opening for a learning disabilities teacher in Temperance and that I should apply since it was written all over me that I was ready for a change.

Jenny tugged at my elbow and pressed her bare leg against me. "If you get that job you can move up here and get out of that crummy Crystal City. I'll even help you find an apartment. A lot of my clients are landlords."

"Actually, I have been thinking about relocating and I wouldn't mind getting a new job, one where I can work with kids one-on-one and help them with some of their behavior problems before they end up in jail."

"The Maharishi says that if everyone meditated the prisons could all be turned into recreational facilities," Clarisse said enthusiastically. "He loves all sports, especially Big Time Wrestling. He taught the Sheik how to meditate, and it helped him win the North American Title."

Frank and I simultaneously excused ourselves from the table and walked to a nearby water fountain. Frank looked around furtively and lowered his voice. "John Lennon was right about this TM business. It's a scam. The reason he split with the Maharishi was that the old goat was trying to fuck Mia Farrow."

Jenny walked over to us and said she was ready to leave. We scanned the area looking for Scott so that we could say goodbye.

"There he is." Jenny pointed under a tree where Scott was flat on his back, briefcase at his side, staring at the mid-day sun through the branches. No message from the Maharishi, no job offer, too many killer women and too much sugar had laid him down with his arms stretched out. It was, as Frank would later write in a poem describing the scene, "A horizontal, solar crucifixion for a man of the moon."

"Maybe I better pass on this party," Scott said weakly, still half-slumped at the table in his living room. "I've got some more work I can do, besides I want to talk to some of the flyers when they come upstairs. Maybe they've heard something from you-know-who."

"Okay," I said, seeing that Scott's mind was already made up. "I'll give you a call tomorrow and tell you how it went."

I left to the faint thump-thumping of the levitators in the basement.

***

Over my shoulder the moon struggled towards fullness as I pushed open the door of the split-level solar house and spotted a woman in a towel rushing down the hallway into a sauna. Reggae music was in the background. The place was packed. I quickly surveyed the scene, recognizing no one and no one seeming to recognize me. The anonymity was a good feeling. Those last few years in Crystal City I felt I was as conspicuous as a giant's cloak on a midget. But walking into this exciting new world – having left the lingering shadows of Crystal City and Lana on the doorstep – I felt brightly unencumbered.

Rumors were flying that all kinds of people were taking their clothes off at the indoor swimming pool downstairs. I descended the stairs for a quick look only to spot a couple of paunchy guys skinny-dipping. A few other men were on the verge of disrobing near a bubbling Jacuzzi.

"A typical party," a woman behind me said in a bored voice. "A bunch of drunken guys taking their pants off."

Writing her off as a cynic and not at all representative of the stimulating, life-affirming crowd just waiting for me, I headed for the sunken living room. A Leonard Cohen album was playing. I decided to absorb the atmosphere and not try to force anything, just let the party come to me. People were sitting on couches and pillows. Some were dancing in a rhythmically willowy fashion to "Bird on a Wire." I eased myself down next to a woman who owned Gourmet Curiosities and was seen from time-to-time on Toledo television morning shows. She was talking to another woman about married men. With an I'm-new-around-her-tone, I asked her why women go after married men when there are so many single ones.

"Single guys are too easy," she half-turned to me and laughed.

Another cynic, I thought, but I was the one who had brought up the subject. Fair enough. I decided to return to my game plan and just lie back and get a feel for the crowd.

A married couple, just returned from Dallas, was sitting on the couch. The woman had attended a Mary Kay Cosmetics convention-she barely missed being awarded a pink Cadillac for sales – while her hubby was at a gathering run by motivational guru Zig Ziglar, known for such slogans as, "You are suffering from stinkin' thinkin' and hardening of the attitude." As the couple leaned forward speaking to different people, their message was the same. "You need a check-up from the neck-up."

On the other side of the room a big butter-and-egg kind of black guy was over-using the word portfolio, while a man of the cloth was talking to a thin nurse trying to get her to sign up for his Funky Fitness, Rape Prevention and Puff Pastry class at the Jerusalem Baptist Church. A woman who managed Calico, Sage and Thyme, a new bar opening at a mall, was lamenting the dearth of men who could perform successful premature withdrawals. A golden oldies album was playing, "Cupid" then "Hanky Panky."

Near the fireplace a bleary-eyed, drawn woman wearing beads and brandishing a Scotch was loudly talking about a book called "The Sexual Contract" she had just read. It was an anthropological study on the roles of men and women. "Men think they started everything," she hiccupped, "but this book says that women were the first to actually use their sexuality. We noticed that we got meat when we were in heat, so we just pretended we were in heat most of the time."

"By the way Helen," another inebriated woman said, straightening herself after doubling up with harsh laughter. "I just love that perfume you're wearing. What is it?"

"It's called Impulse. It's supposed to make you instantly innocent. Ain't that a crock."

Maybe I was being too overly somber and maybe I was still a trifle traumatized by Lana's leaving, but I found myself offended by this boozy female negativity. I knew things were rough all over, but didn't they believe in stuff anymore? It wasn't easy, but it certainly wasn't impossible.

Feeling a bit woozy I decided to stretch my legs, so I went back upstairs – past a group of young guys, posing with hips cocked at studied angles – and into a small game room that was overflowing with EST members and bookstore employees. I leaned against the wall, feeling as if I were watching one of those scenes in a movie where the camera shifts quickly from one person to another – facing getting more animated, voices getting louder, everything accelerating – as one of the EST women, a retired belly-dancer and author of "Winning Through Enlightenment," was talking loudly about a man who had made a pass at her downstairs.

"How did you feel?" her friend asked.

"I felt flattered, confused, hopeful, sad," she clicked off her feelings. "I guess I'm just not used to men who haven't been through the training."

Right next to her a local televangelist was insisting that his performing the "Gator" was the only thing that could save the party, while a few feet away a woman with a crew cut was arguing about penis envy with a guy wearing a Wine, Women and Walleye t-shirt.

"It's not so much penis envy," she hissed, "as urination envy. We just like the way you piss."

"At least we don't have to fake orgasms," he countered defiantly.

Fearing I might break into a scream, I considered mingling for a moment but chose to remain braced against the wall after spotting a dancing pair of Women's Studies instructors from Crystal City University. They were one-time friends of Frank. He had unsuccessfully pursued first one then the other, then referred to them as the Bitter Biddy, Sour Pussy Sisters. Out on the dance floor they were rug-cutting in a stiff and perturbed manner – eyes shut, faces contorted, as if they were in the process of taking a crap. "The Thrill Is Gone" was playing. "The thrill was never there," they both yelled to no one in particular.

I turned towards the presumed safety of a half-looped ex-nun, who opined, "What I really want is some kind of weird intellectual with the body of a factory worker," in the general direction of a group of middle-aged men, dressed alike in tweed jackets with drooping pockets, bemoaning the vagaries of being broken down romantics.

"If I were his mother," the crewcut woman whispered in reference to the guy in the Walleye shirt, "I would have shoved him back in when he was born."

I was about to make a break for the exit when a voice rose above the din.

"Now there's an angel," trumpeted Peter, a fresh-faced, broadly-smiling guy wearing a Banzai Cycle Shop t-shirt and a Perry Como patch-sleeved cardigan. Most of the evening he had been softly speaking of the Lord.

The secular object of his attention was a tall, blond-haired woman in conventional heels and a simple black dress. She appeared to be in her late 30s and was alongside a serious-looking, wavy-haired fellow of around 25. She walked with smooth aggressiveness – her long, straight hair spilling all over her shoulders and back.

Peter devoutly watched her nimbly negotiate the stairs to the pool. "I think I'm in heaven," he cried before heading down to the water.

I was right behind him.

"I know it's kind of corny to say," the blond angel began in earnest, "but Three Mile Island changed my life." Her name was Emma. She was 40 and a grandmother. She lived with her ex-husband who was now "just a roommate." They owned a concrete business. He had custody of their 10-year-old daughter. "I don't sleep with him or anything." She brushed her lap clean. "But since we live in an energy efficient house, I decided not to move out. I've been dating Jimmy for about a year. He's 26."

Jimmy fidgeted his hands as he watched us.

"I just got back from a solar-energy meeting in Athens, Ohio," she said. "There were some really intelligent women there."

A lacquer-haired woman in an army jacket glowered down from the top of the stairs and held her nose as a couple half-naked real fat guys- the kind with no asses – staggered slowly by. "What the hell's wrong with the women around here?" one of them yelled, mincing his steps as if his balls were killing him. "All they want to do is bitch about men and dance with each other."

Emma smiled warmly at the men and said they don't know any better. Jimmy excused himself to take a whizz. Peter took off his sweater and kicked off his shoes. I whipped out a joint.

"None for me thanks," Emma said. "That stuff makes me sleepy. You know, I spent 15 years trying to figure out why Ralph, my ex, didn't want me – worry, worry." She laughed as if certain that worry were a thing of the past. "I moved out, then moved back in because of the business and our daughter. Now he wants me, desires me, and he's got plenty of girlfriends of his own. Oh well, enough about him."

We talked about politics. I told her I used to be pretty active in Crystal City, but lately was trying to focus on the personal rather than the political.

"I'm just beginning to realize a lot of things." Her eyes narrowed and the tone of her voice sharpened. "No offense to you, but male dominance is behind most of our problems."

I told her that no offense was taken and that I basically agreed with her, but I cautioned that dominance in relationships was pretty much an illusion and always a matter of complementary factors.

"It's a 50/50 proposition," I said smoothly. "I think most women don't realize what part their behavior plays in creating a relationship. They don't want to acknowledge their own responsibility. It always takes two to tangle."

"That's cute. I never thought of it that way, though. There's a lot in what you say." She played with her necklace and took a deep breath. "You really are nice. I'd like to make a date with you but I'd hate to break it."

"Well, it's the thought that counts. I'll give you my number and if you feel like it, give me a buzz."

She carefully copied my number into a unicorn address book. I flashed on Lana and my heart started beating a little faster. "I'm finding out that you bachelors are a lot of fun," she said. Jimmy came back and they left.

I hummed a that-was-a-little-more-like-it tune to myself as I went upstairs, relishing the fact that I was just about to leave when I spotted her. That had a bit of the old when-you-least-expect-it-Lana-at-her-best feel to it. I liked that, as long as it didn't get out of hand. Which, of course, the newly emerging Ray would not let happen.

"Don't Let Me Be Misunderstood" was playing. Only a few people remained at the party. Peter came by, sans both Perry Como sweater and Banzai shirt. He took his pants off and assumed the lotus position near a chubby woman in a red Danskin top and Calvin Klein jeans. Peter had donned a pair of frameless glasses and put most of his earthly possessions at his side. Serenity was written all over him. The woman put aside her glass of wine, agreed that much of what we possess possesses us, but refused to take her clothes off.

As I was leaving, a defiant voice rose from the sauna. "Well excuse me for having an erection! You know you could take it as a compliment for Christ sake."

***

The next afternoon I chaperoned the school Christmas dance, and that's where I saw Judy for the first time. It was her huge, flashing eyes that riveted me as she shimmered and whirled in and out of the darkened gymnasium with a girlfriend. I almost asked her to slow dance but figured that might cause some trouble, what with me being a 30-year-old teacher and her – I found out later - having just turned 17. For the rest of the day I blinked and saw her eyes.

I called Scott that night to tell him about the party and how it took me awhile to get in the swing of things and how I was initially disturbed by the harsh tones of many of the women.

"That's a sensitive area for you," he counseled. "You're still grieving the loss of Lana, which is perfectly normal. Soon you'll lighten up, which is precisely what I need to do for my problems with the Maharishi. It's all a matter of maintaining perspective. I understand that now, perhaps that's what his message is to me."

"Actually the night turned out great. Right before I left the party I met this grandmother and we seemed to hit it off. She even asked me for my number."

"Oh my, a grandmother taking your number. That's a healthy sign. You need a good woman to get your mind off that killer."

"Yeah, I'm feeling better already. I even saw this gorgeous high school girl at the dance this afternoon."

There was a moment of stark silence on the phone.

"Ray, for God's sake be careful." He abruptly wished me a happy holiday and hung up.

As far as Scott was concerned, under no circumstances were teenage girls to be discussed. As far as I was concerned, it was just a matter of maintaining perspective.

***

On Saturday evening, January 3, Frank showed up at my door. His father, an administrator at CCU, had dropped him off on his way to visit his latest graduate assistant girlfriend.

"This holiday season almost finished me," Frank moaned as he slung himself on the couch. He was trying to get over a bout with the flu during the holidays and was doing okay until he suffered a relapse on New Year's Eve. He blamed it on a lengthy French kiss he had given to a bisexual woman at the stroke of midnight.

"I could taste the pussy juice, but I was bound and determined to kiss her like I meant it, just for auld lang syne." Frank hacked with pride. "If I die I deserve it. That's fine with me."

He laughed demonically then cringed as he spotted a Rolling Stone cover with Lennon fetally curled up with Yoko. "There you have it," he wheezed with disgust. "Everything that guy's been through and he ends up in a mommy-please-help-me-trip, for heaven's sake. I guess that's what the late '70s were about for a lot of guys. These women have really been cranking it into high gear. It's like they want to start another era of the goddesses, where they sustain themselves through blood sacrifices."

Frank waved off a glass of juice I offered him and gathered himself a bit. "Well I can't speak for anyone else but I'll tell you what, I for one totally reject any and all sensory knowledge kinesthetically programmed from my mother and deviously designed to keep me operating on some umbilical yo-yo." He rocked his still-fevered frame up to the edge of my couch. "And I don't care how many bruising romantic interactions I've been through, or no matter how severe some of my female-spawned insurrections have been, I swear I'll never sink to the mommy-please-help-me level. I'll slit my fuckin' throat first."

"C'mon Frank, you can't blame everything on your mother. You know there's more to it than that."

"You're right, it's a modern societal thing." He sat back frowning, working his body around and trying to get comfortable. "In simpler times there'd be someone to teach you about ceremony and ritual and show you practical skills and help you figure out what your role should be." Frank reached for my blue-checkered comforter that was folded near the end of the couch. "The only thing my old man ever taught me was how to chase after every God damn co-ed that moved, and the rest of the men in my family were just a bunch of drunken hillbilly yahoos that fucked like polecats before passing out every night."

The fevered memory of his upbringing moved Frank to secure himself under my comforter and he grew quiet, so I told him what I had done over the holidays. It had snowed hard the day before Christmas and I was unable to drive home to Cleveland. It was the first Christmas Eve I hadn't been with my parents my entire life. The symbolism of that, in conjunction with other recent events, was not lost on me.

"Lana's gone, I'm out of the womb of Crystal City and I've even finally distanced myself from my parents," I said as Frank nodded weakly. "Everything that seemed to sustain me for so long is gone and I feel like I'm really out on my own for the first time. It's scary but exciting."

I explained that I had been alone again on New Year's Eve and that it had been that way most of life. And that even as a child I would make sure to disappear at the kissing hour, content to hide in the coat-room or wait in the bathroom until the coast was clear and I was safely withdrawn and remote. And how I always had felt, until this New Year's, vaguely inadequate and ashamed unless I was with a woman to ring out the old and bring in the new.

"There's a reason that the Hindus defined women as MAYA – illusion," Frank whispered, clearly conserving his energy. "All these mystic opposites like goddess/demon, virgin/whore, nurturer/devourer are just a bunch of unreal, shadowy phantoms designed to confuse and dominate us – and divert us from the reality that in many ways we're better off by ourselves." He blew his nose for about 30 seconds, entombed the tissue in my wastebasket then reeled back in exhaustion. "And I ought to know, I spent the entire past decade doing a phallus in wonderland trip."

Frank's first marriage took place in 1970 when he was so much in love with his high school sweetheart that he would pump gas into the trunks of Volkswagons at the gas station where he worked in southern Illinois. That marriage lasted two years and his second one – which featured wild courtroom scenes, 30 days in jail for Frank and copious infidelity on both sides – lasted three years. At that point he moved to Crystal City, where his father was dean of students at the university, and eased himself right into a third marriage, which ended in spirit if not in fact two years later when he was 26. After that, and up until his declaration of celibacy in mid-1980, he continued to lace on the gloves in one relationship after another with barely an unattached day in between.

Frank meticulously unwrapped a throat lozenge and forced it into his mouth. "This summer did it for me. The combination of that Republican Convention and that string of women I went through finally cured me."

During that steaming hot July week when the Republicans nominated an aging actor for president, Frank carried out a blitzkrieg of romantic activities. He whirlwinded through an Edgar Cayce reading-group leader who wore a neck brace during her period, a redhead who flipped out at the cemetery during a 24-hour marathon therapy group, two roommates who were always threatening to move out because each believed the other was casting a spell, an ex-wife, and a woman from the touring Chicago Knockers mud wrestling team.

As we watched the convention on television in my apartment, he would explain to me how each of these women represented a new dimension or possessed a quality no one else had and that was the reason he was convinced each was the answer. He was taking a fearsome beating and by Reagan's acceptance speech had been pared, sliced, diced and gashed to pieces – finally declaring himself a celibate and beginning a path that would bring him remarkable clarity. No one was fooling him now.

"This knowledge may lead to my grave," he conceded, burrowing under my comforter. "I just may be vacuumed out of this place. My body may be telling me that I just can't handle these women in conjunction with this Reagan thing. All this slit-skirt decadence and creepy Moral Majority fascism makes my skin crawl. It must have been like this 50 years ago in Berlin right before Hitler took over." He suppressed a sneeze. "All I want is my health."

Frank was particularly distressed by his lingering sickness because it had come when he seemed to be on the verge of getting a job. He hadn't worked for nearly a year and his income for 1980 was $284. However, he had interviewed with the Pine Manor Nursing Home, and they needed a custodian. The woman practically assured Frank he would have a job, since he was on welfare and she was hiring off the rolls. He was supposed to go in for a second interview Friday but was too sick to get out of bed. He feared the job was in jeopardy all because of that New Year's Eve kiss.

I flicked on the TV. Frank rolled over and flashed on the "Solid Gold" dancers shaking their flanks. They were clad in tiny leotards, snaking around guest hosts, the Oak Ridge Boys. They slingshot their hips. "Why don't you take your fucking clothes off," Frank yelled, hand on forehead. "You've won. Why bother with the skimpy attire?"

He was definitely on the ropes so I switched the channel, but not before he rallied to blast the media. "They're just perpetuating sexual gamesmanship, finding the lowest common denominator for human interaction. There's every flavor of cosmic cunt imaginable on TV. The knockout-with-the-good heart, mmm, yummy. There's the give-you-shelter-from-the-storm soulmate, wow, nice tits. We're being bombarded and perverted in every way imaginable." He held up a finger and announced dramatically. "Human life has never been cheaper."

I scanned the channels. A commercial featured the Schlitz Malt Liquor Bull with some mistletoe on one of his horns. Frank emitted another groan. I clicked to CNN which was doing a story on Marshall McCluhan, who had just died. "He must have seen it all coming whether he admitted it or not," Frank nodded, his teeth chattering a bit. "Deep down he had to know that eventually the media would create a passive society of voyeurs, unable to think for themselves, just sitting there ready to be endlessly titillated and led around like sheep." Frank blew his nose into a tissue, then leaned his head back and stared at the ceiling. "Maybe it's better that he didn't live long enough to see how bad it's really going to get, especially now that we're about to have a telegenic sociopath in the White House."

I found a local talk show where a bearded, professorial-looking fellow was being interviewed. Frank glanced apprehensively at the screen and lost what little was left of his color. "Oh no, it's Allen Koch," he shrieked. "He very shrewdly executed my second divorce. The first time I saw him he looked like a hard-on waiting to happen. He's got a beard now, but he's not fooling me. I think he ended up fucking my third wife." Enemies were jumping out at him through his fever, and he was ready for the fight of his life. "As my last act I may snuff that Zionist moneygrubber, just so he won't be alive after I'm dead." Frank turned his back to the TV, whimpered, "He's giving the A.C.L.U. a bad name," and passed out.

I made sure Frank was covered for what was certain to be a fitful sleep. There was definitely something to his point about getting away from women, but I had to admit to myself that I wasn't quite ready to go as far with it as Frank had. In fact I still felt a bit like Gatsby, living in a state of romantic readiness. True, I was operating on new ground in a new year and I wasn't about to plunge into any madness. Yet I definitely felt on the verge of something. It was in the cards.

The Union and the Club

A surprise snow cancelled school on Friday of the first week after Christmas vacation, so I decided to drive to Crystal City.

The day before at school Judy had come to my room to take my picture for the yearbook. She was the staff photographer. It was fourth period and there was only one kid, Bill, in my room. He was wearing a beat-up brown pilot's jacket and was reading an article on the "Dukes of Hazzard." Bill had a bad case of acne and a missing front tooth. He only made it to school about twice a week.

When Judy walked in Bill let out with a loud groan. She wore a white blouse, tight Chic jeans and medium pumps. She was about five-seven with honey-colored hair mid-way down her back. She had ample breasts and just the tiniest hint of baby fat which, I quickly surmised, would melt away forever with one week in the summer sun.

"Just relax." She aimed her twin lens at me.

"That's not easy," I suavely countered. Bill snorted a no kidding.

She snapped, then set for one more, and flashed again. I was momentarily blinded.

"I really liked that green dress you had on at the Christmas dance," I croaked as her pumps clicked to the door.

"It wasn't green," she said with over-the-shoulder disappointment.

"Oh well, maybe I wasn't looking at the dress." Precisely as I was saying this, Bill echoed, "Maybe he wasn't looking at the dress." We looked at each other and Judy turned and looked at both of us with a confused glance before backing out the door.

"That did it," I said after explaining the scene to Bert as we sat in the Crystal City University Union, a place I had frequented for the past dozen years. "I can't afford to be making suggestive comments to these young girls at school. A little playful flirting is fun, but I've got to set a better example." Bert was nodding absently as I went on. "There's a

New Year's resolution for me. I'm not going to treat these girls at school like flavors of candy. That's not my attitude about women." At the mention of New Year's I noticed Bert wince and droop his shoulders. "By the way, how was your New Year's Eve?"

"A disaster." Bert sighed, beginning to slowly remove his peacoat and French beret, his favorite winter attire. He was also wearing one of his 42 identical golf shirts – most of them white, some pale pastels- purchased over the years at various K-Marts; a Montgomery Ward, brown sweater vest, and chino slacks. Around his neck was an oversized "I'm Proud to be Slovenian" medallion.

Bert rubbed his eye with a knuckle then allowed a thoughtful frown to settle on his face. It appeared he was contemplating a lifetime of New Year's Eve disasters so I decided to grab some coffee and let him regroup. As I walked to the coffee line I passed the huge round table that had been the traditional meeting place and focal point for all the radicals and crazies during the late '60s/early '70s.

Though I had only left Crystal City a few months earlier I felt a strong flush of nostalgia as I – a stroll-by visiting alumnus now – gazed at that circular icon of the Revolution. It was there at that round, dull-pink table that Stoney, loose-limbed symbol of the local peace movement, organized acid-flowered festivals of life and sang arias from his opera about a female Christ who had been crucified on an upturned bunk bed. It was there where Hawkeye, a legally blind speed freak with Coke bottle glasses and a Colonel Sanders goatee, would table-beat out lengthy Cream drum solos and belch out anti-war slogans. It was there where Rodney and Ralph, two warring Jesus Freaks, would exchange Anti-Christ charges, each claiming that he had seen the double-edged flaming sword of God come through the Union's ceiling and cut the other's heart in two. It was there where Weathermen-on-the-run would whisper about bombs, visiting Rainbow People and White Panthers from Ann Arbor would talk about the inalienable right to ball in the streets and soft-voiced poetesses would give spine-tingling accounts of war's chilling human toll. But above all it was there – where now scowling members of Women Now sat flanked by wispy frisbee players and a right-wing railroad worker strumming a guitar – that I once conjured eternally hopeful dreams and proudly wore my heart on my sleeve.

Balancing two cups of coffee I returned to where Bert was sitting and noticed him talking with an old arch-enemy of mine, Dr. Ricardo Milora of the Rehabilitation Counseling Department, from where I had received a Master's degree in '74. Set up to train students to counsel people with disabilities, the "Rehab Program" back then was getting a lot of federal money and had become a veritable magnet for hangers-on and professional slackers, most of whom seemed to possess severe physical and mental problems of their own. Some limped; some were deaf or blind; some of the women acted like Carol Channing; many exhibited odd twitches and unusual fears; some took acid all the time and barely spoke; some put down Prince Charles as a reference; and most introduced the rights of animals into every classroom discussion.

And what classes they were – each featuring sobbing confessions, shrieking accusations and, finally, firm resolve by everyone to pick up the pieces of shattered psyches and learn to reach out to one another across the abyss of human suffering. All of this occurred before the break. After the break there was a movie. It was during one of these cathartic sessions that I had referred to Dr. Milora as a sexist pig for insisting, while not even attempting to conceal his boner, that a different woman light his cheroot during each class. Being a self-proclaimed liberal he gave me an A for my honesty but had really never forgiven me, especially for exposing him before he had a chance to get one of the ex-nuns in class to fire up his tiparillo. As I sat down next to Bert, the senor vamoosed.

"Okay, tell me what happened New Year's Eve."

Bert sat back on his heels for a moment then hunched forward over the table with his arms. "I thought I finally found someone so I drove back here on December 31st." Before Bert left Crystal City to return home for Christmas vacation he had met an English grad student at the Recreation Center. "It was Saturday night, and she was kind of crying in the TV lounge. She was watching 'WKRP'." He moved swiftly to her side and found a plain, quiet, recently-divorced, unattached, on-the-rebound, shy, depressed and insecure woman. "Just perfect, I figured, after checking for artificial limbs."

There was a time when it seemed that the only women who would go out with Bert had artificial limbs or floating knee caps or were nearly bald. But this one seemed whole. He sympathized with her during "WKRP," got a little better feel for her near the end of "Flo," courted her in his own boyish way during "Love Boat," and – in the middle of "Fantasy Island" – asked her what she was doing during the holidays.

"She goes, 'I don't have any plans over the holidays. I won't be doing anything or going anywhere. I probably won't even leave my apartment.' I say 'Maybe I'll run into you sometime or give you a call.' I was playing it cool. She goes, 'Okay, have a nice time.' I'm thinking it's fate. Here I was ready to write off the year and – boom. I was in a good mood for a change over Christmas and figured why don't I drive back and spend New Year's Eve with her. She said she wasn't doing anything. She said it was all right to call. She said so right when Tattoo was doing the hula with Charo. I got back to Crystal City around five o'clock that afternoon and called her, introduced myself with a Russian accent and asked her if she was free that night."

"What did she say?"

He paused and his whole frame sagged. "She said she had a lot of studying to do, plus it was that time of the month."

Blasted by this pair of excuses, Bert retreated, Visa Card in hand, to the Oriental Sauna to wring in the New Year. Actually, he had already made this particular journey to the East around 30 times since June, hurling himself into serious debt.

"It's no big deal, though." He pushed himself away from the table and folded his hands behind his neck, flapping his elbows freely. "Besides, she had this funny lisp when she talked." He moved his chair closer to the table and smoothed down his hair. "Did I ever tell you my Martina Navratilova story?" One night in Cleveland Bert had decided to take a shot at Martina, who was playing for the Cleveland Nets' pro tennis team. He figured that he wasn't the handsomest guy in the world, but maybe she'd like him because she wouldn't have to worry about pretty girls stealing him away. "Anyway," he sagely pointed out, "she's no trip to Hollywood herself."

She was also Eastern European, probably lonely and they both were a little on the chunky side. He could look after her, show her the ropes, be unaffected by her fame and wealth – after all, he had a few credentials of his own. Sure, their careers would sometimes conflict, but the bond could overcome the differences. They could work it out. Of course he had heard the rumors about her bisexuality but wasn't convinced at all. He knew they didn't have that kind of stuff in the Old Country.

"I finally got up the courage to trail her after one of her Sunday night matches. I even had my binoculars with me."

"What happened?"

"My Pinto couldn't keep up with her Corvette," he said while rubbernecking a rather husky woman talking to a German prof by a water fountain. "I love those athletic-looking girls." He rose from the table and began to approach the stout woman – now bent over, drinking – but stopped as if hitting a brick wall and quickly sat back down when she limped away adjusting a knee brace.

Bert shook his head and contorted his mouth as if he were getting rid of a bad taste in it, before confiding that, sure, there were women who were mesmerized by him, who were ready for romance, who were dying to get a call from him. But they hung out in bars or smoked cigarettes or were nothing like his ideal of a blond, Slovenian girl who spoke French and played golf.

"Karen Carpenter would be perfect too," he conceded as he checked his watch. He had a busy afternoon scheduled. First, he had to go to the travel bureau and set up an internship doing volunteer work in airline ticket writing. He was constantly trying to get a job on the airlines, in order to meet stewardesses, but was always turned down because he was overweight. Then, at six, he had a rendezvous to play racquetball with the only girl who had warmed up to him in Crystal City. Unfortunately, she was engaged to a guy who was six-five and lifted weights regularly.

As Bert was talking about his plans to use his travel bureau experience to get a job in the theater world of Europe, two Russian exchange students walked by. One of the reasons Bert had returned to campus was the Russian Exchange Program that had just been started at CCU. He leaped to his feet and exploded with an outburst of Russian. The women smiled and kept walking, giggling at a tight-jeaned frat boy a few feet in front of them. Bert sat down and put the Czar Nicholas coins back in his pocket. He had bought them specifically to show to the Russian women who were invading campus that quarter.

"If I don't get some dates pretty soon," he said, accordioning his fingers nervously on the table. "I won't have a chance to use my formula." His date that afternoon didn't count. She was engaged.

His formula was to take a girl out for racquetball or golf and afterwards pizza. If a lull in the conversation would occur, he had three surefire topics to discuss. Medical advances in the area of aging; U.F.O.'s; and Hootenannies. The latter's particularly short-lived era was Bert's favorite cultural time period, and he loved to relive it over a pizza. Following the conversation it was back to his sin bin, where he might even produce his guitar and croon a Lettermen or Chad Mitchell Trio medley.

Unfortunately, for courting purposes, the women on campus in the early '80s were not only not interested in him but, for the most part, looked at him in total disbelief, even before he mentioned Hootenannies. The result, thus far, was in Bert's own words, "Eleven stand-ups. And that doesn't even count cancellations."

Bert went up to the serving line and returned with a can of Tab. A group of sorority pledges clattered by. "Look at the girls around here," he said, sitting down and yanking at the pop-top. "I don't believe I can't get laid."

"When was the last time?"

Bert spoke wistfully of a romance that spanned the latter part of the Watergate era. She was a waitress at Long John Silver's. They dated for over a year, but it ended somewhat prematurely while she was giving him a blow job. Bert came in her mouth. They were never the same again.

"I guess what really pissed her off," he intimated sheepishly between sucks on his Tab, "was that I hadn't been able to get it up for a month before that, and then – Wham."

He knew it was over when in an attempt to make amends he bought her a scarf at Uncle Bill's Discount Store, the kind the Pirate Girl used to wear on "Treasure Hunt," only to have her hurl it back at him and say she was breaking it off in order to find someone who could at least get her clit warm.

"How on earth was I supposed to know what a clit was?" Bert whispered.

Shattered, he refused to date for a long time and when he started to try again, he couldn't get anyone to go out. Finally sensing that he must not understand women he tried to learn about them. He read books on the feminine mystique, pored over Cosmopolitan and Redbook, watched the "Phil Donahue Show," and cruised cosmetic counters in department stores. He went so far as to go through the express line at Krogers six or seven times a day, rubbing elbows with women, watching what they bought, grabbing the National Enquirer or Reader's Digest and anything to do with Elvis or Liz or Jackie O. He even purchased some tampons.

"I thought I might get some idea about the clit from them, but no dice."

It was then that he became obsessed with credentials, something to impress the gals with. True, he had Berlitz accreditation in four languages. But of his six degrees, five were associate degrees from Kosciusco Community College in Cleveland; his golf pro certificate was from a retirement resort in Arkansas; his brown belt in karate was from a Universal Life Church type place – he had to check a box promising to practice six hours a day for six months – and his pilot's license was coin-extracted from a Cedar Point Amusement Park machine.

"I guess I always wanted to be James Bond or something," he laughed.

Just then Scott Nelson appeared, briefcase in hand. He was wearing a new London Fog raincoat. His black, feathered fedora was tilted slightly. He nodded, sat down, opened his briefcase, took out a notebook and jotted down some notes. Although he was now living in Toledo, Scott rode the commuter bus to Crystal City each day. He had been a student his entire life and, unlike Bert, his credentials were quite legitimate. He had two Master's degrees, one in mathematics, the other in philosophy, had done extensive work in computers and had, of course, found time to study with the Maharishi, both in Switzerland and in Iowa.

I hadn't spoken to him since I told him about the grandmother and Judy but had received his Christmas card requesting that I not inquire about the Maharishi since the new year would find him devoting less time to worrying about the Maharishi and more time to job interviews and advancing his own work.

"How's your job going, Scott?" I asked.

"Unfortunately, it keeps my mind off my work," he sighed, removing his raincoat, and revealing a smart black blazer, an open-neck blue shirt and medium grey pants.

Scott's job was to abstract books and magazine articles for Crystal City University's "Philosophy Journal." During 1980 alone he had read nearly 2,000 pieces on philosophy from the ancients to the contemporaries. He saw threads everywhere, many of which he could apply to his life's work, to combine the philosophy of Immanuel Kant with computers and the principles of the Transcendental Meditation in order to develop a central nervous system for the world.

"Did you have a job interview this week?"

He slowly nodded his head. "I think I blew the guy away."

Scott had signed up for an interview with Bell Labs. They were looking for graduating seniors interested in technical writing. "The interviewer asked me what someone with my background had to offer Bell Labs." Scott flicked a piece of lint from his cuff. "I told him I was glad he asked that question and traced my intellectual lineage back from Milton Friedman to Adam Smith, brought in the Kant connection and speculated that even Hegel would argue that I would be of more value in the private sector."

"You didn't," I said. "What did this guy say?"

"Well, he seemed quite impressed, but when I called Bell this morning to follow up, I found out that there were no records at all of my interview."

Scott's job pursuits had again proved fruitless, so he once more found himself scanning the Union, as he did most days, for women with whom he could engage in polite conversation. This was where he was most at home and at his best; gently squeezing and kissing the hands of foreign students; waxing philosophical and poetic with women from the humanities; offering to go for coffee, perhaps even spring for lunch with his meal coupons; commenting on the decor of this or that; and eventually complimenting a lady on her choice of rouge or, especially, heels. In the proper mood Scott could work a crowd in the Union or at a party like no one else. Smallish in stature, greying – yet boyishly handsome – with well-chiseled features, always maintaining a philosophical soft presence; briefcase and notebook in hand, working mathematical equations with initials, developing digital mantras with area codes, he could, without working up a sweat, extract anywhere from five to fifteen phone numbers a day. That morning, however, he seemed in a reflective mood.

"How did you spend New Year's Eve?" I asked.

His eyes glowed. "I was in Columbus, just leaning back thinking about that killer from a couple years ago."

"Which one was that?" Bert inched closer to the table.

"At 16 she managed a 2,500 unit apartment complex. She was a real powerhouse and a homecoming queen."

On their first date Scott got down on his knees in front of her while she pulled her skirt up and her rich-bitch panties down to mid-thigh. "She pulled my head close to her pussy and kept clicking her brown spiked heels and swiveling the chair just enough to rock my nose in pursuit."

A compromising position? Certainly, but how he loved her then, licking her hose, whiffing her mobile muff.

"Then there was that time during Hell Week when she seduced me in Harshman Quadrangle on the cold linoleum floor," he shuddered, smiling.

She was a Chi Omega, proper, tall. Scott was particularly enamored of tall women. She told him "I want to get on top of you and go crazy," pushed him down and worked him over among the perfumed stationery, pastel-colored toilet baskets, Greek beer mugs, carefully discarded sanitary napkins, pictures of beefy boys back home, "Today is the first day of the rest of your life" posters, unlimited checkbooks with seaside designs and the imminent arrival of her roommate, the Boomer.

"She was my little cobra then," he sighed wistfully. "But she ended up brutalizing me. I would call her house and her mother would answer and tell me that Randi said she never wanted to see my wrinkled brow again. She actually used the word wrinkled." Scott shivered at the memory. "I wore a gold wedding ring, third finger right hand, to remind me of what she did to me. I finally took it off New Year's Eve."

"In other words you just spent the night thinking about her," I said.

"No, after I took the ring off I was holding it up to my flying saucer lamp when the phone rang."

It was Sara, a tall redheaded Leo whom Scott had met at the same party where he had met the killer Chi O. He hadn't seen Sara since then, but she asked him if he was doing anything. When he said he wasn't, she offered to stop over for a few drinks to celebrate the New Year.

"When she arrived she insisted on putting on the Columbus soul radio station." He shut his eyes and swayed rhythmically in his seat. "A Barry White song was grinding in the background. I was reclining on the couch wearing my father's grey smoking jacket and maintaining a soft presence." As he continued the tale Scott leaned back and folded his hands on his flat stomach. " She was sitting on the floor. Her hand and face were near my crotch. I took her hand and moved it towards my lap."

That was all he'd had to do. She peeled off his clothes first, then hers. Then she jumped right on top of him. Scott was astounded. "In my experience I knew that most women didn't go right on top, they'd wait a time or two before assuming their, uh, proper position."

When she climbed on top, Scott explained, she actually jumped straight on his cock, hitting it right on the nose and rode him for awhile. He knew he would never see her again. It didn't matter.

"It was both mystical and primal," he explained, the memory giving him a dreamy look. "And, just as importantly, it re-affirmed to me that there's definitely more than one way to receive a message. And more than one person that can send it."

"That's a whole lot more exciting New Year's than I had," a somewhat awed Bert interjected. "I ended up jacking off at the Oriental Sauna. I can't figure out why I can't get a woman."

Sensing that Bert needed advice, Scott decided to share some insights gleaned from his own past. Scott explained how during the late '60s he had lived with three different women but never came close to making it legal, simply because he wasn't spiritually satisfied in these relationships and didn't have the confidence to pursue the women he was really attracted to.

"I was involved in perpetual cheating," he said, tapping a pencil on his notebook. "Not because I had a basically deceitful nature but because, in my relationships, I was dealing from weakness and insecurity."

Scott gaze rested on a woman in the food line and he quickly excused himself. Bert's hand was moving slowly across his face. He was clearly bewildered. He had just met Scott the summer before and really didn't know too much about him or his world. I filled in some of the details of Scott's past for him.

In 1971, Scott had flipped out on acid. It had something to do with a fear that somehow all the vaginas of the world would shrink, and he would, despite his modest penal dimensions, be unable to enter any woman. He began seeing various counselors, explaining to them that his earliest and most persistent sexual fantasy was that he was so small that he could easily insert his entire body into a woman's womb. Near the end of his therapy, he even owned up that the only parts of a woman's body he'd ever been able to consistently relate to were from the knees down. The counselors couldn't help him as he neared total collapse.

It was then that he embraced the culture of the East, getting heavily involved in TM, studying and instructing at the Maharishi International University in Iowa, then to Europe, then to San Francisco, before finally heading back to Crystal City in '78, to immerse himself in the study of philosophy, mathematics and computers. He returned as a man with a vision.

"Holy shitski," Bert said.

Scott re-appeared with a tall woman in a drab brown skirt, plain cotton sweater and old-fashioned heels. He helped her into her chair, perfunctorily introduced her to Bert and me, then fished into his briefcase and produced a page from his thesis.

"This is what I wanted to show you, Doris," he began excitedly. "I'll read you the key parts. Thesis: To provide a unified data processing and communication network for the world. Antithesis: To avoid any anti-Utopian situations of Orwell's '1984'." Scott's hand was gently glazing over the sheet, which had been heavily marked with red ink. "Syntheses: To construct a privacy respecting, unified data processing network as the world's central nervous system. That's it."

Doris stared at the sheet for a few moments before finally speaking. "When do you expect to finish this?"

"Probably not in this lifetime, but I do hope to have the first chapter, which will lay the groundwork for the project, completed this year. You know, 1981 is the 200th anniversary of the publication of Kant's 'Critique of Pure Reason,' western philosophy's magnum opus."

Doris said that she wasn't quite aware of that, then got up to get a napkin from the food line. Scott's glance lingered on her as she walked away, then he turned to me, his sky blue eyes crinkling, and spoke excitedly. "She works in the voc ed research program. She reads Greek on her lunch break. She had two years of it. She's blowing away the Ph.D.'s she's working with. Jesus, I've got to learn Greek."

Doris returned with Scott's eyes riveted on her shoes.

"If you were with me," he said, leaning close to her as she spooned at her yogurt cup, "I'd insist you wear those heels."

"All the time," she teased.

"Only in bed," he countered, a smile creasing the corner of his mouth. "That's when I think the woman should be on top, where she belongs."

Doris gulped and the yogurt squirted down her chin.

"Scott, you're awful," she punched at his shoulder, then wiped her mouth.

Scott sat, a bad boy, blushing, then quoted Francis Bacon. "Mother Nature is commanded by obeying her." While she busily finished her yogurt, Scott rambled on using words like undercoat and buttressed; he spoke of relaxed animation and limpid timbre before concluding by saying, "I really enjoy being with a woman I can look up to."

"You're a breath of fresh air," Doris said and got up to leave. "Why don't you give me a call at the office next week?"

Scott stood as she left, then sat down and sighed. "Two years of Greek. You don't know how that excites me."

Bert's mouth had been agape during most of Scott's conversation and he had taken on the glazed look of someone who had been hypnotized during a Las Vegas lounge act. He finally came to, shook out the cobwebs, groggily checked his watch and realized he was already a few minutes late for his travel bureau appointment.

"I've got to get back to the Doc Center," Scott said, folding some papers into his briefcase. "I'm abstracting Dane Rudyar's 'Planetization of Consciousness.' He's got some interesting theories about Adam and Eve."

Bert and I agreed to meet at Jensen's later. I wanted to see what happened on his racquetball rendezvous. Scott would be much too busy that evening to join us.

***

With a few hours to kill I drifted around campus for a while then decided to drive around town, which didn't take long because Crystal City is a tiny community-just a couple dozen blocks-tucked away in conservative Northwest Ohio's farm land. The university dwarfs the town and in the late '60s/early '70s it served as a cozy, Oz-like home for so many of us, with politics and youth and magic and exploding ideas everywhere. Though 50 percent of the students come from Cleveland or Toledo there are literally people in Crystal City from all over the world. Because of the size of the place you could really get to know everyone, almost as if they were under a microscope. We all stuck out of the horizon of the flat land like Easter Island totems. Everyone was famous in Crystal City.

After doing a quick lap around the town, I pulled my car into the parking lot that was built when Manville House, strike headquarters during the Kent State massacre days, was torn down in the late '70s. A retired, shaggy-haired political science professor was walking aimlessly among the meters and directed me to a space that was close to where the living room had been of that legendary political house, which is where I had first met Lana.

It was April of 1970 and Lana was lounging on the beat-up purple velvet couch, drinking herbal tea and eating cinnamon toast. "Fire and Rain" was on the stereo and Far Out, the orange and white house cat was curled up next to her. She was wearing a rust-colored down vest that she had brought back from Colorado. It was the first time I had seen one. "It's real toasty, " she said, wriggling her shoulders. "You should get one, it'd look just outrageous on you."

A group of us left that day for a rally in Washington – marking the 50th anniversary of Women's Suffrage – where Gloria Steinem carried a picture of the My Lai Massacre with the caption, "An Example of the Masculine Mystique." On the way back Lana fell asleep with her head nuzzled on my shoulder. Occasionally she would half open her eyes, smile through a stretch and moan ever-so-softly.

A few days later Lana headed back to the Rockies and that summer I moved into Manville House for a few mind-boggling years. During that time William Kuntsler slept there overnight. So did Abbie Hoffman and Jerry Rubin. Right down the street was the House of Joy, the women's political headquarters. The doors on both houses were always open. There was a constant parade of brothers and sisters in and out back then. No one had a lease at Manville house. Guys slept in their cars in the driveway, pitched tents in the yard and crashed all over the living room and kitchen.

There were gimpy-legged Marxist guys who were constantly presenting local grocery stores with lists of non-negotiable food demands; beyond Zen kind of guys who claimed to have never stepped into the same river once; any-spare-change guys who said things like, "Show me a dog with a wallet and I'll show you an animal lover"; guys who had lived in a cave in Utah and spent most of their waking hours trying to convince everyone that Walt Disney would live forever and rule the universe from underneath Disney World; large-dicked, dope-dealing guys who looked like Fritz the Cat and sold Oxydol for $5 a hit, claiming it could re-connect you with your ancestors; hefty, bib overall-wearing guys who insisted that if you gave a feminist a credit card and an orgasm she'd leave the movement; glaring Jesus Freak guys who rode around on Harley Lambs of Steel and perpetually asked women if they knew the difference between being touched and felt; and frail, stringy-haired guys with bulging Adam's apples who explained away each suicide attempt with the words unrequited love.

Getting out of my car and buttoning up for my two-block walk to Jensen's I had to admit to myself that as crazy a place as it was I never really felt as connected to things as I did when I lived at Manville House, and that I should have left town when, almost simultaneously, it was torn down and things began to sour between Lana and me. Yeah, I should have left when they turned it into a parking lot. Even my old friend the professor emeritus – who was now arguing with himself on the sidewalk – would probably find himself in agreement with that.

***

Jensen's was the typical college town over-21, fake elegant place – decent food, good-looking waitresses, a casual atmosphere and a secluded back bar where the braying coaching staffs of area high schools would gather. A winding stairwell led to a party room upstairs. Everywhere

– the doors, the walls, the planters – there was the garish coat-of-arms of the Jensen family.

Wading through the bar crowd of familiar faces it felt like yet another typical revolving door night at the circus in Crystal City, with images jumping out at you, fun house style, flashing your life past your eyes every few minutes or so. Distorted mirrors and tinny, canned laughter.

As I moved through the bar's swinging doors, I spotted Bert and Frank at a corner booth in the dining room. Frank was bundled in a red, white and blue jacket and a Pierre Cardin scarf, a gift from his father. Bert appeared crestfallen.

"How did the rendezvous go?" I asked Bert, sitting down next to him.

"A disaster," he muttered, tumbling a salt shaker in his hand. "I had everything set up but it backfired."

"What happened?"

"I got her into the locker room and kidded about both of us taking our pants off. She says, 'Oh Bert, you're so strange' and I thought hey, that's a good answer so I say, 'Close your eyes and don't peek,' and I whipped my clothes off and stood there for at least three minutes. I couldn't believe it, she didn't peek, no curiosity at all. Finally I told her it was okay to peek, and as she opened her eyes I put the towel over my face and just stood there hoping for the best. I could hear her walking out. I don't know. I've tried everything with women. I don't know what they want." Bert's usually cheery countenance had taken a decided downturn.

A blood vessel throbbed on Frank's neck. Bert's approach to women had always enraged him, but he also knew that Bert had not evolved to his level of healing celibacy and was still living in bad faith as far as women went. Convinced that we all must crawl before we can walk and that when the student is ready the teacher arrives, Frank opted to present Bert with a common sense perspective and some practical guidance on a level Bert could handle.

"You haven't come to grips with being your own mother," Frank began loudly, hacking between words, then lowered his voice to a whisper as a nearby waitress dropped a dish. "That's why you were incapable of communicating your feelings. Look, women want communication, emotions, soulful looks in the eyes. You had the towel over your face. She probably didn't know what to do."

"Well, she could have grabbed my dick instead of walking out," Bert snapped.

Proving that we all preach our own struggle, I chimed in with some advice, telling him it was doomed to get involved in a deceitful situation with an engaged woman. "Also you need to pay attention to some of the intermediate steps between saying hello and taking your clothes off."

"Ah, you're probably right." Bert settled back in the booth and appeared resigned to his fate of being at the mercy of un-compliant women. "It's not that important, but if I don't make a move like that they just play games with me."

"Standing there naked with that towel over your eyes is just letting the mother dominate you," Frank said testily, momentarily abandoning his role as serene sage. "You are powerless, unable to see her reaction, hoping only for her approval of your pee pee. Toweled in womb darkness. Totally defenseless."

"Look, all I wanted to do was play with her tits or something. You guys are getting carried away. I'm fed up with everything."

Sensing Bert's growing frustration Frank patiently returned to square one. "It all comes back to becoming your own mother. If you can pull that one off, then you don't have to worry about the woman taking too much power, and you don't end up on the short end of that dyadic experience."

"I don't know," Bert countered weakly, "at this point I'm just trying to get laid."

Frank cleared his throat and patiently proceeded. "Once you get this mother thing straightened out with a woman, then you can both grow as individuals and the sexual relationship that comes out of this can be free from games and maybe even guilt."

Bert looked lost.

"Don't be too eager," I said, then quoted a line I had heard Caine say on a recent "Kung Fu" show. "As you seek you push away, so simply allow things to flow."

Bert weighed this wisdom with a squint then summoned our waitress. "Give me a couple sausage sandwiches without the bread and a rum and Tab." As she walked away he looked her up and down, sighed and shrugged his shoulders. "I've been trying to get laid for six years. I've tried to get them into the Jacuzzi, into games of strip racquetball. I've offered them massages. I've used my flash paddle" (a paddle he has in his car with phrases like, "You're cute," "Do you want to party?" and, "How 'bout a date?" that he uses while driving or at a stop sign). "I give up."

"You can only get it once you give it up." I said, paraphrasing Caine.

"That sounds great," Bert shouted, jerked his arm and knocked over his pink can of Tab.

"It's also a matter of credibility," I cautioned, mopping Bert's spill with my napkin. "When women see you alone all the time, they think you're weird. It takes women to get women. That's why married men are successful. A woman has them. They are desirable, safe. If you're alone all the time you get a reputation, and you can't get a date. It's a vicious circle."

We all grew quiet for a few minutes, the convoluted-ness of the evening's subject matter rendering us mercifully mute. The waitress brought over Bert's food. He picked at his breadless sandwich and studied it intently before taking a bite.

While Bert chewed Frank slowly tried to tie the whole thing together. "If you develop your own mother, then the completeness you'll feel will set off good vibes and make you appear to be satisfied in a relationship which, in a sense, you are. Women will be attracted to you, not threatened by you. Mom and dad together are never really threatening, you know they will balance." Frank scratched vigorously at the back of his hand as Bert nodded his head in dull agreement. "Ask her out, after all, what could be safer than having mom along as a chaperone? Women sense this intuitively and, since most women have come to grips with their own mothers, one reason why they have an edge over men, the four of you can go out. The mothers have each other to talk to, and you're left alone with her. If she's father deficient you can easily slip into that. If she doesn't need a father you can let the old man go fishing and since, at that point, you've finally got it reduced to an essential animal level, you can get down to some monkey business – if you're so inclined."

"Yeah, monkey business!" Bert squealed and waved his arms. He ordered a hard-boiled egg in Russian, showed the waitress a coin magic trick and eagerly asked her to play racquetball with his mother and he the next day. She said she would love to. Some other time.

Frank leaned toward Bert and cupped his hand to his mouth. "It won't work with her. She's an orphan."

"What's the use," Bert winced and pulled out his Visa Card. "I think I'll head up to the Little Red House and get their oil bath special."

"I'm going to turn in early," Frank said, stretching his arms and yawning. "I got that nursing home job and Monday's my first day. I need to rest up this weekend."

I decided to stroll to the Club.

***

The Club was two blocks from Jensen's. These two joints were the poles of the downtown strip. Jensen's catered primarily to the townsfolk who were over 21 and wanted to drink and dine in comfort. The Club was a legendary bohemian place. People who had been all over the country, including San Francisco, would say, "I've never seen any place like the Club." The Jensen family owned both places and two or three other watering holes in town. The only other people who seemed to own anything in Crystal City were ex-drug dealers gone semi-legit.

As I began my walk down Main Street I stared at the Jordache-jeaned model in Macy's front window. She was always good for some eye contact. I glanced at my reflection in the window of the Parrot and Peacock, one of the newer bars in town. I had only stopped in the place a couple times. With its high ceilings and half-filled happy hours it struck me as the downstairs of a whorehouse. The cocktail waitresses were mostly poetry grad students and 30ish divorcees. The word was that most of the women who hung out there were not cheap, but certainly reasonable. It looked like the kind of place where people should rise from their own ashes.

"Gumball Rally" and "Slumber Party Massacre" were showing at the town's original movie theater, the Cla-Zel, named for Clarence and Zelda, Jensen family cousins. Acne-faced guys in Crystal City Cougar High School jackets milled around with 15 and 16-year-old girls that they had absolutely no right to be with. Lots of pickup trucks and Jeep Broncos cruised the streets, horns blaring. Just as I was carefully maneuvering across the now dangerous four corners main intersection, a fraternity fire truck roared by with a guy hanging out the window sporting a huge fire hat. The hat signified that the wearer's penis was the largest one in his house. It was common knowledge. Even the dimmest sorority babes knew about it.

Unimpressed, I moved along. An old townie walked by searching for the money, so the story went, that he had lost 30 years earlier. The loss had ruined his life. He was still looking, though. His Ben Hogan hat and his tobacco-stained, now wrinkled face, crept through the streets, darting glances from curb to curb, hiding his face from passersby. I wanted to say something to him, tell him to stop looking – that the search was futile, just like mine had been along this same path so many nights in pursuit of Lana's footsteps. But before I could speak I was jostled by a quartet of freshman girls singing "Love Stinks."

Regaining my balance I passed the Downtown Bar and its upstairs adjunct, the Uptown – a newly-opened, disco-type place. The Downtown was a small bar, owned by the Jensens, that had undergone quite a revival since the Ross Hotel burned down. The Ross had been the flophouse in town, but few people knew that it was funded by the Mental Health Board to be used as a halfway house for county residents who had been released from the Toledo State Hospital but had no immediate family to live with. Everyone from miles around who had been released from local nuthouses and had no place to go ended up at the Ross and could usually be found drinking in its surreal Tiffany Lounge. The Ross had burned in December of '79, and the residents, while scattered all over town, were reunited almost daily at the Downtown to howl and drink with the local Hispanic population.

"Live Music Tonite" read the sign in front of the Club. There never used to be music, except for local jammers who would play for free during university vacation breaks when business was slow. There were no happy hours or drink specials. The Club never used to advertise, it merely relied on its reputation that spanned two decades and began when it was just a small neighborhood bar across the street, on the spot where the Wood County Library stands.

Ah, the Old Club." Cramped booths, multi-level creaking floors, a back bar that shotgunned into a mysterious, dark room. An alleged Cherokee Indian, Dirty George, dwelled upstairs. "Scotch and Soda" by the Kingston Trio was on the jukebox. It meant something then. As long as there would be a Club, that song would be on the box. Poets who ran with Kerouac played in jug bands there. Reek the Freak ate urinal cakes and shit in girls' purses when they went to the ladies' room. Sprayman brought in stag movies from Cleveland for Sunday afternoon showings. Dave, the squat, nearsighted manager of the Club, threw wild after-hours parties at his farm house, where the guests shot up cars and fucked right on the hardwood floor. Rumor had it that an assistant manager burrowed a tiny hole through the ceiling of the women's john. Lots of girls knew about it, some even got off on it. Hawkeye drummed interminably on tables and belched out Coasters' songs there. Narcs had the shit beat out of them outside, while "Maggie Mae" played inside. Townies mingled with college kids and argued about Vietnam.

The last night of the "Old Club" was January 20, 1973, Nixon's second Inaugural. The regulars tore the place apart board by board, fixture by fixture. Some took souvenirs home, cushions from the booths, toilet seats, pieces from the bar. Many wept openly and unashamedly, vowing never to set foot in the new place across the street.

"How's it going, Ray?" asked Harry, the short, balding manager of the new Club, as he greeted me at the door. He had put it in his time at the old place, but disdained any kind of nostalgic discussions, preferring instead the pleasures of today. Once featured in a documentary about servicemen of the '60s who were against the war, Harry had changed since his protesting days and was now into outlaw music and employed bikers as bouncers. Harry smiled away his old protest days. "You can't fill your nose with slogans," he would say while stroking his chin and listening to Waylon and Willie on the box.

A band from Toledo called The Greatest was playing.

"Are they any good?" I asked.

"They're better than their name," hyped Harry.

Business was dipping a little and the place was getting rough. To maintain order Harry had hired, along with the bikers, a couple wild-eyed vanquished Ross Hotel dwellers to work the door. Several of his employees looked like lupine country and western singers. With Harry's staff creating tension, the college students were starting to stay away. Its reputation, earned mostly in the '60s, was no longer carrying it, but the Club was doing well enough, although Harry now had to advertise a little, have some drink specials and occasionally bring in live music during the middle of the week. The one-dollar cover charge idea that he had been toying with was for now out of the question.

Ducking through the door, I made a quick left – past a group of clucking freshmen girls with glistening braces who were squeezed together at a picnic table like baby chicks in an incubator – and headed for the corner of the bar referred to by the undergraduates as the geriatric ward. I looked at the old-timers huddled around me and interspaced along the bar and was thunder-bolted by thoughts of the last few tortuous years, especially when that lesbian contingent began to assert itself with Lana right there in the middle of it.

With "It's a Heartache" or "Dust in the Wind" playing in the background, she would dance with members of the women's softball teams that steamed it up at the Club during the torchy and weird summers of '78 and '79. Lana wore terry-cloth shorts, drank Mai-Tais and danced slowly on the tables, all under the watchful eye of her doubleplay partner, Carol. Most of the time I avoided these scenes. The women would congregate on Thursday night, women's softball night in Crystal City. Lana would get loose and sometimes, so the stories went, she would practically play with herself while bumping and grinding alone near the pool table. Carol would angrily yank at her if too many men were watching. God only knows what went on went on in the girls' john. One rumor had enema pictures being posed for. Guys who were good dancers were sometimes allowed in to watch.

When I asked Lana about this wildness she would neither confirm nor deny, saying instead, "If you would ever bother getting out of your room and showing up at the Club, maybe I wouldn't get involved in that craziness." I had to admit a certain culpability due to the undeniable fact that, rather than venturing out to face her, I chose instead to spend those nights just like I did as a ten year-old: my mother would be late getting home from work and I, faintly suspicious something was up, would be sequestered in my room, heart pounding while I listened for car sounds in the driveway; or would venture out into the empty living room in hunched anticipation of headlights illuminating the Venetian blinds, hoping and praying she would show and when she did I would lie awake for hours, trying in vain to assure myself there'd be no more nights like this.

Dylan's "Tangled Up in Blue" snapped me out of my vivid flashback.

"How you doin' there, big boy?" Bonnie the barmaid chirped, looking sassy in newly-permed curly red hair.

"Just fine there, gorgeous," I smiled as she moved away to serve some customers.

In my four-year affair with Lana, Bonnie was the only other woman I had made out with. Lana and Carol had gone to Kentucky. While she was gone I met Bonnie, and we ended up parked in her driveway necking in my Vega. Then, my thoughts were on Lana, while hers were, more than likely, on her droopy-mustached, married sculptor pal. He was from Canada, which seemed to get him laid a lot. Bonnie saw him once a week, a little more often than I was seeing Lana. There just wasn't room in our lives for each other.

Bonnie was too busy to talk so I moved towards the back room and saw Karen Collins, a saucer-eyed brunette with a pixie hair cut, standing near the popcorn machine talking to a young guy in a Boston Bruin hockey shirt. Karen was born and raised in Crystal City and had gone with the same guy since high school. They made it legal in '74. She had had her share of flings but seemed content to stay with her hubby, who managed the local International Harvester outlet.

"Hi Karen, what are you billing yourself as tonight?" I asked in reference to the recent tendency of the married women in town to go either by their married name, their maiden name, or some other symbolic name – depending upon where their head was at. Apparently they reasoned it was easier than taking a ring on and off.

"Oh, tonight I'm just Karen," she said, pushing away the tickling hand of the youthful Bruin and gathering up her purse. "I've had a rough week, but tomorrow night I'm thinking Wonder Lust or Strawberry Moon, maybe both. I'll have to sleep on it."

"Last call" rang through the Club. "We don't give a fuck where you go, but you can't stay here," yelled a pony-tailed bartender wearing long earrings and a police badge. The lights came on as college kids streamed by me. Younger sisters of women I was six years older than 10 years ago passed. Girls I had coached as sixth graders when I worked for the recreation department wobbled past. A Ponderosa waitress was being escorted out the door by a black guy who had come to Crystal City in the late '60s, studied sociology, and spent most of the '70s arguing that the killings at Jackson State were more significant than those at Kent.

Outside a friend of mine was sitting on a bench, shivering, while waiting for a woman to get off work from the pizza place across the street. He had recently purchased a head shop in town. An ex-state shot put champion, he had been married for ten years before he and his wife grew apart when he got into pot in '77. In '78 he got into the Beatles and in '79 the Moody Blues, and on his first acid trip went to the Toledo Sports Arena to watch the Northwest Ohio Tough Guy Contest.

"You're out a little late, Chuck, what's going on?"

"Well, I took a couple of 'ludes, turned on the video cassette and sat down to watch some porno flicks with Betty," he began, obviously perturbed. "She didn't want any part of it. I mean, if Linda Lovelace taking in twelve inches or a chick getting tied up and a gun held on her while four black guys fuck her doesn't loosen my wife up, I don't know what will. I mean, Jesus Christ." He shook his head slowly. "Now I'm waiting for Lisa to get off work. She's 19. I told her I might give her a job in the head shop this summer." He paused, thinking hard, still trying to piece together the puzzle of his marriage. "You know, maybe if I get a flick with a woman and a dog or something. I've heard that even some really conservative chicks get off on that."

I told him I was no expert on matters such as that and moved down the street, opting to take the back route to my car. Undergraduate women were hitching back to their dorms. It used to be that guys would pick them up, act unthreatening and hope for a blow job. Two black women whistled at me from their sorority house, near the remnants of the Ross Hotel. An ex-girlfriend of sorts, two dates then she announced her engagement to the guy back home, walked her German shepherd near three high school girls who were talking like "Dating Game" questioners. A goofy, head-bobbing guy – who had come to Crystal City as the trembling, pimply-faced 13-year-old son of a divorced gay professor and was now the charismatic leader of a reggae band – was walking with four gorgeous women hanging all over him to an after-hours party that was revving up three houses away from one of my old residences.

Crossing the street to avoid having my aloneness accentuated by rubbing elbows with his obvious in-demandness, I veered through a darkened gas station and thought of how much I had isolated myself, while obsessing over Lana, during those last few years in town. Orbiting in the background and frozen on the fringes. Avoiding people and being self-conscious about still being there, still hanging around, yet not knowing how to extract myself.

The courthouse bell struck three as I arrived at the metered and brightly lit lot located in the back of a laundromat and pizza parlor. I got into my car – which was faithfully awaiting me where Manville House had once nobly stood and where, in the spring of 1970, I had seen Lana for the first time – and drove away from Crystal City.

Slipping out under the cover of darkness, in a kind of romantic retreat, I peered into the distance trying to figure out how to move beyond the memory-shadows that haunted me. I didn't see any solution on the horizon that night, but at least I was still looking.

Part Two Initiation

> To live is to feel oneself lost.
> He who accepts this
> Has already begun to find himself
> And instinctively, like the shipwrecked,
> Looks around for something on which to cling.
> — *Kierkegaard*

The Men's Group

"Before Ray gets into the second part of his journey, I need to share," Gary said quietly, his just over five-foot frame seeming to have shrunk appreciably in the week since I had told the separation part of my primal story. "I had a pretty bad slip this week, but thankfully I came out of it, partially because I thought of what happened to Ray's friend."

Gary explained that he was deejaying a wedding reception in Bay Village, a fairly well-to-do Cleveland suburb, when disaster struck. Just as he was beginning his trademark candlelight champagne toast-where he turns down the lights in the hall and has the bridal party hold candles and softly hum "Moon River" as he steps from behind his sound system to deliver a dreamily romantic toast he has specifically composed for the newlyweds – the drunken best man decided to get a laugh at Gary's expense by yelling, "Hey chrome dome, why don't you stand up when you talk."

"Of course I was standing as tall and proud as I always do during that part of the evening," Gary sniffed, tucking his legs up under him on the couch. "Look, I don't have to tell anyone in here that marriage is an antiquated institution that can enslave men just as much as women, but kids deserve a romantic send-off. I can justify that mythically."

Gary's eyes moistened but he brushed off an offered tissue. "I'm sure the guy who made that comment is living in an early stage of denial, but he made me feel, or I allowed him to make me feel, like crawling in a hole. And to make a long story short. . ." Gary stopped abruptly and his eyes searched the room to see if anyone was laughing at his height, "a shame spiral hit me, I packed up my equipment and on the way home my sex addict took over and I rented 'Romancing the Bone,' one of my favorite porno movies."

"This group is about discovery, not recovery," said Dale, who chaired the meeting in Gary's absence and was a leading candidate for the non-leader position. "What did you learn from this experience?"

"Well, I watched it a bunch of times and found myself looking at the guys and getting more and more depressed."

"Because of the size of their penises and their sexual prowess?" I asked.

"No, they all had wavy hair," Gary sighed wearily, stroking his lengthened forehead. "I've long since come to grips with my penis size. In fact I used to joke that my dick was just as big as anyone's but on me it looked bigger." A moist-eyed smile creased across Gary's face. "Anyway, after each time I watched the movie I would stare at my head in the mirror and invariably began to question, not just my baldness, but my whole journey as a man. Was I receptive, sensuous, nurturing, yielding, decisive, initiatory, playful, rational and aggressive? I couldn't answer that question."

Gary's narrow shoulders sagged under the weight of his perceived inadequacies. "Suddenly there was a knock on the door and I froze and all I could think of was that I couldn't be seen in this condition. That I never wanted to be seen again." He breathed deeply and gathered himself up. "Just then I flashed on Ray's friend who blew himself away because he didn't want anyone to see him, and I knew I couldn't allow that to happen to me. At that moment I chose life." Gary nodded his head with slow resolve." By the time I opened the door whoever was there was gone. Who knows, it may have been a spirit-guide. But whomever it was I owe them. I took 'Bone' back and canceled my adult video membership. I think I've finally let go."

"Every letting go entails a transformation, a passing from what was to what will be," Dale said and motioned to the group to congratulate Gary.

One by one the members approached Gary and gave him manly hugs. Dale, adjusting his ever-present backpack, placed a noisy kiss on Gary's forehead. Clearly lump-throated, Gary waved to Dale to get on with the meeting. Dale nodded in my direction.

"You mentioned transformation before, Dale … well getting ready to talk about when this initiation stage of my story took place, I couldn't help think of what a unique time period it was, especially for men."

I then went on to speak about how the late '70s/early '80s was a post free love/pre-AIDS pocket of time when the feminist consciousness was really beginning to touch everyone and the sense of male lost-ness was just on the verge of reaching epidemic proportions. I theorized that men's roles were becoming a mystery and we seemed clueless-and that it was a painfully transitional time when something magical was definitely ending and something very new – a kind of psycho-sexual battleground - was beginning. I concluded by calling it a unique and toxic time when the battling in the so-called sexual revolution was perhaps at its fiercest.

"Bag the overly dramatic socio-political garbage, Ray," Gary snapped, then covered his mouth with his hand before removing it to speak in a strained voice. "I'm sorry Ray, but you remind me of that guy who told me to stand up. He was tall with broad shoulders, a beard and short brown hair. I guess I'm still angry."

"It's not about anger," Dale corrected him in a barely audible voice. "It's about grief."

What Dale told us then was something we all knew but still needed to hear: that while the women's movement was fueled by anger, the men's movement was foundationed with grief; that since as boys we were told not to cry, as men we must weep; and that the path to a manly heart must invariably run through the valley of tears.

"My whole initiation stage was nothing more than a grief-walk from one coffee house to another," Dale said softly in reference to the several years he had spent drifting around after suffering the separation of having his favorite hangout, Grounds For Thought, burn down. Thrust out of his home away from home, he tossed his backpack over his shoulder and began a lengthy search for a coffee house where he could feel that sense of community he had experienced at Grounds.

"I went all over Cleveland looking for a coffee house to settle in. Brewed Awakenings, the Phoenix in Lakewood, Common Grounds, all the Arabicas. I was nothing more than a hollow, frozen man grabbing at straws and mugs." Dale allowed his furrowed brow to relax a bit. "I was nearly paralyzed with grief and the people I met seemed one-dimensional – it's not just women whom we look at as cardboard figures during this stage, it's everybody – because I was incapable of relating to them as complex human beings, so wooden with grief was I." Dale took a moment to silently forgive himself. "But I managed to get through it and learn some important lessons."

What he learned was that he couldn't find the perfect coffee house because there is no such thing and that a coffee house is a state of mind and he had to carry his concept of a coffee house paradise wherever he went.

"Just last night I broke my guitar out in the Englebrook bar by the Ford plant," he said proudly. "During their happy hour I sang 'Dance of Grief' and one of the retired autoworkers requested I sing 'Far, Far Away'." Dale blushed and smiled as if admitting he was finally learning to take himself less seriously. "I told him I'd put the guitar away if he would buy me a cup of coffee. We ended up talking until the Cavs game came on." Dale snapped his head away from the memory and got back to the task at hand. "What I want you to keep in mind through this initiation stage, Ray, is that you've just been separated and you're grieving, confused and very unsure of yourself, in a kind of spiritual wilderness. But that's where you acquire the tools to pass from adolescence, if you will, into true manhood."

"Actually it was just like being a teenager in high school," I said, settling back into the couch's cushions, "I felt awkward, like I was just trying to learn the ropes, especially when it came to dealing with Judy."

Dale removed his backpack and placed it on the floor. "During this stage everything familiar has been taken away as part of the symbolic return to a state of humility and innocence. You are like un-worked clay suited to be molded."

"That's a cool way of looking at it," I said.

"Quite honestly, I can't take credit for that," Dale admitted. "It's something I found in a fortune cookie at the Panda Wok Chinese restaurant in Lakewood. I'm trying to convince them to have a special men's movement night there. Maybe get into some after-dinner weeping." He drew his backpack close to his leg. "Now tell us about your journey into the wild."

"I don't know how wild it was, but there were some pretty ornery animals around at the beginning."

The Donkey Basketball Game

"What's long and sleek and full of semen?" asked Mr. Zielinski, a stumpy Civics teacher. No one answered. "A submarine full of sailors," he said, opening his checkered sport coat to reveal a colorless sansabelt curled beneath his belly.

I sat pinned in the corner of the teachers' lounge near the Coke machine and tried hard not to listen to the conversation of the staff members. Aside from the usual adolescent humor, vilification of the students and thinly veiled self-loathing for having chosen teaching as a career, bizarre politics dominated the morning discussion – especially the Iranian hostage situation.

"George Wallace had the right idea," Mrs. Lany, a three-fingered science teacher said in reference to a newspaper story about demonstrators opposing the United States policy towards Iran. "Love it or leave it."

"Well, underlying his simplistic rhetoric was the very valid principle of states' rights." Mr. Raintree, the gaunt business law teacher, argued in between puffs on his non-tobacco cigarette. "No one can dismiss that." He shot a quick look at me. I had not been directly invited into political discussions since Raintree asked me, about a week after the election, what I thought of Reagan running the country and I told him it made me wonder where Lee Harvey Oswald was when we needed him.

"We shouldn't give the Iranians a penny," chimed in Mrs. White, a brassy, dishwater-blond math teacher who smoked a pipe and whose recent marriage to a timid black man seemed to have somehow elevated her to the status of expert on all things noteworthy.

"Ve shud haf sent all de Iranians back de first day it happened," said Mr. Jenkin, a post-Nazi Germany immigrant who taught American History and bore a scary resemblance to Henry Kissinger.

"Right, think about all the families back here. We should lie, pretend we're going to give them the money, then bomb 'em," offered Mr.

Pacheski, a skinny, bowtie-wearing former assistant principal, who had been relegated back to the classroom in '79. The kids smoked joints in his class, set paper airplanes on fire and shot pencils at the ceiling. He just locked them into his room and tried to weather the storm until retirement. He had 11 years to go.

"What does Ted Kennedy have two of that Jimmy Carter wishes he had one of?" asked Mr. Binkley, a 40ish bleach blond English teacher and self-proclaimed swinger. "Dead brothers," he horse-laughed, got up and struck a swashbuckling, hands-on-hips pose, the same one he had used while modeling for the Montgomery Ward catalog that he carried in his briefcase and passed around to his classes. "They call me coffee because I grind so fine," he growled to a couch full of female staff members before intimating that he was nothing less than the "boss hoss with the hot sauce" as he led the teachers to the meeting room for a speech given by the principal, Mr. Nott. It was the end of the first semester, and there was a teachers' meeting in the morning and a donkey basketball game for the students in the afternoon.

After gaveling the mid-year meeting to order, making a lengthy, disjointed pitch for Shaklee vitamins and telling a couple slightly off-color anecdotes, Nott grew serious. "Act like you care because whether you do or not, you can probably fool 50 percent of these kids." While attempting to conquer a stray thread from the sleeve of his rumpled brown sport coat, his voice took a philosophical turn. "Sometimes you've got to spoon feed these kids, throw out a few carrots but don't put the cart before the horse."

"What about those test results, Ronny?" asked Mr. Henning, the school police liaison officer, who most of the time didn't concern himself with educational issues, needing all his energy to handle the tough discipline cases. Always dressed in black he fancied himself as a modern Wyatt Earp and had recently taken to wearing an "I Shot J.R." button.

Nott candidly admitted that the school's standardized test results were among the lowest in the state but shrewdly reasoned, "We could interpret these tests another way, for God's sake. Maybe these kids are so bad we're doing a helluva job." A few teachers edged to leave and

Nott acknowledged with an agonized expression that he wanted out as badly as they but had one last word. "Handle you own problems, just use your common sense. Don't make me come around your room and be a jerk. I don't want to be always sticking my goofy head into your business. Don't make me act like any more of an idiot than I already am." He laughed good-naturedly. "Let the games begin. 10-4."

The biggest event of the winter at Temperance High was the donkey basketball game. They prepare for it for months. There's an afternoon game for the students to watch and an evening one for the townsfolk. I volunteered to take tickets for the afternoon game, the most painless duty. The game pitted the faculty against the students. The donkeys had special protection on their feet to save the gym floor. Players rode the donkeys and didn't have to dribble. The referee had a prod for the more obstinate donkeys. While ticket taking I concluded — after reflecting on my colleagues, my chosen profession and how I seemed to be frittering away my precious time as if I had a million years — that a strategically placed prod might serve me well.

My duties made me miss the first half action, but I was able to find a bleacher seat to catch the last part of the game. Judy was taking pictures for the yearbook but looked a little bored. I hadn't talked to her since that day she snapped my picture. Catching her eye I motioned and made room for her. She came over and plopped down next to me.

"I'm getting tired of these games," she said, fiddling with her camera. "They're pretty boring after the first five minutes."

The score was tied, but the faculty seemed in control. Several players were off their donkeys and pulling mightily while the referee made judicious use of his prod. Judy sprang up to snap a donkey head-butting Mr. Nott who loudly proclaimed that someone must have fed it Shaklee vitamins. Sitting back down she carefully smoothed her French-twisted hair, the way Lana used to do when she wore it that way.

"Do you have many more pictures to take?" I asked, looking away from her honey tresses.

"I've got more than enough," she replied, hazel eyes flashing.

While the game went on we breezily talked. She was a junior, was interested in becoming a professional photographer. She wanted to attend the Art Institute in Ft. Lauderdale.

"I love it there," she said, closing her eyes. "I've spent my last couple of summers staying down there with my uncle. It's really wild. I love it."

She burst out laughing at the action. The football coach, who once had a tryout with the New England Patriots, was off his donkey pulling madly. His glasses fell off. He brushed them to the bench and was straining at the leash. He was way out of shape.

"The coach is being cruel to his mule," Judy giggled, raising her eyebrows in fun. She and I laughed like kids.

"How come you're not out there?" she asked, poking at my elbow.

"Well, I really don't know how to ride those things, plus I'm pretty shy."

"You should try new things," she lectured. "You might be surprised at how much fun you can have."

That made sense. We talked about ourselves. I told her I was an old hippie. She figured that. One of her friends' dad was at Woodstock. She had read a little article about me that was in the school paper. In it I said I was into rock-n-roll, was single and my favorite TV show was "Kung Fu." The article also had me saying the women come and go. It was a misquote and I told her so. I didn't want her thinking I was some kind of Don Juan.

"What I really meant was that I had a hard time figuring women out," I explained, feeling my brow furrowing.

"I think I know what you mean," she laughed. "Men are pretty confusing too. I got set up for a New Year's date with a guy who's almost 30 and he acted more immature than some of the high school guys I've been out with." Judy stretched her fine legs out in front of her and slowly cranked her ankles. "It's funny you mentioned that 'Kung Fu' show but I like it too. Everybody makes fun of that Caine guy but some of the things he says really make you think." She turned towards me with a serious look. "It would be neat to actually know someone like him."

After a lengthy pause which found me somehow unable to produce even one remotely relevant "Kung Fu" quote, Judy continued on about how she loved all kinds of water sports, spent a lot of time alone just daydreaming, wanted a candy red Corvette and loved Neil Diamond music. I responded that I didn't know how to swim, was pretty much of a loner and dreamer myself, wasn't really into cars, but liked Diamond's earlier stuff.

"Oh yeah," she said. "Another thing. I don't talk about politics or religion."

I told her I did, but usually ended up wishing that I hadn't.

As we were chatting, a small child of one of the teachers appeared and asked Judy for her camera. Mom followed and said no, even though Judy didn't mind. The little fellow grabbed at the camera, missed, and his hand settled on one of Judy's breasts. She looked at me. Certain that nothing in my Caine repertoire would be in any way appropriate for this particular situation, I looked up and began humming Diamond's "Kentucky Woman."

Out on the floor, the coach had his glasses back on and was adjusting his tank top. He was an extremely hirsute man. Judy motioned toward him with her camera. "I like hairy chests but that shoulder stuff is a little much. And that gut is gross."

I motionlessly sat in smooth-chested, slender silence.

Behind us, the principal climbed the bleachers to root out a kid who was distracting the donkeys with some well-timed hee-hawing. The crowd hooted him. Nott good-naturedly mugged, tripped, and landed in the lap of a girl who was AC/DCed all over. "Nice going, slick," a kid yelled. The crowd roared.

"That Mr. Nott is a real card," Judy said, reaching behind her to scratch her back, causing her breasts to jut tantalizingly.

My hands pressed palms down on the bleachers. She moved a little closer to me. My right hand was against her thigh. Neither one of us moved.

She told me she grew up pretty fast and used to work at an Arco gas station by the Interstate that had turned out to be a front for prostitution. She had begun serious dating when she was 13 but wasn't sure she wanted to get tied down with anyone because there were too many people to meet and things to do.

"Now me and my friends hang out at Bronco Billy's, it's a new mechanical bull place where the old Narcissus Disco was. I'm glad there isn't much disco left, I think it's boring."

"You and me agree on that one, Judy, but I have to tell you I'm not too big on this urban cowboy business either. I mean, 10-gallon hats on the Michigan-Ohio border? Give me a break."

She tilted her head slightly. "It's a little silly, I guess, but people just want to dress up and have a good time. You shouldn't take it so seriously."

"You're right," I conceded. "I tend to get too serious about things. In fact, one of my New Year's resolutions was to lighten up a little." I popped her on the knee. "I'll tell you what, if you catch me getting too heavy just shake your finger at me. That'll be our sign to keep me in line. I could use it." I smiled and extended my hand. "Deal?"

"Deal." We shook on it. Her palm was sweaty. Or was that mine?

"Do you work any place now?"

"Yeah, at the Sports Arena for rock concerts and special events like the Auto Show. I run into a lot of winners there." She rolled her eyes. "All kinds of weird guys are always trying to pick me up."

"Well you can't knock their taste," I said, certain I was suave beyond belief.

Her face flushed, reminding me of how young she really was.

"I meant you're really nice and friendly."

"That's okay," she smiled warmly, gulping as she looked down.

The game was almost over. The faculty was safely in front. Nott had retreated to his office. The school police liaison officer stood in the gym doorway, readying himself for the post-game rush. He carried a gun in a shoulder holster. A donkey stampede would not catch him unprepared. The busses were fuming outside. Judy's sister, a seventh grader, came from the opposite bleachers and asked for a ride home but Judy was staying after school to work in the photo lab. Her sister said hi to me and ran away squealing.

"If that little brat takes my lipstick once more I'll. . ." she began, then quickly composed herself. "I better be going." She stood up and adjusted herself with a slow shake.

"It's been really nice talking to you," I said.

She looked me right in the eye. "Yeah, it's been really nice talking to you." Slinging her camera over her shoulder, she turned and walked away.

Following her through the door, I found myself blending – quite comfortably and without self-conscious analysis thank you – into the high school crowd.

***

"It was really great just talking to her," I said to Bert the next night. "After being locked in with Lana for so long and mentally tying myself in knots all the time with ruminations and speculations, it was nice just to relax and have a simple chat."

"I know exactly what you mean. Those young girls are just so friendly. I'm glad I'm going back to the Little Theater, lots of high school girls work there."

Bert had decided to cut short his sabbatical year. He had contacted his former supervisor who was glad to have Bert back. The woman they had hired as a substitute for him was having problems. As two-time Mr. Lakewood Theater, Bert was a tough act to follow. He had already moved out of his room in Crystal City and would be heading for Cleveland the next day. Bert insisted we have a night on the town. He felt I needed some practical experience at how to function away from what he referred to as my "ivory tower cosmos world." This would be his last chance to show me the ropes in the real world.

Our first stop of the evening was Max & Erma's. It was a loud, garishly decorated hamburger and beer place that had old-fashioned phones at every table. You could call anyone and harmlessly flirt. Women could call guys from the dance floor upstairs. Bert had never been here before. When he saw the set-up he took on the look of a man who had just died and gone to heaven. Before we were seated it was clear he already had a phone strategy figured out.

"I think I'm gonna go by my initials, B.J.," he said, swiveling in his chair and scoping out the room. "I'm feeling pretty self-actualized today, but I still need a new image. B.J. sounds like a mischievous guy. That's how I'll introduce myself." Bert's hands were a blur as he rubbed them together. "It wouldn't hurt you to take some notes," he said, slapping me on the back and letting out a whoop.

Before executing his game plan, Bert carefully cracked each finger as he recapped his sabbatical year at CCU. Admitting it hadn't been the social bonanza he had hoped for, nonetheless there were some undeniable bright spots.

"I talked to a 15-year-old bus girl in Jensen's yesterday and told her I'd meet her in four years in Europe for a pizza, so I guess I ended on a good note."

The waitress, a rail-thin woman named Olga, came to the table. Bert noticing her nameplate, ordered in German. Olga didn't understand.

"You know what my biggest disappointment was this year?" Bert continued after ordering, in English, a breadless sandwich, double order of fries and a Tab. "I ran into two girls who were in my junior theater ensemble. Right after they graduated from high school I would visit on weekends and buy them pizzas. After a year or so I got them to start calling me by my first name. Now they're grad students and they won't even speak to me."

The phone rang. Bert knocked over the condiments to answer it.

"Oh yeah. My name is B.J.," he said, squinting up at the dance floor. "I can't see you. Sure, I'll be right up."

Bert briskly scuttled up the stairs only to return in two minutes.

"She sounded great and said she wanted to dance with me, but it was just a joke." He sat down and decided to double his order.

"Don't worry, Bert. It wasn't personal."

He just shrugged and took a hard slug at his Tab.

"What made you decide to go back to your old job?" I asked.

"Two things really did it," he began glumly. "I went over to this girl's house a couple of weeks ago and when I knocked on the door the lights went out. She knew I was coming. I thought maybe it was a power shortage so I kept knocking, but no dice." Two women walked by in designer jogging suits. Bert shook his head slowly and raked his hand over his face like Lou Costello. "But I guess the last straw was about a week ago when I saw this bald girl playing pool alone at the rec center. I asked her if she wanted to get a pizza, but she said no and acted kinda mad. I figured I'd give her a break, and she ends up getting pissed off. That did it."

He also confessed that he had made a farewell appearance at a couple of his favorite massage parlors that afternoon.

"Are you going to use them in Cleveland?" I asked.

"Nah, they're all in bad neighborhoods, plus I'm afraid to run into guys from my church. Anyway, most of the places are Korean. That pidjin English drives my crazy."

He craned his neck, looking around for someone to call. "I've got to be careful living at home. Over Christmas my mother noticed a Visa slip for $50 with 'Oriental Sauna' written on it. She told me not to work out there anymore."

The phone rang and Bert quickly grabbed it. Women's hands had been all over his body that afternoon, and he was eager to do some sweet-talking. The caller was one of his former acting students, and he began speaking Russian and gesturing wildly. He appeared to be telling some off-color jokes. Finally he hung up and ordered a drink to be sent to her table.

"Sounds promising, Bert."

"Nah, her boyfriend's coming in 15 minutes, plus her left ankle has always had a funny colored thing on it."

"Are there any prospects with women from the theater?"

"Well, there's Esther, my old standby. If I don't get anything I'll marry her in four years when I'm 35. There's also this real athletic lighting director. She's 32 and aggressive. Kind of a women's libber type." He paused pensively. "The only problem is if I don't make it with her, if I can't get it up or something, since she's so into it, it will be my fault. If I don't make it with Esther I can always blame it on her kneecap."

"Just ask that lighting director out and then go to her apartment," I said. "You'll electrify her, you're a man of action."

Bert partially agreed but claimed he had a better idea for tonight. "We could tell the girls we meet that we just got out of prison." He darted a glance at the woman at the next table and lost himself in thought for a few seconds. "You know, most of them aren't exactly what I'm looking for, so I'll tell them that I'm not interested in any heavy commitment and just want sort of an intimate friendship." He leaned close to me and lowered his voice. "After a while we can give each other massages. I'll just tell them to think of me as a girlfriend with a dick." He sat back, content. "If I start off by letting them know they're not my ideal girl maybe they won't be afraid of me and will at least go out with me for a pizza."

I told him that particular approach seemed a bit convoluted – even by my legendary standards of circuitousness – and suggested he simplify his tactics, much as I planned to do in the future.

Citing my naivete, Bert would hear none of my advice. Besides, he had noticed that the woman at the next table was ring-less. He dialed her number. She picked up the phone. In an effort to be inconspicuous Bert pulled his seat away from the table and looked in the other direction, but the woman knew who it was. He asked her if she came there often and introduced himself as a movie director, adding that he was a good slow dancer who also did magic tricks. I was trying hard not to listen. The conversation was short. When he hung up he shot a quick glance at her. She didn't look back, asked for her check and departed abruptly.

"I told her not to worry," Bert said, looking genuinely puzzled after she scurried out the door, "that my ideal girl was blond and Slovenian. I thought it would set her mind at ease. I don't know what they want."

He took a bite out of his breadless sausage sandwich and grew stone silent.

A huge TV screen at the side of the bar broadcast the Miss Universe Pageant. Bert and I watched quietly for awhile, but during the swimsuit competition he finally spoke. "I've got a couple of tickets to the

Golden Cherry burleycue, lets go there."

I was reluctant, but since it was his last night in town and I knew he viewed introducing me to the quirky side of nightlife as part of my real world education process, I agreed to go. We left with Bert in his car and me following in mine. On the way over I noticed a Mazda wagon filled with kids swerving near Bert's car. Middle fingers were exchanged, suddenly the Mazda's door opened and a moon was shot at Bert's Pinto before the Mazda sped into the night. He slowed down, pulled into a gas station lot and motioned me to follow.

"What was that all about?"

"I just blew a kiss to the girl in the front seat," Bert began, a little breathlessly. "She was looking at me and smiling. All of a sudden these guys started giving me the finger. They had long hair. I thought they were all girls. Did you see that guy shoot the moon? I mean, all I did was blow her a kiss. She looked like Olivia Newton-John."

***

"Live Girls" the sign on the marquee said. The Golden Cherry was actually the recently remodeled Soap Opera Laundromat. As we walked towards the theater, a wiry, darkly-clad preacher stood on top of a car railing against sin and drugs. "I just do a line or two of the Lord and come out preaching. I don't need no drugs or pornography." Spotting us heading towards the entrance he yelled, "Don't expect your clothes to get clean in there, brothers."

Just inside the door, a plump, 50ish woman with purplish hair teased into cascades of ringlets took our tickets. Her huge breasts were molded by her bra into bullet-like projectiles and she maneuvered them in the direction of the stage. "Park it wherever, fellas."

Bert and I chose to sit near the back wall. Cigarette smoke contributed to the room's dimness as I looked around at the audience. It was made up mostly of old guys with flashlights. They looked like 15th Century popes and would flash their lights between the dancers' legs. For a buck the girls, who appeared to be not much older than Judy, would come down and sit in the customers' laps. I remembered when I first went to one of these shows in the late '60s. The dancers looked old and hard and unapproachable, and the crowd seemed to be middle-aged. There were comics with names like Willie Dew who had worked in vaudeville. I hadn't been in one of these places in at least 10 years. They now featured "Continuous Entertainment."

A glistening-with-sweat black woman ground to "Hot Child in the City," then a petite white girl – with frizzy red hair that shot out like solar flames during an eclipse – writhed to "Dirty Deeds Done Dirt Cheap." A cigarette puffed out of a vagina drew warm applause right before a black widow woman welcomed everyone to her nightmare. "Only Women Bleed" was followed by "A Little Bit of Soap." Bert's eyes were glassy and his mouth partially open. He looked at each successive performer as if he were gazing upon the Beatific Vision. As I eased back into my seat, a dryness in my throat and a bulge in my pants, I was only mildly surprised to find myself no longer feeling holier than thou.

An old guy tussled with a filmy gown while another greying, partially bent-over customer tried to fit into a broken seat next to the runway. During "Who Was That Lady?" a tall, wispy blond grabbed at a guy's lap and said, "Honey, you better do something about that," before quickly gathering her discarded clothes and exiting. Next, with "Let's Get It On" thumping in the background, a grotesquely obese patron yelled, "Come here baby," to a full-figured southern belle. She squinted at his crotch and asked, "Is it soup yet?"

No one laughed. We were all much too titillated and tantalized there in the dark, lusting at a distance for the women in the high heels and exotic lingerie. Who, one by one, pranced onstage to disrobe and masturbate; then pranced off, winking and blowing a kiss; then, just before disappearing, turning to bend over and moon the already over-mooned audience; then wobbling down the creaky stairs, like exiting girls at the high school dance, having shown but not really connected with the half-hidden and throbbing boys in the shadows.

The stench of cheap perfume was getting to me and I was ready to leave. Having been raised a Catholic, heaven knows I enjoyed a dirty show as much as anyone and – as Caine would point out, the chains that bind us most tightly are those that we refuse to acknowledge – I had no problem at all admitting the elemental power of this type of entertainment. But I was starting to get nauseous – and a little frightened. If this were, as Bert would say, part of my initiation into the real world, where would it all end? The one-handed magazines, the porno tapes, the life wrenched into a tissue or down the sink. Then what? Life-sized dolls? "Inflatable Amy never gets a headache." And, by the way, why aren't real women like that?

I nudged Bert and motioned toward the exit.

"Nah, let's wait for a couple more," he said in a perturbed tone. "I finally get someone to go to one of these places with me so I don't have to sit here alone, and you want to split. I mean, what's the big deal about waiting a little longer."

Suddenly the announcer said, "We've got something for the ladies," and a Mediterranean-looking fellow got up and began to dance. The female dancers, who were the only women in the place, gathered around the undulating amateur hoofer and seemed prepared to pay him the deference usually accorded patron saints of small Sicilian villages.

"That's it for me," I said and got up. Bert had to reluctantly agree, even though he himself had planned to strip on male amateur night, figuring he could get around the "no masturbation" rule by turning his back to the audience while surreptitiously whacking it a few times.

When several members of the crowd, including Bert and I, began heading for the door before the lanky Neapolitan had even removed his pea-green jacket, the women made a fuss and tried to lure everyone back.

"They're begging us to stay," Bert said, visibly moved, as he lingered near the exit. "That's kinda neat."

***

Bert slept on my couch that night, but when I awoke he wasn't there. A note on the table informed me that he would meet me at noon at the

Original Pancake House.

He arrived around 12:15. He had on his "good" brown pants, a golf shirt and a sweater vest. He looked like one of those older guys coming home from Mass that I remembered from my neighborhood.

"Where did you take off to this morning?"

Bert waited for the waitress to finish pouring coffee before he spoke.

"I stopped off at the Little Red House for a quick bath."

It was the cheapest place in the area, and he wanted to make a last visit before heading back to Cleveland. He had a "Grand Finale" idea, which was to jack off early during the half hour bath time so he could produce another hard on at the end, when the girls always rubbed you dry with a towel.

"The last thing they rub is your dick," he said in an almost clinical monotone. "I figured if I had it ready she'd get the idea and help it along a little bit, kind of as a going away present or something, but she acted like she didn't even notice the thing."

I was glad that the massage parlor subject had come up since I was feeling quite uneasy about where my friend's life seemed to be going.

"Bert, you've got to straighten yourself out. You can't keep going to those places. That burlesque was bad enough. I had nightmares about it all night, places like that are one-way tickets to nowhere. You don't need all that crazy stuff."

"Ah they're not so bad, but I know what you mean, though," he sighed wearily and smoothed down his hair. "If I'm ever going to fulfill Maslow's Hierarchy of Needs, I've got to discipline myself more." He examined the bottle of Tabasco sauce and found it empty. "I will, though. No problem."

The waitress came over and Bert ordered eggs over hard, two side orders of sausage and toast not sliced.

After she walked away Bert berated himself for not requesting more Tabasco sauce before something else dawned on him. "Hey," he said, snapping his fingers. "I know what I wanted to show you. I've got my scrapbook in my car. I'll go get it."

While I watched him making a funny, rubbery warm face at a toddler as he ambled down the aisle, I was reminded of something Caine had said in yesterday's "Kung Fu" episode – "That which is not sought will remain unfound" – and how Bert, starving for love, spent so much time seeking blow jobs.

In a moment he returned with the brown book, a carefully kept record of his life. It opened with his resume and a list of his special accomplishments and skills: Golf Party Entrepreneur, Greater Cleveland Theater Man of the Year finalist; an award from the governor for raising money for charity; and a notice in the Lakewood Post of his graduation from the Tommy Bolt Golf School, one of only 6,000 to have ever done so. There was also a copy of a letter he and a friend had written, while in the reserves, to President Nixon, expressing confidence in their leader but pleading as "good loyal Americans" that he do something about world peace. There were pictures of Bert in college and in Europe; gleefully jumping with the Eiffel Tower in the background; pensively posing near the Berlin Wall; a slender handsome Bert with a fraulein.

"I could have made it with her if I would have played my cards right," he said, blowing a speck of dust off the picture. "But I felt sorry for her because her dad died about a month earlier. What a schmuck I was."

There were pictures of girlfriends in college. Pretty girls. Knockouts even. A belly dancer. Girls, hands cupped under their chins, lying close to the camera. Roommates' girls. Girls of best friends who had come on to him, but he didn't do anything.

"I never touched her because she was going with my buddy," he reflected proudly. "She mentioned something to him about liking me, and he blamed me when they broke up. He never spoke to me again. Neither did she." He closed the book.

"Would you like some more coffee?" the waitress asked.

"Nah, but how about a large Tab," Bert answered, again forgetting the Tabasco sauce and again mouthing a curse.

He continued to reminisce. How he almost became an conscientious objector in order to get a girl. How he and a friend used to fence during his junior year in college – and how that was the best year because by then you knew the ropes, there were lots of underclasswomen, and you didn't have to worry about going out into the world like seniors did. How he would never tell a girl he was in love with her if he wasn't, even though a lot of guys did it to get laid. How he stood on the seal in the middle of campus at CCU, and how that may have been his big mistake because they said if you stood on that seal alone you'd never get married. How embarrassing it was when one of his sister's girlfriends had pantsed him when he was 10 and how he wouldn't mind it now. How if he'd ever propose it would be after singing "Time in a Bottle." How I was so lucky to be tall, and if he were tall he'd join the Skyscraper Club in Cleveland and have lots of dates. How, because of his language skills, he could turn off the light and be a different lover each night. How one advantage he and I had, as older, never-been-married guys, was that we had gotten all the roving out of our system and would be good hubbies. How he'd like to jump out of a birthday cake nude at a bachelorette party, or wear a Lone Ranger mask and be a rent-a-streaker at a girls' softball team get-together. How no one could discount the influence of the Old Country, and how he'd be in-like-Flynn once a Slovenian girl's mother found out what his last name really was, and how it would sure be nice to be a daddy, and how he'd never even look at another woman if. . .

The waitress delivered our breakfast. Bert finally asked for more Tabasco.

"Did you notice that pretty blond over there?" I asked. Bert didn't even glance up.

"Don't point, Ray," he snapped. "I saw her when she came in. I've already life-guarded her."

"You've already what?"

He looked over his shoulder and lowered his voice. "It's called the lifeguard technique. I got the idea by overhearing some waitresses talking at an L&K. They said they really got turned on when the head popped out. That's when it hit me."

His idea was to take his dick out, and he agreed to let me in on how he did it, in case I ever wanted to try. It only worked in warm weather.

He would wear shorts into a Big Bob's or a Denny's or a pizza parlor and single out a girl he wanted to impress.

"It's a sure-fire method but you've got to be careful or else you'll get arrested," he cautioned. "What you do is look out the window, but actually you're watching the waitress' reflection. You pretend like you're looking at another girl outside but you're really watching the waitress. When you know she's looking at you, you start scratching around at your dick. Then you just let the head pop out. They love it. Plus, you're not looking in their direction so they can't nail you for flashing. Lifeguards have been pulling this for years. Each time I've done it I got a good reaction. You ought to give it a shot."

It took me a while to gather myself for a response. "Are you out of your mind, Bert? Aside from bringing new meaning to the term indirect approach, you are really asking for trouble." Bert winced and motioned for me to keep it down. I lowered my voice. "If that's part of showing me the ropes, it's also letting out enough rope for you to hang yourself. Promise me you'll forget about the lifeguard technique."

"Maybe you're right," he said, stroking his chin and nodding. "Besides, girls like that romantic stuff, just like they eat up that astrology business." He paused for a moment, thinking hard, his fingers dancing on the table. "I'll have to work on that. But let's get out of here before that blond recognizes me."

His undetected escape seemed to brighten Bert's mood. "You know modern science is going to conquer the aging process and everything," he said as we walked out into the hazy January sunlight. "I saw on 'PM Magazine' where they got these computer chips that can grow hands back. Maybe even if you've got a defective dick you can get a new one."

Instead of his life slipping away, Bert reasoned as he raised the hood on his Pinto and started it with a screwdriver, he had lots of time.

***

On Tuesday, January 20, right around the time Reagan was taking the oath, I walked over to the school library to look for a magazine –

and Judy. I knew she hung out in the library from time to time. As I scanned the periodicals rack, I heard that voice.

"Find what you're looking for, sir?" I had been thinking about her for the six days since the donkey game, but Judy had caught me off guard.

"Uh, yeah, no, not really." I stood straight up, picked up a magazine, put it back, put my hands on my hips and forgot the question. She had on a pale blue sweater, painted-on black jeans and black boots. She was carrying an American History book and had on strawberry lipstick. Within fifteen seconds I had a hard-on. I picked up Tiger Beat magazine and nonchalantly held it over my crotch. Thinking of the male librarian naked made me reasonably limp, and I regained my composure.

"Uh, I was meaning to ask you," I stammered for something to say. "What's your sign?" is what I came up with.

"Scorpio."

"Oh boy," I smiled. "I'm a Taurus. We're complementary signs. Scorpio is a powerful sign. It's all about rebirth and renewal. Contrasts, too."

"Oh," she said and appeared to be thinking real hard for a comeback. "My dad is always laughing at astrology, but I think it's kinda neat. He's the assistant prosecuting attorney in Monroe County so he's kinda cynical."

My mental eyebrows rose.

"We don't get along so I'm gonna move out as soon as I turn 18. I've got a married friend who lives over near Sylvania. I baby-sit for her son Gregory, who's a little doll. I could move in now if I wanted to. I stay over there a couple of weekends a month and sort of come and go as I please." She tucked her sweater into the back of her jeans and waited for me to say something.

"That's nice that you have a place to go to get away from home," I said, casually leaning against the magazine rack. "Uh, you know it's a full moon out tonight. Do you pay any attention to those kind of things?"

"Not really."

My heart had finally stopped pounding. Holy shit. This is ridiculous, I thought, I'm literally going to pieces here. I thought I had some control, especially after that disaster with Lana, but I'm gushing like one of the Brady Bunch. She looks totally composed while I'm babbling about the moon.

"Well, Judy," I at last said. "I can teach you about the moon, if you want. You'll get a feel for it in no time. It's nice to believe in things."

"I'm up for just about anything," she said as the bell rang. "I've got to go to journalism class. I hate it because Mrs. Davis is a pain in the butt. She doesn't teach us anything, and I think she picks on me. Well, talk to you later."

She clicked away and I breathed a sigh of relief. At least I hadn't made a complete fool of myself. Several kids were staring at me as they filed into the library. I was still covering myself with Tiger Beat.

***

For the next few weeks I waited for Judy every day after third period. I stood in the hall, pretending I was acting as a hall monitor. In a way, I suppose I was. When the bell rang she would come clicking along and stop and talk. She had a free period in the library and was supposed to be working on yearbook stuff, but the librarian didn't mind if she talked to me. Sometimes we stood in the hall – our eyes entangled – and talked the entire 50 minutes, which seemed to go by in a flash. My one student for the period, on the rare occasions when he would show up, would sit and work word puzzles or read. The female teacher whose duty it was to check the girls' rest rooms would walk by four or five times and glare or smile. Other teachers would peek down the hall and look at us. The slinky school secretary would sometimes walk by, but she never acknowledged us.

I would tell Judy about my friends in Crystal City, and how I really hadn't met any people in Toledo. She complained about living conditions at home, and that she had learned long ago not to tell her 13-year-old sister anything. One day she told me about a 19-year-old "friend" in Florida.

"His hair is kinda like yours," she said, twisting her head as she regarded my long curly hair. "He's a musician, but now he just mows lawns. His mom is in her late 30s and is dating one of his friends who's 21. I went down there one time on his birthday as a surprise and popped out of a cake with my bathing suit on." She put her hand over her face, embarrassed at the memory, then removed it to reveal a resolute expression. "I'm gonna have to go down there this summer and settle some unfinished business."

I'm sure it was clear to her that I was much too mature to pry for details, so I didn't ask.

She would also talk a lot about cars. "I'm driving an old Gremlin now, but when I get out of school I'm gonna buy a motorcycle, until I can get my candy red Corvette. I'm gonna call it 'Beautiful Loser.' I really like that song, especially where it says, 'You just don't need it all'." Her head would bob rhythmically and the bell would ring, and she would swirl away, and I would stand in the hall for as long as her perfume would linger.

Sometimes she arrived at my room during my free sixth period and she'd tell me how bored she was with school, and how she had taken all the tough classes by the end of her sophomore year, and how she might be taking some college classes when she was a senior. Sometimes she would sit on the table top and put her heels on my desk while I sat back and desperately tried not to look between her legs – since her eyes always followed mine – as she told me she was jogging regularly trying to get in shape for swimsuit season. Funny, but earlier in the term I had shut myself in my room with my stomach-cramping memories of Lana, but now I found myself leaving the door wide open and listening for Judy clicking in the hall. Sometimes while I waited I actually whistled as my tell-tale heart pounded so loud I expected Edgar Allan Poe to materialize before me.

Our meetings went on nearly every day for almost three weeks when suddenly I didn't see her at all for a couple days, and I really missed her. I asked Scott for some advice, but he refused to get involved. He would not entertain any discussions of 17-year-old Scorpios, citing health concerns. So I called Jenny to ask her how I should handle this situation.

"Just talk to her," she said. "Seventeen isn't that young, believe me. When I was in the eighth grade there was this math teacher who was always telling me how great I looked in hot pants. I knew he wanted me. I even went over to his house a couple of times, but nothing happened. I ran into him a couple of years ago at the Intensive Care Lounge. He was really loaded and didn't even recognize me. I couldn't have gotten into it back then, but it was nice just being friends. We could all use more of them."

When I hung up the phone I was still confused and didn't know what to say to her or how she would react. Was I abusing my position, even though she wasn't a student of mine and I had absolutely no intention of having sex with her, despite that spontaneous erection in the library which could have resulted from the magazine pictorial on the "Solid Gold" dancers that I had spotted when Judy surprised me? Or was it more important, for my own growth and hers, to simply be straightforward and unashamed of my feelings – something I'd always struggled with, believing that somehow it wasn't appropriate for me to even have feelings like other people? And what if I fell flat on my face and the whole thing turned into a disaster? Unable to think of a solution I decided to randomly open my spiral notebook to the Caine section and see what surfaced. "Where you stumble and fall, there you find the treasure" was the quote that made up my mind – just as all the others in there would have – to say something to her.

The next day I intercepted Judy as she was heading to the library and invited her to my room where a doe-eyed ninth grader with a glittery I'm Baby Soft t-shirt was sharpening a pencil. She blew on the lead, said "Hi" and left. I motioned for Judy to sit down at a circular table and sat across from her.

I'm really attracted to you," I blurted out before even clearing my throat. Her eyes opened a little but not much. "I mean I find you very appealing and I love talking to you, and I guess I'm a little confused by it."

"I'm glad I'm sitting down for this."

"Do you believe me?"

"Yeah. You sound real nervous. You must be telling the truth. I'm getting kind of used to this though." Her eyes searched my face.

"Was it very obvious to you? I mean, I'm not going to jump you or anything like that. I just had to say something."

"Well, I figured something was up," she said, pursing her lips ever so slightly. "I don't know what to say."

Neither did I, but I felt a lot better. We looked at our hands until Judy stood up and cradled her Civics text to her chest and began speaking hurriedly.

"You know, Mrs. Davis gave me a C on a journalism project I did. I mean it wasn't great, but I know I didn't deserve a hook. If she gives me anything below a B in that class I'm gonna drop it. I don't care what my dad says. I can't get any C's, plus she's not teaching us anything. She doesn't proofread our stuff and when something comes out bad we get embarrassed. I did this little story about changing women's roles and I think, like, she purposely mixed it up so I looked bad. She's always cutting down the clothes I wear and asking me stuff in class when she knows I'm not ready. And she didn't even let me use the rest room pass the other day. Boy, was I mad."

The changed subject eased me into a counseling mode. "Don't be intimidated by her, Judy. You're the best photographer in the school, and they really need you on the paper. Don't let her push you around."

I was ready to go to bat for her, put my coat over a puddle, defend her against all foes foreign and domestic, joust a dragon or tell off a teacher. Sometimes it seems that being a knight in shining armor is the most natural thing in the world.

The bell rang. She stared into my eyes and smiled. "Bye," she said in a soft, soft voice.

As she walked out the door, all pink and silver frost waiting to melt into spring, I didn't even consider looking at her jeans.

Valentine's Day

There was a heavy snowstorm on Tuesday, February 10. Temperance's schools looked like they'd be shut down for the rest of the week. The road crews had been cut, so the back-country roads weren't cleared enough for the busses to get through. I was glad to have some time off but hoped to get back to school by Friday since Valentine's Day was Saturday and I wanted to see Judy before then. Plus, there was a dance Saturday night sponsored by student council. Judy was on the committee for the dance, and I'm sure she could have talked me into chaperoning.

Actually I had no problem viewing what was happening to me, in terms of being excited about Judy, as the logical filling in of a stage of development I'd missed growing up. There was a Mack truck-like social intercourse gap in my teenage bio that wasn't about to disappear, no matter what the capricious calender might indicate. I had attended an all boys' school, had never gone to a dance during high school, and perhaps never even talked for more than 20 minutes to a girl during those years. Then I followed that up with living in a college town like Crystal City (where no one grows up) and going through the ethereal '60s and early '70s in a kind of enchantment haze before climbing aboard for a careening magical mystery tour with Lana and hurtling out the other side of all that as a still remarkably youthful, albeit developmentally arrested, 30-year-old quasi-innocent who's understandably and refreshingly awkward/tentative about his first meaningful Valentine's Day since the nuns in seventh grade screened all cards not addressed to the Virgin Mary. It all made perfect sense why I was doing what I was doing. It should have been totally obvious to even the most casual observer – let alone, of course, someone as keenly aware as I.

Thursday, without a second thought, I bought her a card. It had a young girl with long blond hair wearing a filmy dress and sitting atop a unicorn. She was reaching down to pick a long-stemmed flower. Her eyes were dreamily half-closed, sparkly stars were in the background and the unicorn's horn glistened in the moonlight. I had had a difficult time dealing with the rush of unicorns in the stores during the holidays since they reminded me of Lana and her pizza-delivery lover, but clearly Judy was helping me get over that. The inside of the card was blank so I wrote.

To Judy,

Dream beautiful dreams,
Always believe in magic.
                    A Valentine's Day wish from a Taurus to a Scorpio.

***

Temperance was the only school in the area not to have classes on Friday, and I decided to return for a visit to a school I had taught at three years earlier. After making the rounds in the lounge and the cafeteria, I stopped by to visit the senior English teacher, a woman the kids called Dusty. Since she knew I was a former English teacher, she asked me to talk to her Creative Writing class about my ideas on writing and literature. I got rolling about my educational experiences and pretty soon somehow had spilled out that I was "kind of interested" in a 17-year-old girl at my school.

Dusty's face froze. The girls squirmed. The guys grinned. Everyone was all ears. I explained that this really wasn't such a big deal; that I wasn't roaming around trying to hit on young girls; that this sort of just happened; and that I was only talking to this girl and hadn't seen her outside of school or anything and that sex, if that's what they were thinking about, was the furthest thing from my mind. I didn't use Judy's name, especially after informing them that her father was a prosecuting attorney. With a few minutes of class time remaining I asked for questions.

"How would you feel if she had a date for the prom?" a girl in stretch slacks and black heels asked.

I told her that I wasn't interested in possessing this girl and that I just liked talking to her. I was certain that this, along with several of my other comments, made it abundantly clear to the class members that not only was I not dangerous, but – if the truth be known – I really had it together in a way that they might consider emulating.

"Does this girl know how you feel?" a voice from the side asked.

"I told her I was attracted to her a couple of days ago."

A few kids whistled. The bell rang. No one moved. I was beginning to sense the potentially incriminating nature of the information I had rather flippantly revealed and volunteered to return another time for a further explanation that would clarify any possible misconceptions. All of the heads in class turned as one towards Dusty.

"We'll see," she said, arms folded. "But I'd like to ask Vicki a question."

Dusty began a slow stalking-like walk towards a hot-looking girl in an oversized letter-sweater and slit purple skirt who had been making disapproving noises during my talk. As the next class was filtering into the room, Dusty shot a glare in my direction and stopped at Vicki's desk.

"What would you do if a teacher who was almost old enough to be your father made a pass at you?"

"I'd shit my pants," Vicki said, gathering her books in her arms and bobbing her crossed leg. "Then I'd tell my boyfriend."

***

On Saturday, Valentine's Day, I headed to Crystal City to visit Frank and Scott. I hadn't seen them for weeks. Scott was holing up with Mary, a woman he had met in the philosophy department. She was a secretary, recently divorced. I had known her former husband for years. In the early '70s he was into dressing up like John Phillip Sousa and marching around campus, disdaining politics. Shortly after his marriage in the mid-'70s, he chose a Leon Trotsky look, switched from music to educational counseling and got into Jung. In '79 he separated from Mary to study at the Jungian Institute of Milwaukee. A recent rumor indicated that he had taken a wife in a collective unconsciousness ceremony at his therapist's office. I decided not to mention this to either Mary or Scott. Anyway, Scott seemed serious about her. In fact, he had told me over the phone that he was getting her into some kinky things with boots and mutual masturbation. He intimated that at first the gangly redhead balked, but that lately they were frequenting the shoe shop in the Stadium Plaza strip mall.

"I've even got her to where she wears slippers during the day and heels at night," he had informed me over the phone, noting he was sure her Stars and Stripes hubby never did anything like that.

I picked up Frank around nine o'clock and told him I wanted to visit Scott and Mary. He reluctantly agreed, then directed me to her place. Apparently he had pursued Mary the previous summer, right before his declaration of celibacy, and one night in July had arrived at her door only to have Scott answer his ring and promise to tell Mary of his visit. The next time Frank saw her she just glared at him and made a comment about him having his "cobra fangs in every woman in town." This, along with several other conflicts between them over women, had produced Frank's deep suspicion of Scott. He also was unrelentingly critical of Scott's desire to "conquer the world while being dominated by women."

Mary greeted us at the door and informed us she had a new rug. I carefully removed my boots after entering the house, but Frank insisted on keeping his battered wingtips on. "There's no mud on my shoes," he said defiantly. "I made sure I was clean before I came in."

As we entered the living room, Scott nodded and inquired if we wanted refreshments. He was a model host, the squire of the domain. Within moments I launched into a confession about Judy and my speech to the English class. I detailed the past few weeks since the donkey game, told of my Valentine's Day card and expressed surprise that, despite a tinge of gnawing, self-conscious guilt, how decidedly natural this all felt.

Scott was eased pensively into a rocking chair while Mary looked a trifle distressed. Frank was a silent celibate. As I went on about Judy and my feelings, Scott listened patiently, cringing slightly at the words "17" and "Scorpio," but adding after I had finished that "in Europe this would not even be an issue."

"But if we are to be properly contrite," he proclaimed, waving his finger, "we don't need the watered down confession of the good Augustine. No, we need to go back to the form, the Socratic-Platonic Apologia." He got up and walked briskly into the dining room. "After all," he said, shooting a quick glance at Mary as an almost imperceptible curl appeared at the corner of his mouth, "since the beginning of time man has had the overwhelming urge to apologize." His gaze lingered on her until she squirmed slightly, then he turned his attention to his briefcase – which he flicked open with a quick, practiced motion – and produced a paper that he claimed was his own paraphrasing of John Milton's Apologia and which he kept close at hand for occasions such as this.

Mary was hunched over on a side chair, eyes darting from one of us to the other. Every now and then she would shake her head, removing the cobwebs. Frank was sitting in silence, uncharacteristically ignoring Scott's willingness to prostrate himself at the feet of women and instead choosing to take umbrage at my use of the term "girl" and railing about the media's perpetuation of youthful images and how women, especially, have been victimized by this propaganda onslaught. It was passionate, sympathetic – and totally out of left field. I needled him that it sounded like his celibacy was starting to get to him.

"No, but it's helping to clear my head," he said, recoiling from Mary's offer of a heart-shaped Valentine cookie. "And I need all the help I can get, especially during this time of year with all these sugar-gushing, vagina-shaped heart symbols bombarding me from every direction."

Scott ruffled his papers and stood up, apparently tired of respectfully waiting for silence. He adjusted the drawstring on his grey smoking jacket, which had apparently belonged to either Mary's ex-husband or her father, and began muttering about soft presence and ambience. I could tell he was itching to read that apologia. He was ready to take the hemlock, then plead insanity – even before any charges were made – but Frank prevented him from speaking by launching into a story about how his crazy career of madly pursuing women had begun.

"I was 13 and I ran away with a girl. We parked our bikes in a cemetery and laid in the grass under some religious statue. We laid there from 11 at night until seven in the morning, just talking and making out. Finally a cop came by and nabbed us. I didn't think of it at the time, but I probably should have asked him what he was doing creeping around a cemetery at seven in the morning, robbing kids of their dreamtime."

Mary was leaning back in her chair as if trying to escape as Frank continued, his tone that of a man speaking about a lifelong malady. "Anyway, she and I were going to steal a boat and head down the Mississippi, just the two of us. We could have made it, too." His voice lowered and he fidgeted with his hands." Her dad came down to the station to get her, then my old man showed up, but at least we got an eight-hour trip out of it. Unfortunately I've spent most of my time since then futilely trying to fulfill what didn't happen with her."

Mary was not moving, Scott was nodding patiently and making more revisions on Milton's work as Frank, a man at last cured, finished his point.

"Now I've been through it all and I'm totally removed. I have no vested interests. Emerson calls it the concept of the 'Invulnerable Essence.' These other guys are always trying to qualify their positions. Jockeying, so they can keep horsing around." He looked accusingly at Scott who cocked his head slightly to indicate he was still listening though reading. "I don't care. I can be totally psychotic and it doesn't matter."

Mary was trying to become part of her chair. Scott hastily crossed the room to check the reference book "Guide, Philosopher, Friend: An End To Technocracy." I asked Frank what women's reactions were to his new outlook.

"That's not the point," he snapped. "But most of them aren't thrilled with the realization that I could very easily get into a caveman approach, just prowling around doing a Neanderthal trip." He scratched at his ribs. "They know I could be perfectly content to swing in from time to time and hit a woman over the head, symbolically speaking, for the sole purpose of waking her up, not conquering her."

"What happens if your timing is off, and you swing down and hit a tree?" Mary asked, seeming to surprise herself. She looked in back of her as if someone else had asked the question.

"I may hit a hundred trees," Frank reasoned. "So what. Sooner or later I'll puncture the target. If not, I'll just go back and hang out at my cave. I'm into being a relaxed primal man with no time for jungle warfare."

After a slight pause he quoted a poem he had written to his third wife. It was an example of a negative, servile attitude he had once had, something celibacy had cleansed him of.

> "If you'd come back to me I'd get down on
> My hands and knees and suck the sidewalk.
> How could I stoop so low?"

"How couldn't you," Scott interjected, then covered his mouth as if he had burped. He put aside his apologia and mentioned that he was thinking of changing the "Moby Dick" quote that had begun his thesis to something simpler, yet still daring. Something that wouldn't be abused. "I'd like to get in there the idea that computers are designed to better accomplish what man has been doing by, uh, hand," he said, shooting another quick glance at Mary who abruptly suggested we go out for a pizza.

We went to Pagliai's near campus. While Mary and I sat at a side booth, Frank and Scott hit the salad bar and at one point, while everyone in the place grew silent, Frank could be heard saying that Scott was living disproof of William Blake's theory that the paths of excess lead to the palace of wisdom because he continued to do everything in his power to "keep playing clitoral concertos."

I asked Mary if this wasn't a rather strange Valentine's night for her. "Well, it's a little different than going out with the women from the office, like I did last year," she admitted with a smile.

After the meal Scott began fading fast. He had on one of Mary's flannel shirts. It was a little big on him and seemed to accent the grey in his hair. Soon he patted his tummy and frowned at Mary as if something were wrong. She acknowledged a similar stomach ache. A touch of the flu possibly. They decided to go. Scott had forgotten his wallet so Mary picked up the tab.

As they left I mentioned to Frank that aside from the fact that Mary was a couple of inches taller than Scott, they could pass for the couple in "American Gothic."

***

Monday morning I waited for Judy to come by. She clicked down the hall waving a card.

"Here," she said, snug in her pink sweater and jeans. "I got a Valentine's card for you. I looked for it for an hour."

It was a simple card to a "Special person. Nice to talk to, nice to know." She signed it "Ms. Judy." I told her I had a card for her, too.

"This is the only Valentine's Day card I gave out this year," I said.

"Me too."

"Yours is the only one I got."

"Me too, except for the one my dad gave me."

I admitted that I had also got one from my sister and confessed that I was bummed out that school was cancelled Friday, because I wanted to give her the card then.

"Yeah," she said almost before I had gotten the words out. "I had a real cute outfit I was all set to wear. I put your card right on top of my camera last night so I wouldn't forget it today."

"Yours was in my notebook before '60 Minutes' yesterday."

I shook my head, stopping short of asking her out for the rest of her life. We both blushed for a few seconds, then she clicked down the hall while a chunky kid in a Pedal to the Metal t-shirt walked behind her and tugged at her sweater. She couldn't be bothered.

***

Wednesday, the day of a full moon, was a half day for teachers' meetings. Judy mentioned that she might come in that afternoon with her best friend, Terri, and her little buddy, two-year-old Gregory.

While I worked out on the universal early that afternoon, I was joined by a couple of freshman girls in shorts and sweatshirts. They were touching their toes and tumbling on some mats. When one of them lifted up her sweatshirt to wipe her brow and revealed two tiny but lovely breasts, I decided I had worked out long enough. I looked out the cafeteria window, saw Judy's green Gremlin parked in front of the school and went into the john to comb my hair. She was standing in the hallway when I came out, holding little Gregory in her arms. She had on a black, flowered Gypsy skirt and a low-cut Danskin top. Gregory was playing with one of her breasts. Judy patiently kept moving his hand.

"Hi, I'm Ray Powell," I said to Terri.

"I think she figured that out already," Judy said.

"Yeah," Terri said. "Judy showed me the picture she took of you."

Terri, a petite brunette in a tight, bluejean slit skirt and an unbuttoned white blouse, wore black heels and hose. She had graduated the year before.

"Why don't you come down to my room and we can chat for awhile?" I offered. They agreed. I got us Pepsis from the teachers' lounge.

"I hear you're into the Zodiac," Terri said as she adjusted her skirt in front of the full-length mirror on the closet.

"Yeah sort of," I replied weakly, my thoughts flashing on what Terri might say to Judy's dad, "Yeah, he's into astrology and talks about the moon all the time. He's really neat." Feeling the need to clarify my views I mentioned to Terri I believed in astrology up to a point but wasn't a fanatic about it.

Gregory was now walking around Judy's legs and playing with her skirt.

"He's been real cranky today," Judy explained as she straightened her skirt after one of Gregory's assaults, then bent way over to wipe something off his mouth. Girding my loins, I decided it would be prudent for me to sit behind my desk for awhile.

Judy said they'd be heading over to this guy Dave's house in a little bit. "We went over there to a party last night. I gotta admit he has a really great stereo system. I don't know about him though, sometimes he doesn't pay attention to me, but the other day I heard he was drunk up at the Crow's Nest and was asking all kinds of questions about me."

I flashed on how Lana used to talk about going to parties and thoughts of Gomorrah would hover in my imagination. Or how she would mention chatting to another guy and I would conjure them in Kama Sutra etchings. But the impossibility of Judy and me as a couple exempted me from flights of jealous fancy and freed me to simply relate to her as a person, thereby enabling me to acquire an essential relationship skill – one that I had, sadly, failed to develop in my formative years. I leaned back and folded my hands behind my head, waiting for the next growth opportunity to present itself, which didn't take long.

Terri removed one of her shoes and was sitting on a desk-top wriggling her toes, her skirt's slit was about three inches from her crotch.

"I think I've got great toes," she said, stretching her leg out. "My boyfriend thinks they're ugly. What do you think?" She turned in my direction, revealing just a flash of her red Valentine panties.

"Terri! God!" Judy said as Gregory almost disappeared between her legs and a hard-on prodded me into a blase' verbal acknowledgement that Terri's toes were somewhat attractive and a silent admittance that Gregory was headed in the right direction.

With her legs outstretched Terri chattered away about how she and Judy got phony IDs and went to bars in Toledo; how they snuck out of their houses in the middle of the night to go to parties; how her father joked that she and Judy could earn a living "turning tricks" on Jefferson Street. "He's only kidding though," she said.

"I don't know about that," Judy said. "Your father is pretty weird. He came into the bathroom one time when I was taking a shower." Both girls laughed. "Plus, he's always telling us we could be strippers at the Golden Cherry. He says he'd sit in the audience so no one would bother us."

I figured I had at least five more minutes behind my desk before I dared stand.

Terri finally put her shoe back on, opening her legs as she did so. I saw it coming and chose to shift my gaze toward Judy and Gregory. The little fellow was playing with Judy's hair while his head was nuzzled on her chest. Judy's eyes were riveted on mine. They decided to leave.

"Nice meeting you, Terri," I said standing up after un-tucking my flannel shirt as a precautionary measure. "You really do have marvelous toes."

Judy yanked Gregory's hand away from her chest. "What's wrong with you," she scolded. He whimpered. "I hope Dave's home," she said, looking in my direction.

"See you tomorrow Judy," I said softly. She smiled and nodded. The girls clicked down the corridor, each holding one hand of the wobbling Gregory.

Even before they were out of sight, I made a beeline for the lounge where I knew Henning, the school police officer, would be taking a lengthy cigarette break. There were some things I'd been meaning to ask him.

"Do you ever see any of these young girls with older guys?" I cagily inquired after sitting down and glancing at a Detroit Free Press, my heady line of questioning seeming as much an involuntary response as the physiological one which had poked at my pants a little earlier.

"Hell," he laughed, "so many of these 16-year-olds are leaving school every day with guys in their 30s it's ridiculous. These young guys can't handle the girls."

I expressed concern as to the legal issues involved, since I should know such things, what with the kind of kids I was working with.

"Hell, we can't do anything unless the girl complains and most of them love it," he cackled.

"What's the legal age in Michigan?"

"17 for girls, they're considered adults then. It's 18 in Ohio."

"What about taking them across the state line?" I asked as if I was worrying about a specific girl in my class.

"Hell, we can't do a damn thing. It's all up to the girl."

"Phil," the slinky secretary from the superintendents office burst in. "They need you down in the shop. Somebody's been stealing wood, and I guess Gordy's got a clue."

"Damn," the lawman said, putting out his cigarette and checking his shoulder holster. "No rest for the wicked." He got up, stubbed his toe on a chair and waddled out the door.

It was time to go home. In the hallway the cheerleaders were practicing for the night's game. They were all in cut-offs and t-shirts, jumping around and practicing splits. "Hit Me With Your Best Shot" was blaring in the background. The music stopped and they began to cheer, "2-4-6-8-tonight we're gonna dominate." When I got to my car and turned on the radio, a song by the Police was playing. It was about a young teacher and schoolgirl fantasies.

***

That weekend I went to Crystal City to hit the night spots. Outside the Club I saw Lana's Toyota wagon with an "I Love Corpus Christi" rainbowed on the back window.

"I just heard Lana ran off and got married to some skinny hillbilly," Bonnie the barmaid informed me after I sat down in the bar's geriatric ward section near the television and at a safe distance from the braying and belching undergrads. "Galen was in here and told me. He's moving back to Texas next month. He just got out of the hospital. I guess he had a rib removed or something."

"Married," I said, half-surprised, half-relieved. "I never figured she'd get married again."

"Yeah, Galen said she and the twins and this guy headed for Kansas in a pizza car."

***

At school, Judy was coming to see me every day, a fact not lost on a growing number of observers.

"How's your girlfriend doing?" asked Georgeanne, my senior aide. She had had a kid the year before. The father was a 14-year-old whose stepdad owned the local pool hall. I told her that whatever girlfriend I may have once had was now married to a pizza delivery man. She raised an eyebrow and dutifully returned to grading my students' hopeless papers.

The newly-appointed basketball coach, a heavy-set guy with a bad perm and Coke-bottle glasses who was always doodling things like "two Polacks walking a breast," nudged me as Judy scurried by selling the school newspaper, the Temperance Titan. "She's really got a pair doesn't she?" I didn't honor his comment with a response but he kept staring at Judy, then at me and popping his thick eyebrows above his thick lenses.

Clearly, the little minds of Temperance delighted in making Judy and me into much more of an item than we were, but I had realized long ago that I couldn't be responsible for anyone's negative interpretation of my behavior. So rather than worry about them, I needed to worry about me. I had already decided to leave Temperance and explore other possibilities, perhaps even a career change. And it was also time to change how I acted toward women. My willingness to just sit there and take what Lana dished out still haunted me. For the sake of my own manhood, if you will, I needed to assert myself and go after what I wanted – and that included more time with Judy, despite how awkwardly that fit into someone's notion of what a 30-year-old should be doing. It was critical that I learn to respond firmly to what opportunities were presented me. Since I only had a few months left at Temperance and then all peripheral teacher/student issues would be irrelevant, the only question now was exactly what to do and when.

It came to me while I was watching TV on a Saturday night. There was a '50s oldies show on. Toledo's own Theresa Brewer belted out "Ricochet Romance." The Four Lads sang "No Not Much" and "Standin' on the Corner." Miss Patti Page did the "Tennessee Waltz", followed by Gogi Grant singing "The Wayward Wind." All the songs were from my very early years, all about love – the search and the magic – and were all the ones I dreamily listened to but was too froze up inside to act on, even clumsily, during my teenage years. Later, on a "Kung Fu" episode entitled "Uncertain Bondage" – which was concerned with the theme of taking risks and chances – the Grasshopper was afraid to give a gift to his master because it might be rejected, and he would feel great pain. "Do you seek love or barter?" the master asked. "What you risk is great pain or great joy."

I made up my mind. I'd ask Judy for a date.

***

The next Monday I invited Judy to stop by my room the last 15 minutes of sixth period. I waited, nervously pacing. Several false clicks went by. A couple of kids opened the door to use my pencil sharpener. With 10 minutes left in the period, the loudest clicking I'd ever heard started. It was her in high yellow heels, yellow disco pants and a ruffled white blouse. She had her hair up, exposing dangling rainbow earrings.

"I guess you could hear me coming," she laughed and looked at her heels. She sat up on the table and took her shoes off. "I'm going to a job interview at a women's clothes store in the North Towne Mall. It's right after school, so I ran home and changed." She examined her shoes. "These are hurting me a little."

Her pants were astonishingly tight, and I almost made a fatherly comment about them, but instead said, "I'd like to see you outside of school sometime."

Her eyes eased open and she muttered, "Well, I don't know."

"I mean, we could go out for breakfast or something. I know you're a coffee hound. We could go to the Original Pancake House. No big deal. Terri could come along. Even Gregory. It would be fun."

I produced a paper with my address and phone number on it. I explained where I lived. "A yellow house, upstairs." She nodded that she knew about where it was, but didn't really say anything, just stared at the paper and put her shoes back on. The next couple of days were teacher/parent conference days. I didn't have any conferences Wednesday. "If you'd like to go just give me a call tomorrow night or Wednesday morning. Don't worry, it'll be okay."

She was out the door. "I better put this back here," she said as she stuffed the paper in her back pocket. Her pants were so tight that she could hardly wedge the paper in.

In the hallway, as the class changed, Journey's overwrought lead-singer droned "Hopelessly in Love" on a portable tapedeck.

***

She didn't call and I ached. The next day I didn't see her in the morning, and she signed out at noon for "personal" reasons. I went home with my ears ringing and tried to take a nap. Lana's image drifted in and out of a surreal Corpus Christi bumpersticker rainbow and I don't remember if I dozed or not, but – lying there in the afternoon light, tears filling my eyes – I realized that my feelings about Judy were a lot stronger than I thought. Could it be that I was losing myself again, despite how I rationalized this experience as simply a near-laboratorial opportunity for intellectual/emotional growth? Maybe. But with someone fresh as a dream wouldn't the equation be entirely different from what it was with Lana? Possibly. She's a fairly mature 17, but not the kind of 17 you see walking on the arm of a star at a Hollywood opening, or in a Woody Allen movie, or on a talk show reflecting on a childhood romance with Polanski or telling what it was like to snort blow with the Eagles.

She's simply a lovely young woman who happened to hit me like a lightning bolt. And who could say how much of that was axiomatically correspondent to the degree of aloneness I felt after Lana? All I knew was that I wanted to be with her, saw her smile when I blinked, was filled with her laughter, listened for hints in her conversation, watched to see if she walked around with any guys, noticed everything she wore, remembered everything she said. Was I coming apart again? Deep down I knew Judy was a sweetheart and I didn't have to worry about her becoming Lana. Judy was just fine. But what about the other half of the equation? What about me?

***

"Sit down, Judy," I said firmly that Friday afternoon. She sat at the table in my room. Her jeans were loose fitting and she had on a floppy, blue flannel shirt. She had been painting on a bulletin board in the library. Her Cedar Point notebook had some stars doodled on the cover and the over-sized bracelet she wore spelled out FLORIDA.

"I was really bummed out yesterday," I said, sitting down behind my desk and folding my hands together, teacher-like.

She looked down, then slowly back to my eyes. It was so easy to look in her eyes. Difficult not to, in fact.

"I don't think it was a very good idea for me to try to arrange meeting you," I said. She nodded ever so slightly.

"I guess I realized something since I talked to you last." I took a deep breath as her head began to tilt. "What I realized was that my feelings about you are a lot stronger than I thought," I paused. Her whole body was slowly leaning to the right, away from me. Gradually. Almost imperceptibly. But her eyes remained on mine.

"What I guess I mean to say is...well...if I don't watch myself I could very easily fall in love with you."

I got to my feet and began pacing in front of the blackboard.

"It's hard to figure, Judy. Maybe I'm vulnerable because the supposed love of my life left a few months ago." I stopped and half-sat on the chalk tray, dusting my pants with chalk. "But it's more than that. I never met anybody like you when I was in high school. I never even had any dates at all." Embarrassed, I looked away. "But you are just so beautiful and so much fun to talk to. . . Well, I've got to be extra careful." She seemed to be locked in an advanced yoga position. "So I don't think it's a very good idea to try to meet."

She looked down. What was making me do this? Why couldn't I just relax and let things flow, like I had resolved for the new year and like every Caine quote I have stuffed in that notebook says? She got up, teetered just a bit, then said, "Well, I guess it's good that I didn't call you," and wiped her forehead in mock relief.

With her humor having cleared the leaden air, I was able to manage, "You should have shook that finger at me during all that heaviness, you know."

"It crossed my mind, believe me."

We both laughed easily and after a not-so-awkward pause, I asked her how the Classic Car Show had gone the night before.

"Great," she said, sticking her thumbs up. "There was a candy Corvette there and a lot of really neat people." She stopped and gulped. "One real winner kept hanging around me, though. He was kind of scary."

If anybody at all bothers you, I began, but didn't finish. The thought of me someday having to confront myself over Judy was not a pleasant one.

The First Day of Spring

Sometime around the Ides of March I took a day off school and visited that Creative Writing class I had stunned with my Judy revelation a month earlier. I had called Dusty and gotten her approval, although she said it was against her better judgement and might end up getting her called before the school board, which would much rather keep issues like teacher/student relationships away from classroom discussions. I countered her apprehension by pointing out that enlightenment does not occur by imagining figures of light but by making the darkness conscious. As a professed champion of free expression she could do nothing but agree and told me she would have the kids write a reaction paper to my visit, thus giving them a chance to creatively explore their feelings. I offered to whip up something myself. "Keep it clean," she said in an agitated tone, "and try not to drool too much."

When I walked into the room the boys nudged each other as the girls wriggled in their seats. Some students from other classes, who were sitting on the ledges and standing in the back, buzzed a little and let out quickly suppressed bursts of laughter. Dusty looked at me as if she were a condemned woman spotting the chaplain striding to her cell. The class had been watching a tape of "American Graffiti" all week. The movie was set in the early '60s, when I was just starting high school, and I mentioned that, hoping to help them possibly see me as I was then and perhaps even grasp the subtle reality that the adolescent in us all never totally vanishes.

Before I could fully execute this potentially invaluable point, Dusty stopped me short and asked the kids if they wanted to read their papers. Most refused but a short-haired, female-jock type raised her hand and offered that she thought I was romantic. A bashful, long-necked guy said I was pretty cool and honest. A square-shouldered girl wearing a Model Airplaners Get High t-shirt said I sounded like her uncle who was always saying that blue jeans were made for teenage girls. A straight-laced, whiny girl, who looked like a door-to-door Mormon, said high school girls didn't like older guys because they wanted someone who could meet their parents and go out with their friends. The "shit-her-pants-tell-her-boyfriend" girl was absent. Several kids didn't have anything, saying they thought the whole thing was a hoax just to make them do another assignment. I told them they were too young to be cynical. Then I read my paper, "30 and 17."

"With her honey hair and hazel eyes she's so beautiful I can't look sometimes. When JFK was shot she was a few weeks old. When Chicago exploded in '68, she wasn't in school and I was ready for the Revolution.

What do we talk about? She mentions her determination to succeed, candy red Corvettes, being lonely a lot, working rock concerts at the Sports Arena, sneaking out at night, popping out of a birthday cake for a guy in Florida and being afraid to go home sometimes because of her parents' arguing. I talk about the cosmos and karma and full moons and empty houses, hinting at – between each line – a lifetime battle with loneliness. In return, as Othello said of Desdemona, she gives me for my pains a world of sighs. While I give the gift of gentle encouragement and the willingness to listen for what's behind her words. I even write her a poem about her '72 Gremlin passing my Ford Fiesta as we leave the school parking lot, each going our separate ways in our respective compact cars, bound together only by blaring radios. She asks me how I knew that she blasted her radio.

Just the other day I spilled my feelings to her, something I certainly didn't do with women when I was younger. She nearly drops through the floor but recovers enough to gently joke about it, relaxing both of us. What's the point, the lesson of all this? That there's no explanation for attraction? That things sneak up on you, and life is full of surprises? That feelings are unpredictable? That the heart is a lonely hunter? Maybe it's just that numbers, whether they be 30 or 17, are no shield against vulnerability or awkwardness or anything."

"Wow! Awright!" several voices yelped in unison. I looked at the girl who made the statement that young girls aren't interested in old guys and gave her a "put-that-in-your-pipe-and-smoke-it" look. She was staring at her fingernails and bobbing her head. Dusty, appearing relieved but clearly taking no chances, thanked me then sang out in her shrill teacher's voice that I would have to be leaving. As I exited a couple of guys beat on their desk tops, and the final reel of "American Graffiti" was cranked up.

***

On Friday, March 20, the first day of spring, someone brought valiums to school. By 11 o'clock the halls were filled with young zombies in Led Zeppelin t-shirts, Speedway Jam insignias and Def Lepperd jackets. Braless girls with "If I told you you had a nice body would you hold it against me?" emblazoned on their t-shirts and unzipped jeans staggered through the halls. The rest rooms were disaster areas. Mr. Nott, who had begun the day yodeling in the teachers' lounge while demonstrating Shaklee's latest line, was barricaded in his office. Chief Officer Henning, who had on a string tie and pants about three inches too short revealing just the slightest bit of calf above his Beatle boots, was beside himself. I thought he was going to call some auxiliary firemen, just in case. He was visibly cracking under the pressure, complained of a touch of the flu and disappeared for most of the day.

I tried to assure some of the staff that what else could be expected on a full moon first day of spring. "That's about as potent a combination as you can get," I said to Mr. Hardesty, a diminutive former barber and current Prefect of Discipline who, it was learned around noon, was suffering from diarrhea. Nott dramatically intoned over the PA system ordering everyone to "stay where you are." At that time roughly one-third of the student body was staggering in the halls, stereo tape-decks blasting, beating on doors and shooting toothpicks at the ceiling. Junior high lunch hour hadn't even started yet. By the time the high school kids got to the cafeteria it would be a combat zone with so much food flying through the air that Frances Scott Key might appear and re-work the "Star-Spangled Banner."

A rumor surfaced that Nott was on the phone with the governor's office. The superintendent was on a lengthy lunch break that corresponded each Friday with his slinky secretary's absence. The supe's wife, who could be seen defiantly adjusting her girdle from time to time, assumed command. She tried to get the drugged kids to stop roaming the halls and gather in the board room to help staple her newsletter together. She ended up leaving in tears when a kid with a "Moses" tattoo wobbled into the room and told her to "staple these," offering his adolescent balls. An example was made out of him; he was suspended for the rest of the day.

I hadn't had a chance to speak to Judy since I told her I could fall for her a couple weeks earlier. She had been absent a few days. She didn't walk by my room anymore fourth period and was signing out a lot. Every now and then I would spot her at a distance, but her eyes no longer sought me out. Earlier in the week Caine had said that "a wise man is governed by what he feels not what he sees." I felt I should try to talk to her. I could have used a valium myself as I tried to muster the courage to seek her out. I spotted her moving quickly towards the library, walking with the shop teacher, Gordy, a mustachioed guy who wore jeans a lot and occasionally sported a brightly-colored "And who's little girl are you?" button. Most of the girls at school liked him. As Gordy and Judy moved gracefully through the lunch time crowd, they looked like they were having a grand old time. She didn't even glance to see if I was standing in my usual station. Gordy, who was wearing a sport coat that day, seemed to be in the middle of a story and Judy was all ears. I figured I needed a reason to talk to her, so I decided to give her a little gift. I wrote on a small sheet of paper:

To Judy on the First Day of Spring,

"Two of the fairest stars in all the heavens,
Having some other business,
Do entreat your eyes to twinkle

In their spheres 'til they return."

Ray

At the school library I sought her out. "Judy," I said. She looked surprised to see me. She was sitting at the librarian's desk in the back room, left-handing a report for Civics class. "How are you doing?" I asked. She looked up with those eyes but didn't speak. Her cheeks were colored with a feverish warmth and her lips were turned down at the corners. I melted a little but went on. "C'mon over to my room. I've got something for you."

"Uh, I'm pretty busy here," she said uneasily, but I was already striding out the door. She clumped – not clicked – after me. Moses, who had opted to serve his suspension in the halls, was draped across the drinking fountain. He saw me, then glanced at Judy following me.

"Awright Mr. P. . . nice." Moses made a feeble attempt at an OK gesture with his nearly useless hands.

Judy and I got to my room and I gave her the paper. "Here. It's from 'Romeo and Juliet'."

She sagged a little as she read it. "It's really nice," she said in that soft, soon-to-be-a-woman voice that every now and then came out. Then she got flustered, blurting, "I really don't know what to do," and literally ran from the room.

A knot fisted me in the stomach. I'd done it again. What in the hell was wrong with me? A familiar pattern was emerging in this so-called growth period of mine that looked to be an endless loop of pointless thrusts and parries resulting in me on an island here and women way over there. Nott came over the PA system and announced that anyone found in the halls would have their parents called immediately. I almost went into the halls, hoping they'd call my mom – who, if nothing else, could at least point out where on the loop I may have entered.

On the way out of the parking lot after school I was right behind Judy. I pretended not to notice that her eyes didn't glance into her rear view mirror. I felt like a creep. We were really becoming friends, the first person I'd found to talk to in that school and I couldn't handle my emotions, try to make a date with her, then tell her I'm on the verge of falling in love with her. Well, what did I expect, for Christ sake? Even though she'd handled my barrage really well she's just 17, I'm a teacher and we'd only been talking for about two months. So then I yank her out of the library and hit her with "Romeo and Juliet," while kids are bouncing here, there and everywhere, and it's all because I'm this lonely guy trying to fill this huge hole inside or something. She probably thinks I'm insane. I scare her now, and I know she used to like me. She needs somebody to talk to just like I do. She's lonely too and probably thought she could trust me and now I've put a dent in that. Well, like Caine says, your trust is as safe as where you put it and despite all my bullshit awareness and allegedly noble intentions, I guess hers is not very safe with me.

A couple junior high kids were walking along the side of the road smoking cigarettes. Their jacket collars were turned up like James Dean. Judy turned left. I turned right. April Wine's "Just Between You and Me" was playing, as it did everyday around 2:30 when school got out. There for awhile I thought it was our song.

Good grief.

***

On a night like this, a full moon on the first day of spring only happens only a handful of times in a lifetime, the romantic monkey rested squarely on my back. I unashamedly longed for an evening of "South Pacific" or at least a gaze across a crowded room; or maybe "Nocturnes" by Chopin or "LA Boheme" or the background music to "Elvira Madigan." I wanted to wait a little long to kiss, the idea being if I didn't kiss I'd perish. I wanted to be naive and tentative. I wanted to hold hands and touch knees and whirl in an embrace. I wanted the whole wonderful burden of romance to be seen through the eyes. I wanted to again kiss – not as foreplay but as romantic gesture – then turn away as if stricken, only to turn and kiss again. I wanted to tell someone I was mad for them, "Je nis fou de toi." I wanted to study album jackets with someone. I wanted a quiet talk with Judy.

Instead, I started this night of nights waiting for a friend in a place called the Main Event Lounge, located in a hastily-constructed strip mall next to the Kowalski Gun Shop. There was a six-foot boxer, who resembled Smokin' Joe Frazier, painted and poised on the door of the lounge. Inside there were all kinds of sports pennants, pictures and scores. "Ohio State 10, Michigan 7." In the john there was graffiti, "Woody Sucks" and "Bo Bites the Bag." They had a small bumper pool table inside a little boxing ring and "Me and Mrs. Jones" type songs on the box. There were two big color television sets and several garish video games. The waitresses wore Adidas t-shirts. This was where my introduction into the Toledo singles' bar scene took place, and where I would kick off a long weekend that would end up wiping the romantic glaze from my kisser.

Ritchie, an old friend of mine from Crystal City, had been calling me frequently, saying I should hop aboard the rodeo circuit – which is what he called the singles' scene – where there were plenty of women who, he insisted, would give me the ride of my life. Unlike Bert, Frank and Scott who thought of me as a kind of sheltered, cosmic lumberer in need of re-education in the world of women, Ritchie was convinced that I could make out like a bandit with Toledo ladies and that my laid-back, analytic personality was the perfect vehicle for scoring. After limping home from school that day, I called him at the radio station where he was sales manager and he suggested we meet at the Main Event

"You finally made it, huh Ray?" Ritchie said after making a grand entrance, saluting, giving a Dutch rub to the bartender, and finally bear-hugging a chesty bleach-blond waitress. "I knew you would. As we say, all roads lead to the Main Event." He carefully removed his black silk suit coat and draped it over the back of a chair. "I'm only gonna tell you this once," he said quietly, leaning close to me, "Your money's no good here." Ritchie had free food and drink deals at many places in town. We ordered a couple burgers and I commented that there didn't seem to be any women in the place, aside from the waitresses.

"Old Smokin' Joe on the door scares most of the gals away," he said with a laugh. "But this is just a warm-up place. Don't worry. They're out there." Ritchie adjusted his gold cufflinks, pausing until our waitress was out of earshot. "All you have to do, my friend, is start spilling out that analytical shit and these women will look at you like you like you're the Second Coming, trust me." He held up a cautionary finger. "Not all of them, mind you. You'll definitely have to pick your spots, especially if you want to use that 'Kung Fu' stuff. That could backfire, but some women will lap it up like you wouldn't believe." He shook his hand with an ooh-la-la motion. "But either way you should be able to get more pussy than Sinatra."

"I'm not trying to get laid, I'd just like to meet some women."

Ritchie held up his arms as if surrendering. "Hey, you got my vote, but I'm not the one you need to convince."

Our waitress delivered the burgers and her breasts grazed against Ritchie's starched white shirt "It's all about tips – nothing more, nothing less," he said with a tinge of sarcasm after she glided away. "Which reminds me, I could use a few tips myself Ray. I'm thinking about getting back with Carol and I need some advice."

With "The Twelfth of Never" softly playing in the background, Ritchie hinted he was tiring of the exhausting single life and seriously considering getting back with Carol, the love of his life, who had called him earlier in the week. Carol had three kids and a live-in boyfriend, Stan, whom she had tried to get rid of once before. She had everything set up, even her mother agreed with her. The kids hated Stan. He never contributed anything, and she was on food stamps because her ex-husband was living on a ranch in Idaho under an assumed name and not paying child support. She was ready to give Stan the heave-ho over Christmas but then he did the dishes and she changed her mind. However, if Ritchie were interested she implied that Stan would soon be on his way; Carol said it was just a matter of time and that since they had been apart she had realized how much she missed Ritchie.

"Absence is to love as wind is to flame," I said, paraphrasing Caine.

"It enkindles the great and diminishes the small." Ritchie looked perplexed so I simplified the point. "You probably need to play this through with her, but I would be very careful."

Having received confirmation for what he was going to do anyway, Ritchie smiled and nodded. "I'm telling you Ray, you lay shit like that on certain chicks near closing time and I don't care if you got gold chains on or not, you, my friend, will be in like gangbusters. Trust me."

"Do you mind if I sit down for a while?" inquired Peggy, one of the Adidas-clad waitresses. She had been given the night off due to a lack of business. We didn't mind so she sat and ordered a Manhattan. She was in nursing school.

"I've got to find another job," she sighed huskily and finger-twirled her stringy auburn hair. "I'm not making it here."

Ritchie nudged me to offer to buy her a drink. When I did, she said that was the best offer she'd had in a week and that she didn't have anything to do the rest of the night. Ritchie leaned out of her line of vision and made a reeling-in-a-fish-motion with his hands, popping back in her sight to mention that we'd be hitting the circuit and asking her to join us. She said "sure," then left to make a phone call to "this guy."

"Strictly a diversionary tactic my friend," Ritchie said, producing an emery board and filing at his lacquered nails. "She's calling Time and Temperature, trust me."

Peggy and Ritchie agreed that I needed to be shown the Windmill, a "Meat Market," so we each drove there in our own cars and took up standing positions at the brass rail with Peggy perched between us. I began to talk to her about Judy – wanting to get her opinion about the situation-but Ritchie's head appeared over her shoulder and he began making a frantic, throat-cutting gesture and loudly announced he had to confirm something with someone and then would be leaving.

"So soon," Peggy said.

"Too many ghosts here," he said, checking his watch and motioning that he wanted a quick word with me. He pulled me away from her and we leaned over the rail a bit. "About the only thing you can say to mess yourself up with this one is to talk about a 17-year-old girl." He said good-bye to Peggy and drew me close for one last bit of advice. "Don't bother to bring out the A material, you won't need it for her. Trust me." As Ritchie headed towards the pay phone by the exit, Peggy said that he was probably calling his own number and suggested we go to the Saddle Inn, where a local group called the Ducktails was playing. That was fine with me.

The Saddle Inn, one of the many Toledo bars owned and operated by Arabs, was jammed, but Peggy and I found seats with a good view of the band. The leader of the Ducktails was a pimply-faced guy with an upturned collar, snub nose and pompadoured hair that appeared ready to fly away. The other guys in the group looked like they were from Lebanon. They played '50s rock. Peggy was drinking tequila shots and blurring around the edges. On the other side of me was a tight-jeaned woman about 21. Apparently her boyfriend was the bartender. His name was Rahsha and he looked like a Cro-Magnon Spanky MacFarland. He kept his animal gaze riveted on his girl's tits while trying to sing along to songs like "Be Bop a Lula." He gripped a towel while he sang. I laughed to myself. Peggy looked at me with glassy eyes and said, "What are you laughing about?" putting her hand on my stool to balance herself.

"Sometimes I wonder why people come to places like this," I said, staring at the tuxedoed, monocled figure of a penguin above the top shelf whiskey bottles. "What do they intend to find?"

"Do you have any intentions for me?"

"No," I said matter-of-factly. "Ritchie thinks I should have, but I don't."

Her hand slipped from the stool, and she sank to the floor and began laughing. I helped her up.

"Ritchie's one of the Windmill's ghosts," she slurred and brushed mechanically at her skirt. "I am too, I guess, but not for long. My boyfriend's coming at 12:30 and we're going to be married in a couple of weeks." She put her index finger to her lips. "Don't tell anyone though. We're going to elope."

I told her not to worry, that one thing I was good at was keeping secrets. That you might say it was a family tradition. I was relieved that she actually did have a boyfriend, both for her sake and also so that I wouldn't have to feel awkward about not acting out some disjointed seduction scenario.

Around midnight her boyfriend showed up. He looked like a rat, spoke bad English and played lead guitar in the Baghdad Blues Band. Peggy pointed at me, put her head on his shoulder and looked like she was going to throw up. He kept not looking at me while Peggy kept mumbling that she "Just wanted to be sure before the wedding."

The tight-jeaned girl was working out on the bar. Her boyfriend was grunting, "yes, yes" at her. The band played "Chantilly Lace." Another Arab bartender made the girl step down from the bar and she plopped on her stool, pouting. I was ready to leave but decided I would comfort her and told her that, in addition to her dancing ability, she had really nice hands. Her boyfriend eyed me, so she didn't acknowledge my comment until he went to the other side of the bar and I turned to leave. She tapped me on the shoulder and said, "A lot smarter guys than old sourpuss over there told me the same thing that you just did. One of them even said I had piano fingers." She extended her hand towards me like royalty. "I'll see you tomorrow, kind sir."

***

"Why don't you meet me at the Betsy Ross Coffee Shop? I want to talk to you."

The Saturday morning phone invitation from Emma, the young grandmother from the Winter Solstice Party, sounded good to me, especially in the wake of Judy's freakout the afternoon before and my grim much-ado-about-nothing night at Club OPEC. I showered quickly and headed towards the Betsy Ross where grandma would sew things up. I could use it.

I had run into Emma at the grocery store a few weeks earlier and we stopped by for a quick bite to eat at the Hungry I restaurant, a place I had occasionally gone to with Lana. At that time Emma had hinted she would call me and we could get together for a movie of something. I had no problem at all with that.

When I arrived at the red, white and blue decorated Betsy Ross, Emma was already seated in the first booth. She barely looked up as I motioned for some coffee.

"I can't see you anymore," she said in a small, narrow tone. Her face was clear and pale as a nun's, the soft curves of her blond hair parted in the middle. "My ex came back early from visiting his girlfriend in Miami, and as part of the interrogation it came out that I had lunch with a real tall guy." She studied her wrinkled hands. "He exploded and said your height was something he couldn't deal with, so I decided I won't see you any more."

I kept waiting for her to burst out laughing and indicate she was doing a parody of some kind, that this was guerrilla theater of the absurd. Then it dawned on me that she was absolutely serious and I slipped into dumbfoundedness – especially when she admitted she was still sleeping with him, something she had told me that she definitely wasn't doing.

"I don't know how he enjoys it," she grimaced. "He sort of forces his way on me. He has custody of our daughter. He's president of our business." She trembled and her ERA lapel button seemed to buckle. "I thought when I moved back in it would be different." Her choked monotone trailed into silence.

I sat there for a moment, my mind blank, trying to figure out what sins of a former life had gotten me to the place where someone who I had had one 30-minute lunch with would call me and raze me out of a tortured, yet welcome, sleep to tell me she couldn't see me again because her ex-husband had problems with my height. Twenty-four hours earlier I had bummed out Judy and now I was face-to-face with out and out surrealsim. Suddenly, I felt like crying. Emma was ready to leave, but I had a few things to say.

"You're allowing him to do this to you," I began, leaning halfway across the table. "Sleeping with him, wasting your precious time and your precious space." If the game was up, fine, I still had a few points to make. If I was supposed to be paying some karmic price for heaven knows what, I could understand that, fine. I wasn't exactly Mr. Squeaky Clean. If I was merely a relatively innocent victim in the turbulent battle of the sexes that marked this time period, I could live with having it coming on a certain random level, fine. Somebody had to pay. But please don't expect me to sit here and take it without launching a few roundhouses of my own. "I mean this guy's your roommate. You moved out on him once before. He's got other girlfriends. You're dating someone else, and the only thing he knows about me is that I'm six-five. So he decides to 'X' me out, and you're enabling him."

Emma probably didn't deserve a tirade, at least she was trying to be up front with her reality, which is more than I could say for Lana, and I'm sure this wasn't easy for her. Maybe she set this up because she needed to hear some things. Anyway, I was tired of trying to be a perpetually retreating nice guy like my dad always was – never admitting anything was wrong, never realizing nothing was right. I was tired of being made to feel, as I had during my emotional valet years with Lana, like something that's not part of life, that doesn't count, that's some kind of asterisk or footnote, that's the last to be considered, that's the fifth wheel or the spare tire, that's the first piece of excess baggage to be tossed out.

"If I don't, he might take my baby." Emma trotted out the ultimate female reason for compliance with any irrational male behavior.

"It sounds like he's already got her. Everybody gets what they want. You want your baby, money, security. You got it. But the price is your soul." I softened my voice. I didn't want her to think that I hated her. I didn't. I knew it was still Lana I was furious with. Lana and this whole sad struggle to make some kind of connection. Emma looked at me and seemed to understand. I reached out for her hand. There was a soggy tissue rolled in it.

"You think it's important to preserve this charade for the sake of your daughter," I said. "You're old enough to know better than that. Plus, how do you ever expect her to have it any any better if this is the kind of example you give her."

"I know, but I'm getting it together slow but sure."

"Look, the more you ravel up in this situation, the longer it will take to unravel. You're looking for a miracle, a break, but what you don't understand is that the longer you go to political rallies and talk about freedom and growth, then go 'home' to this masquerade, the longer the road back is going to be."

She blew her nose into a napkin and put some sugar and cream into her already cold coffee.

"But I've got little Chrissie and the business and so many other things to consider. It's all so complicated."

"No it isn't." I said. "Life is pretty simple. You're just complicating it with all this business about security and considerations and variables. What it really gets down to is.....What do you want?"

"You're life is so uncomplicated. You're free."

"So is yours and so are you, whether you like it or not. That's Karma 101."

She got up first and pecked me on the cheek. Leaving me there seemed to be important to her, like it was symbolic. I followed her outside.

"I'm really going to miss your little car," she said as she ducked into her Volvo wagon. "Big cars turn me off."

Driving home I passed the Korean Sauna where a woman was pulling an empty "Star Wars" wagon. Out of the blue I began to feel a battle-weary kind of anger welling up inside of me as my mind lodged on a diatribe about women our age that Frank had delivered to me a week earlier. How these women have got to start getting it together and begin acting like women, responding like women and get away from these little girl avoidance games of glancing away before eye contact, then giving you points based on your ability to read their minds. How they're so quick to blame men for everything but when someone comes along who's playing a different game, or no game at all – who's not just following his cock but really thinking about things – well he's to be avoided like the plague.

I drove past the magic shop where I had bought Lana her crystal ball, Frank's words still rumbling in my head. How women always talk so movingly about wanting to see a man reveal his vulnerability. But God forbid you reach deep inside and talk about self-doubt or the darker things that are eating away at you. That isn't quite what they had in mind. What they want to hear instead is how you cried, at age seven, when your dog died. That's so sweet. But anything that might make them really uncomfortable, like your lingering, choking fears and dry-heaving insecurities, the kinds of scary things that shake their tidy conceptions of what a man should be and how much security he can provide, you'd be wise to keep that stuff to yourself. As Frank had so aptly put it in summation, "We don't want this vulnerability business to get out of hand. Better stick to 'Old Yeller'."

Before turning down my street I passed the Westwood Adult Theater, where "Deep Throat" was playing, and came to some conclusions of my own. I know no one's to blame, blah, blah, blah; that they're all victims, blah, blah, blah; and that the late '70s were rough on us all. Say hallelujah! But some women are so smug and think they've heard everything, so they begin to smile at you in mid-sentence, as if shrewdly recognizing yet another con job, and never really listen to a word you say. Well, I've never lied to a woman or manipulated one, and I know a lot of guys who are in the same category, and I'm sick and tired of this collective guilt bullshit!

I could hardly remember what had happened to me in the past 24 hours, from the catastrophic "Romeo and Juliet" note to Judy, to the preposterous rejection at the Betsy Ross by grandma. What was going on here? What had seemed such a heroic quest had deteriorated into me losing ground while shuffling back and forth on some cheesy treadmill. Maybe it was time for a change in approach. Maybe it was time for me to quit bending over backwards with my eternally empathetic homilies and my semi-space cadet glow and hit the nightlife blazing, like a militant romantic.

The Men's Group

"I know it's against the rules, but I've got to take a water break," I abruptly announced to the group midway through relating the initiation stage of my journey.

No one moved. The lights had been lowered during this part of the story to signify the shadowy, darkly symbolic nature of the people inhabiting my "wilderness," but I could see Dale look at Gary and Gary look back at Dale with confusion. No one had ever requested interrupting any part of his primal story, let alone the vital initiation stage when most of the critical learning takes place with such painstaking tenuousness.

I was already deep into the process of beating myself up for making the request and for not remembering to put a glass of water at my side, which was a blatant example of the kind of self-sabotage that had earmarked my life, when Gary spoke out clearly and firmly.

"Let's take a quick five. And remember Ray, don't speak with anyone and don't judge yourself. Mentally and spiritually stay where you were."

I hastily headed downstairs to the water fountain with a million mental lashes whipping me for not getting all the way through this stage like everyone else did. And for being such a lummox with Judy, and for not being able to see through the sad silliness of my three obviously misguided friends, and for not choosing a better primal story than the somewhat troubling tale of fevered futility and misplaced anger that was unfolding upstairs in the near dark.

"Psst, Ray." I turned around and saw Dale peeking over his shoulder to see if anyone had followed him. "Listen up, I'll be brief." He quickly took off his backpack, put it on the floor and knelt one leg on it, as if he was about ready to break into "Mammy." "Keep in mind that during this stage you're frozen with grief – following both a loss of ideals and a specific person – and you're operating in the darkness of believing that some specific thing or some specific person can save you. That's all natural." A dull thud from above found him covering his head, as if experiencing an air raid, before resuming his lecture. "To remind folks of this frozenness I've recently included Hank Williams' 'Cold, Cold Heart' into my discovery medley, just to keep the focus on the process and to diffuse any shame connected with it." Dale stood, strapped on his backpack and ascended the stairs.

I took another drink and began heading up the steps when Gary emerged from the shadows of the first flight stairwell.

"Some might say I shouldn't be doing this but as men at times we have to break the rules and do it without apology." He positioned himself three steps above me and looked directly in my eyes. "I know you're scared, so was I when telling the initiation stage. It's the most confusing part of the journey." Gary stretched out his arms, put them on my shoulders and drew his head close to mine. "But remember, big guy, if you're not terrified by the process, you don't understand the nature of self-exposure and you're not digging deep enough to make it worthwhile." A flushed toilet caused him to duck but he quickly rose back up. "Just think of it as passing through the fire on the way to becoming purified and healed." He paused and allowed a joyous expression to envelop his face. "I've started playing Johnny Cash's 'Ring of Fire' for my newlyweds just to remind them of what they'll be experiencing." Gary turned abruptly and strode up the stairs.

As I walked back into the room the lights were lowered. I maneuvered past Dale, who was softly humming "Cold, Cold Heart," and thought of becoming un-thawed. Sitting down next to Gary, who was gently whistling "Ring of Fire," I thought of becoming purified. Feeling as if I needed to choose between flames and ice, I quickly reassumed the mental state I had been in just a few minutes earlier – and found I was still pretty hot under the collar.

The Face of Fire

There was no sense wasting any time. I had a three-day weekend coming and I sure as hell intended to make the most of it. If Emma and Judy wanted to run away, so be it. I was getting a little pissed at myself for just standing, or sitting, there without either going after them or heading in another direction. After coming back from the Emma debacle that afternoon, I concluded that an entirely new approach was needed and the Toledo night life was a perfect venue to try it out.

I visualized bold charm and controlled cockiness during my post-supper meditation, which focused on the concept of that which you seek is also seeking you. Deep breathing exercises accompanied my evening's tube viewing. Inhale. A '40s movie called "The Great McGinty" was on. A wizened political veteran was advising a young candidate to, "Get married. Women don't like bachelors and won't vote for single men." Exhale. Another classic flick featured Alan Ladd looking into Virginia Mayo's eyes and saying, "Every guy has seen you before, but the trick is to find you."

Find her, Find Her. That was my mantra for the night's mission. I knew there was no formulaic way to produce magic, but I was nonetheless determined to try my hand at some new tricks.

When I walked into the Windmill that night, the first thing I noticed was a prostrate guy licking a skinny woman's heels. She had a gigantic hairdo and was sitting on the rail, teetering, while her attendee was on his knees lapping away. I walked over after he had departed.

"Do you let everyone do that?" I asked.

"No," she laughed as the bootlick returned with a drink. "I know him. I'd beat the shit out of anyone who tried anything like that."

"What if I said your heels are driving me crazy?" I leaned close to her, bluejean ad-like.

"I'd say go for it," she burped and her bulky hair looked as if it might snap her neck. The now fully upright fellow yanked at her arm, spilling a little of her strawberry margarita on her chartreuse blouse.

"You asshole," she yelled, tagging along.

The Windmill was the premier singles' bar on Toledo's west side and was a luridly resplendent masterpiece of tackiness. Hanging ominously above the bar was a message board, like the one on Times Square only much smaller. It advertised drinks with names such as "Sneaking Suspicion"-which purportedly removed all doubts – and intermittently hyped special events, like the "Drink a Beer/Smash a Car" promotion the next day. Evenly spaced around the rectangular bar were upside-down spittoons that resembled imitation brass slabs of meat. The overhead bladed fans seemed to be reminding everyone to keep circulating, which I did as I scoped out the patrons.

The crowd was between 21 and 50 years of age, with most appearing to be in their 30s. The ratio of men to women was about three-to-one. There seemed a disproportionate number of checker-panted, leather-jacketed, frosted-haired guys who called men and women both "babe" and nursed lean phallic drafts. Two excessively made-up, tight-jeaned women sat in a booth and stabbed at each other's tater-tots as if they were finishing off still stirring murder victims. And lots of guys acted like movie Italians as "Two Faces Have I" blared over the sound system.

With the anticipation of a kid entering a candy store, I lit by two attractive 40ish women who were talking near the phone booth. The taller one was saying that her husband was screwing someone else the night her son was born. "You have to expect that," said the other. I made a quarter turn and heard a pock-marked, faded blond boast, "When I want to get fucked, I'll get fucked" while "This Magic Moment" played and a Mr. Universe caliber body builder ballooned around the bar like the Michelin Tire Man.

"If somebody says something odd, just keep moving," a matronly woman with large breasts, that were shaped into pointed cups like party hats, advised her friend as they headed towards the powder room past a guy, standing like a sentinel, wearing a button pleading, "Just breathe on me, don't make me come." This wasn't a place for the faint of heart, I noted with mature resignation, and the bloom had faded off many of the roses here. I could deal with that, perhaps extract some wisdom and possibly even thrive, if I learned to play my cards right. Besides, sticking my nose in the middle of all this might even be fun, something that hadn't exactly been my middle name lately.

I wedged into the crowd at the bar. The barmaid had a sassy look and punk rock sparkles on her face. The guy next to me said to her, "Would you be offended if I told you I'd like to lick those sparkles off your face?" She smiled demurely. Another guy in a starched white body shirt called her over and explained how a silver washer in his shoe was making him limp. It was a joke. He pointed to his crotch and said, "Limp, get it." She finally got it, grinned at me and made a circular index finger-to-temple gesture, indicating that the jokester was one crazy guy.

After singing along, with gusto, to the lyrics of "How Long to the Point of No Return?" while leaning against the waist-high rail, which dissected the bar like a brass tightrope, I struck up a conversation with one of the waitresses. She had electric blond hair and was wearing an Oil is a 10 button. We had talked for just a few seconds when she said to me, "Look, I'm taken" and skittered away.

Instead of allowing myself to be rejected into sulking silence, I waited less than a minute and motioned her back. "You know, you can only be taken if you want to go for a ride. Remember, that which gives you comfort also chains you." She walked away and went over to one of the huge male bartenders and talked to him, shaking her head vigorously. I read the question on her lips. "What's he doing here, anyway?" I answered by mouthing at her, "Any port in a storm, honey," then turned and surveyed the bar.

"When Irish Eyes Are Smiling" was on the juke. They still had some green beer left from St. Paddy's Day. A short jut-jawed, baby-faced son-of-the-sod was leaning against the bar intently listening to the lyrics. When it came to the part, "But when Irish eyes are crying, sure they ste-heal you're heart away," he talked the lyrics, certain of his vulnerability, his eyes a tad misty. Then he dutifully snapped back to the business of being a man. What choice did he have? The next tune was "Love Stinks" and brought rousing choruses from tables of women, a sentiment which no longer seemed to surprise me. With a tinge of nostalgia I flashed on how I had gone to the Winter Solstice Party just a few months earlier, as an introduction to the exciting new world of Toledo, and was so stunned by the tired cynicism of the women there, being almost naively raw at the time, and how now I was beginning to feel so much at home in the cold comfort of this particular firing range.

As I leaned against the pinball machine, a very drunk woman with long dark hair tapped me on the shoulder and asked me if I was married. With a glimmer of hope I told her I wasn't. "Well, if you at least pretend you're married I'll play kissy-face with you," she offered in a low voice, tossing her hair out of her eyes with a jolt of her head. I told her that I wasn't into games and that playing kissy-face with her was just about the last thing I was interested in. She countered, "If you're not willing to play the game that's just a sign of your immaturity," then as she began to walk away, she hissed over her shoulder, "I'm 10 times smarter than you anyway."

Bowed but nowhere near beaten I drew energy from the combative atmosphere, steamed around the curved corner of the bar and eyeballed a couple of serious looking women brandishing engagement rings. They were leaning close to each other, talking at the same time, fiddling with matchbooks and smiling broadly at a lumbering bartender who was doing tricks with ice cubes. He looked like Jethro Bodine. I overheard one of the women say, "Right now, I'm into security." I tapped her on the shoulder, told her security was an illusion, then quoted Caine. "The web can be brushed away by a flick, but to the spider it's a secure haven."

She stared at me contemptuously before finally saying out of the side of her mouth, "I'll keep that in mind, buster."

"The Wanderer" was on the box and I commenced circling the bar with the carefree air of a tumbling tumbleweed. That is until I heard a shrill voice say, "Never take your bottom off before your top, for Christ sake. That's rule number two. Rule number one is never go out with a man over 30 who's never been married," and I found myself stopped dead in my tracks – just as a group of five guys entered like a string of cut out paper ghosts and began to do a lap and intensely search the faces of everyone as if they were looking for signs of life. They breezed past some women in the corner who were dancing in front of the flames of a faux fireplace, waving their hands and swaying like perdition's lost souls. A voice from behind me whispered, "At least casual sex isn't a terrifying as intimate sex." Feeling as if I were hurtling down a vortex, I careened into a woman and profusely excused myself. She smiled a nonchalant "no problem," but her eyes, like a deer surprised, seemed ready to run, and so – suddenly and out-of nowhere – was I.

But the jukebox stopped, keeping me locked me in place. No music. Freeze frame. Circuit malfunction. Aside from the tinny click of glasses the place was totally silent. The customers were just staring in the general direction of one another, as if they had been assigned to watch each other in order to develop an across-the-room kinship and give unspoken approval or disapproval to new wardrobes or hairstyles. They seemed to want to wish to whisper encouragements, offer condolences, share a life. But, instead, like me they just remained in place and stared. Frozen searchers. Still lookers.

Then the music returned in a jarring fashion. The animation started anew as did the groping towards the next bar stool.

Even in this place of strangers who knew each other all too well, my numbed senses told me I had worn out my welcome, and I headed for the door but was stopped by a loud, "Ray, Ray." I turned and saw a face out of the past wading through the packed bar. It was Kent Davis, a student I had had at North Baltimore High in the early '70s. His family owned a plastics' factory. They were extremely rich and Republican. Richard Nixon slept at their house during the '68 campaign.

"How's it going there big guy?" Kent asked with inebriated interest as he stuck out his hand. "I hardly recognized you with that beard. What are you trying to do, look like Jesus Christ?" He had an infectious laugh.

I hadn't seen Kent in several years. Clearly, he was on the prowl "I'm looking for bruised knees," Kent said, circling his eyes like binoculars. "I just ask 'em if they want to go back to my place. I live right on the 17th hole of the Findlay Country Club. I tell them I'll take 'em for a plane ride. If they don't go, who cares." He laughed again. "You'll never believe this but Walter's here."

"Oh my God," I plopped against the wall. Walter was Kent's younger brother. When I first saw him he was at recess in the seventh grade. Even when I left North Baltimore in '73, Walter was in elementary school.

"There he is right now," Kent howled. "Look at that head." Walter had exactly the same head he had when I saw him on the school playground. It was the kind of grotesquely huge head you see on the football mascot for the Spartans of Michigan State. I was glad to see his body had caught up.

"How you doin' Ray?" Walter, now somewhat egg-shaped with prematurely thinning hair, extended his paw and immediately went into a Plasticman routine of reaching to caress just about every woman that passed by, just like it was recess on the last day of school. Within a moment he was locking arms with a slim, aerobically-toned blond who looked like a stationary tango dancer about ready to twirl out of her flowered skirt.

"Psst," Kent leaned over. "She's 35 and fed up with Toledo guys."

Walter had a claw-twisted Nazi death grip around her waist. We were all standing close to the jukebox. I kept looking at the petite blond. She wouldn't look at me. Walter was whispering in her ear.

"I remember all those quotes you taught us from Shakespeare," Kent said, wiping his nose on his sleeve. "I've really gotten laid a lot using them."

I thought of the quote I had given to Judy just 36 hours earlier and the purity of my motive and how my student had befouled my teachings.

Kent snorted. "Yeah I've bullshitted a lot of babes with them. I've got 'em written down in a drawer right next to my water bed."

I felt the need to change the subject. "Look, there's a guy walking around with a dick in his hand." I pointed to an elongated gentleman in a plain suit and tie who was carrying a hair dryer kind of flashlight with a condom pulled over it. He was billing himself as "Dr Feelgood" and was walking around getting women to tilt their heads back and say "ah" while he flashed down their throats. "I think I'm having an LSD flashback," I monotoned.

Kent doubled with laughter. "You were always a riot."

It wasn't that funny.

I kept staring at Walter and the blond. Every now and then she would whisper in his ear and his eyes would bulge. I was standing there, a statue, and this kid I'd known since he was 10 was apparently making out like the proverbial bandit. It was yet another in the night's string of instructive moments that somehow kept failing to move me closer to, at most, enlightenment or, at least, the exit.

Walter began telling jokes about the Atlanta child murders. The blond was tittering. I told him to knock it off or I'd start telling Alfred E. Newman jokes. That's what the kids called him in the fifth grade. In response, he mechanically pecked the blond on the cheek and pushed his crotch against her frame. She still hadn't acknowledged me until I loudly proclaimed to no one in particular, "I heard about older women hitting on young guys but this is one step beyond." Then I glared directly at her. "I guess you're just looking for something comfortable to slip into."

As Walter swivel-hipped to the bar with his fly half open, the blond countered me blankly, "I'm not hitting on him." She hiccupped then placed her hand in an armpit and produced a farting noise. "Slip into that, mister know-it-all."

Walter returned. Kent pointed to his fly. Walter looked down, gasped, casually dropped the drinks and quickly zipped up. The blond's look could have killed him as he stormed the bar for more drinks. Before he got back she left with the guy with the flashlight dick.

On this, my maiden militant mission, I decided it was time to cut my losses and retreat, so again I high-tailed it for the exit only to be nearly stampeded back into the fray by a large group of costumed revelers screaming about an equinox party. I found myself re-entering – having been turned around by the throng – right behind a thin, sexy girl in a tight, pussycat leotard. Her ass cheeks were showing. She sported a tail, whiskers, four-inch heels, and was arm-in-arm with a geisha. Feeling the need to yield to what appeared to be the flow of fate, I followed them back in and a couple of guys gave me approving glances. I stopped. The ladies sashayed on. I stoically reclaimed my station at the cigarette machine.

An under five-foot woman in a Victorian outfit asked me if I was trying to look like a lumberjack. I was wearing a flannel shirt, jeans and a hooded sweatshirt. "Really, you ought to be a bodyguard," she giggled, reeking of cheap wine. "No, seriously, what are you supposed to be?"

"I'm a blessing in disguise," I said placidly. Caine would have humbly approved.

I found refuge at a stool next to a guy dressed as Sherlock Holmes. He claimed to be a visiting writer from England and was telling an all-the-way unbuttoned Maid Marian that he was writing a singles' bar play called "The Heart in Motion." She moved on.

"It's the same all over," he articulated around his swizzle stick. "In London even the fox has become an urban animal, searching the pavement for a mate. I've written a poem about it. 'The fox, sleek, harried, hurried, running near the neon'."

As he finished, a couple of regulars walked by obviously perturbed at the costumed contingent. The first threatened to get a bunch of people together and "Take over Steak and Ale," while her friend stumbled, looked down at Mr. Goodwrench lying on the floor and said, "If I were a man I'd piss on him." Just then the pussycat sidled up next to me.

"How would you like to go out for breakfast?" she asked brightly.

"Hm, I don't know," I responded with measured deliberation.

Her geisha friend popped out from behind her. "How would you like to pay for breakfast for both of us?" They both snorted and coughed, trying not too hard to suppress laughter. "You just looked like a guy who should be interested." They roared and the pussycat twirled her tail near her mouth and licked at it. "We're broke, come on, you're hardly gonna get any better offers." Her voice high-pitched on "hardly."

Their presumptuousness provided me with a second wind and in order to illustrate to them that they probably had no idea who they were dealing with, I leaned between them, squeezed their shoulders real tight, and volunteered, "Didn't your mothers ever tell you that you could catch more flies with honey then with vinegar. Seriously, you ought to try the sweet and soulful approach, the aggressive bitch is out this year."

I eased my grip, backed off and began inching towards the door when I heard the geisha say sharply, "What the fuck is with that guy?"

I whirled and quoted Caine. "Not to know a man's purpose does not make *him* confused."

With that I finally busted my way out of the Windmill and into the parking area. I checked myself to see if all my body parts were intact and started a somewhat tortuous, stumbling search for the faithful steel steed I had safely tucked away before entering the night's fracas.

"What are you looking for?" a female voice queried from behind.

I halted, raised my arms in surrender and answered with something akin to name, rank and serial number.

"Magic," I replied, peeking over my shoulder.

***

The next night, a stale and dreary and drizzly Sunday, I was sitting in my roll-back chair, between my Pink Floyd and Cleveland Indian posters, watching the tube.

On a "Solid Gold" rerun, 1958's "It's Only Make Believe" was the featured classic, followed by Blondie pleading to be thrown into designer sheets, after which Madame, a horny old puppet, begged for the loosening of the immigration laws in order to improve her love life. The show concluded with Rod Stewart, on his knees, informing everyone that even the President needed passion and the Plasmatics, behind the closing credits, busting up a large TV. I pressed the remote. A commercial exhorted viewers to videotape their own wedding since it could always be erased. Click. On a talk show Mickey Rooney was complaining that after eight marriages his heart probably looked like a piece of cauliflower. Click. On another talk show Ann Landers acknowledged that things were getting better as far as social acceptance for singles, but added a final cautionary note, "If you're uninvited and unexpected, you are also unwelcome."

I finally clicked the thing off in disgust. A single man in the '80s was not uninvited, unexpected and unwelcome everywhere, that's for damn sure. Didn't Ann Landers ever here of the Fine Line Lounge?

The Fine Line, where Jenny sometimes tended bar when she wasn't working at the massage parlor, was about the size of a small railroad car and was located next to a White Hut – Oasis in the Night. There were stevedores at the Fine Line and women who looked like Hermione Gingold. A couple of regulars had cerebral palsy. Everyone played the bowling machine. As I walked in that night Dean Martin was warbling "In the Misty Moonlight." Jenny was doing shots with a guy sporting a Dockwalloper tattoo. She was wearing painted-on, faded jeans and a fuzzy white cotton sweater. I told her she looked terrific.

"Thanks" she said, smacking her lips from the tequila and reaching into her bullet bag for a cigarette. "How's that 17-year-old chick doing?"

"All right, I guess. But I may have gone overboard with her. I think I'll be backing off a bit."

"That's cool." Jenny sucked the smoke into her lungs and let it out with a gush of breathlessness. "You ought to come over here and see me a little more often," she said in a funky Mae West voice. "I'm no spring chicken but I ain't over the hill yet." She winked and stroked her braid.

A woman at the bar, who had craned her neck in outrage when Jenny said 17-year-old chick, belched loudly and began muttering about jailbait. She had that common, flirty, way-beyond-30, gap-toothed look, and was wearing a Dial-1-800-EAT-SHIT button. "Did you break her in right?" She squinted and slurped her drink.

"I never touched her," I snapped.

As I accepted her slobbering apology, Rhonda, the co-manager, made a grand entrance and began hugging the regulars. She had just returned from San Francisco. Wayne Fontana and the Mindbenders' "Game of Love" was on the box and I had assumed my usual position at a bar, silently standing and trying to balance coins. I had on an LSD – Better Living Though Chemistry sweatshirt. Rhonda regarded it approvingly.

"Right on." She made a fist.

She bought me a glass of wine and started talking about having smuggled mescaline across the Mexican border and how she had some kind of ship's captain certificate that had enabled her to perform a wedding in the bar three weeks earlier. In fact, the bride herself was on hand. Rhonda introduced me to her.

The Capri-panted bride, smelling like a Kessler's distillery, hoisted her glass towards me. "You ain't that good looking but you got a great body."

"I'd give you a 10 as a person," Rhonda interceded and leaned her breast against my arm.

When the Fine Line closed at 1:00, Jenny went home with one of the stevedores and Rhonda asked me to meet her at the High and Dry Lounge for some pool. While we played she asked me if I liked coke. I said that I thought it was okay but I'd never buy it. She said she had just bought some, whispered her address and told me she'd meet me there in five minutes.

"I didn't want anyone to see us leave," she leveled with me in front of her house. "Zam, the guy who used to live here, is out of town. Not that we're real tight or anything."

Once inside Rhonda quickly began laying out the powdered lines while hurrying through the salient details of her life. In the early '70s she was a born-again Christian but now was an agnostic spiritualist. She was married at 16 to a hillbilly guy but they split up two years later. He got custody of their son Zippo.

"I never touched drugs until I was 25." She stroked at Popeye, her Doberman pup. "Look, I like to have a good time, you know. I swing a little too. But don't get me wrong I usually love my man."

I told her I thought that was a good trait.

She informed me that she was a victim of incest and had been raped by two black guys. "I told them, 'Hey, do your thing, but leave me alive'."

She was worried about her older sister who hadn't been acting herself lately. "She left tonight right in the middle of the bowling game. She was winning, too."

We snorted her coke and smoked her pot.

"You really are shy," she said, seeming both surprised and charmed. "Why don't you take your shirt off then we can go upstairs?"

A dull twitch of anticipation just barely inched aside the dark detachment that shadowed my mechanical ascension to her second floor bedroom for my first sexual encounter in the nether world of Toledo single life.

She insisted on having Popeye in the room. "Popeye stays. Don't worry, he's always here when I make love. The only time he's ever got worked up was that first time when he thought I was being hurt, but he's gotten used to Zam by now."

I finally convinced her to put Popeye in the backyard. She donned a Frederick's of Hollywood outfit, saying, "If I don't acknowledge you in the bar, don't worry."

I told her that I wasn't worried.

"I may give you a call," she said, "but not after Wednesday."

I had no problem with that.

"Do you come quick?"

"It depends."

She licked at my lips. Her feigned open-mouthed passion seemed to contain the absence of everything.

"Now I want you to fuck me," she growled.

During the act of lovemaking she stuck a tube of amyl nitrate under my nose, which woke me up enough to simultaneously generate fear of a heart attack and eliminate any anxieties about duration of performance. I gladly finished fast.

"That was super," she heaved a long sigh and smiled beatifically. "You know, out of all the drugs we did the natural was the best, but I won't call you after Wednesday.

"That's fine."

Daylight was almost breaking through the drawn curtains. She put on a blue bathrobe, fished a cigarette from its pocket and tossed a new cover on the bed. "The problem I would have with you is becoming emotionally involved."

She had me gone and Popeye back in about 10 minutes. As I began to drive away Ricardo Montalban's voice was on my car radio, seeming to sum up the night's romantic menu. "Another name for love at Zantigo's is. . . combination platter."

***

"Is Rachel there?"

Like a haunted, muted bugle, Milton's voice over the phone interrupted my hungover half-sleep.

"Oh man, she's probably still in Honolulu for Christ's sake. You know that." I hung up the phone and rolled back into a curled up position under my comforter. The last thing I needed on this head-pounding morning – after Popeye and Frederick's and coke and amyl nitrate – was Milton's gravelly, lost love bleating for Rachel.

Every year for nearly half a decade Milton called. Always around the the first day of spring, and always to ask the whereabouts of Rachel. His obsession with her was one of the great legends of Crystal City lore. Milton, a university professor's son who had allegedly never fully recovered from making his own acid, had met Rachel in the early '70's, when she had just turned 17, and was smitten and maddened at first glance. A wispy, brilliant artist with curly, strawberry hair and volcanoes in her eyes, Rachel was all he could talk about when I first got to know him in a Melville study group he and I attended at that time. Back then he would softly and endlessly rhapsodize about the passion-fueled nobility and mythic nature of romantic fusion.

After she got married and moved to Hawaii in '75, Milton's tone turned grave and he would gloomily lecture that the whole business of romance was far trickier than anyone could possibly imagine and that one had to be constantly on guard in order to prevent getting beaten down or totally lost in obsession. It was then that he began dressing periodically like Captain Ahab, gimping around town in a long black coat and pipe stem hat – and that was when the phone calls had started, inquiring if Rachel was still around or had dropped back in the area for a visit or maybe had never really left at all.

Feeling guilty about hanging up on him, I tried to call back but the line was busy. I hadn't actually seen him in over two years but Frank had mentioned to me just a week earlier that Milton had shown up at a recent poetry reading, loudly lectured that the women's movement was taking a fearful toll on society and shouted, "Death to Moby Dick," before disappearing into the night. And around Valentine's Day I could have sworn I recognized his voice on a national radio talk show railing about how women entering sports' broadcasting was one of the signs of the end of the world.

Perhaps his re-emergence on the periphery of my life was not a coincidence and – given my involvement with a 17-year-old, something Milton could definitely identify with – perhaps I should take this opportunity to consult him. If I were billing myself as a seeker of new adventures and approaches, there was no reason to shy away from his unique perspective on the whole battle of the sexes in general, and the dangers of teenage girls in particular. Frank was always saying that Milton was a modern prophet. Maybe it was time to re-examine the lessons to be gleaned from Milton and his somewhat offbeat lifestyle.

Milton's house was in the exclusive residential section of Crystal City, where most of the profs lived. A huge inheritance had enabled him to pay cash for the large Victorian dwelling and for many years he lived quite comfortably on the rent collected from his four or five tenants. But last year the university had prohibited students from living there because of numerous complaints about Milton's aberrant behavior.

As I pulled into his driveway I noticed he had once again put on his annual spring poetry display, a practice he had begun right after Rachel left. Each spring Milton would put out all the poetry he had written about her on a small card table in his front yard. He would perform this ritual in the hopes it would mystically draw her back. He claimed that poetry's power spanned the dimension of time and space. When she didn't return he said that at least the exercise prepared him for another seasonal cycle of rejection.

I brushed aside a gnarled branch that guarded his back steps and knocked on the door, which immediately creaked open a few inches.

"Oh, it's just you. Long time no see, c'mon in." Milton appeared almost emaciated in a blue terry-cloth robe with chicken legs sticking out and was sporting a straggly beard and had a shaved head; 40 going on 60.

"What's with the bald look?"

"Rachel loved 'Apocalypse Now.' That's what her cousin told me when I ran into him last year. I was going for the Marlon Brando character's look thinking maybe that might lure her in this direction." He shrugged his shoulders and gouged a thumb under his collarbone. "But just this morning I remembered she hated Telly Savalas, so I'm going to start letting it grow back."

"Have you ever tried contacting her directly and finding out if she's even considering coming back?"

"Nah," Milton muttered, "it's better left to destiny."

"Sorry I hung up when you called this morning."

"Don't worry," he said, slapping me on the back. "If Rachel wasn't there, she wasn't there."

"Uh, say Milton," I began uneasily, "there's something I want to talk to you about."

"I know," he said darkly. "Nobody comes by here anymore just to shoot the breeze. What's troubling you?"

"A 17-year-old girl."

Milton erupted into a violent cough and sunk to his knees. I maneuvered his contorted body into a wobbly kitchen chair and when he had regained his composure, his eyes settled on me with the kind of look you would imagine upon the face of one doomed soul gazing at another as they stood before the gates of hell.

"There's nothing I can say, but there are some things I can show you." He rose and cleared his throat. Pausing dramatically, he beckoned ever-so-slightly with his hand. "I encourage you to watch me closely tonight and just let things gradually sink in, but don't over-analyze like you usually do." A baleful glare flooded his countenance. "Keep in the back of your mind, however, that you may be seeing your future."

I gulped at the prospect that turning out like Milton was on my horizon but made a pact with myself that I would try to absorb his actions with an absolute minimum of mental dissection. Poised to be a here and now kind of guy tonight, I would simply let him do his thing and wait for another time to piece it all together.

Milton yanked open his refrigerator's door, grabbed a bottle of Old Style, twisted it open and escorted me through the living room toward a small utility room guarded by a velvet curtain. He stopped at the entrance, turned and stared, Svengali-like, into my eyes. "No one has ever been in here but me. Now you, too, must come in."

Following him through the funereal purple curtains I didn't know whether I was entering a witch doctor's hut or a confessional. Instead what I discovered was a freshly decorated, if a tad cluttered, suburban-type den.

Lighted by blinking neon beer signs and papered with posters from classic romantic movies from the '40s, the room was strewn with videotapes and audio cassettes, flowery Hallmark greeting cards and Sears catalogs. I cleared the brown Naugahyde couch of lists of scrawled phone numbers, a book about how Stanley found Livingston and a copy of the Watchtower, its cover story on masturbation, as Milton rummaged through his audio tapes before extracting one with ARMAGEDDON printed on it.

"This is what you need to hear." His voice boomed like a doomsday preacher, then quieted to a whisper. "It's a tape of female sportscasters I've recorded doing broadcasts since Rachel left and I started noticing these things." Milton sank to his knees in front of his tapedeck. "Listen to the way they describe a guy missing a shot or striking out or blowing a field goal. The delight in their voice is unbearable."

Try as I might I couldn't hear anything unusual, but Milton reacted as if he were listening to survivors' accounts of the Holocaust.

"I play it over and over. It gets more painful every time." Milton dabbed at his eyes with a balled up candy wrapper and sniffed, then brightened with resolve. "I must make some calls. I must locate her."

He grabbed a phone list off the couch and feverishly dialed four or five numbers, asking each, just as he had asked me, if Rachel were there and hanging up abruptly when the answer was negative.

"I can't lose my resolve, not now, not ever," he blurted defiantly, gazing at a photo of Rachel above the television, transfixed. She was wearing a polka dot blouse and had a tiny ribbon in her hair. Right beneath her perky little turned-up nose was a full inch of tongue licking over her upper lip. Milton used both of his hands to wrench his head violently away from the picture, then slumped to the floor coughing loudly into his fist before turning in my direction.

"Do you want to see my master tape?"

"Fine." I was on emotional automatic pilot as I sunk deeper into his couch. The hazy, flickering light from the beer signs had almost hypnotized me. I was struck by how normal and almost commonplace everything appeared to be in what in reality was a bizarre setting. I mentioned this to Milton.

"You're finally beginning to understand." He smiled sadly. "If you're not careful, soon just about anything seems normal. That's what those young ones can do to you."

Milton lurched to his feet and slid a videotape from behind Rachel's picture. He blew off the dust, inserted it in the deck and thrust himself backward into viewing position.

"I get this out every spring." He scratched at the bumps on the back of his hands. "I call it 'The Face of Fire.' That's from a quote by Ishmael after he's stood on the deck all night watching a burning whale." His voice grew faint and distant. "He starts hallucinating demons leaping from the flames but finally snaps out of it when dawn breaks. Ishmael then warns us to 'Look not too long into the face of fire' lest we forget the beauty, life and warmth of the natural light." His bloodshot voice was now barely audible. "I can't seem to follow that advice. Without Rachel I can't stop looking into the fire."

Milton stretched out his bare foot and turned on the tape. I was expecting whips, chains and bestiality, certain that only the darkest of the dark would be presented. Instead what I saw was, again, the all too familiar. It began with short clips from "The Dating Game." Each one showed the winning guy eagerly bounding around the curtain and the woman showing a clear sign of disappointment coupled with body language that stiffly screamed "Keep your distance." Periodically, Milton would freeze-frame on a disapproving expression or wooden hug and whimper.

Next came a short collage of clips from daytime talk shows, each with a woman guest dominating the conversation, the host nodding agreement with her, and the male "victim" unable to get a word in edgewise. In the midst of this segment Milton leaped to his feet and shrieked, "Don't let them get away with it," before sinking back down for the following section, featuring snippets from commercials, during which he occasionally stopped the action to savor a panty-hose ad or roar like the MGM lion as the Doublemint Twins peddled their trim little butts away on a bicycle built for two.

The conclusion of the tape featured dozens of women in tenderly romantic poses, clearly being adored and protected by their men, interspersed with clips of female news anchors reporting on men being handcuffed and carted off to jail for various sex offenses. By this time Milton was content to hold his hand over his eyes and peek furtively through his fingers.

He clicked off the tape, got to his feet and held up his hand to stop me from asking any questions. "There's nothing to discuss," he said sternly. "It's time to go out."

I rose unsteadily and followed him through the velvety curtain, flashing on how I used to feel as a teenager leaving the Saturday confessional on pins and needles feet. A sense of deep relief accompanied me, but my firm purpose to sin no more was overshadowed by a lingering certainty that I'd need to be back the next week.

For the rest of the night everything seemed framed in an off kilter blur, as though I were looking through squinty eyes. I remember Milton peering into a mirror in his living room and rubbing his hands across his face. Not unlike his hero Ahab, who disdained the traditional whale maps and charted the pursuit of his obsession on his brow, Milton chose to read the lines on his forehead to guide his course of action.

"It will be quick and relatively painless tonight," he said somberly as he pulled on his long dark coat. "We'll swing by the Don't Die Wondering lesbian bar, they know who I am there, then I'll drop off a treasure map at the Convenient Store." His tongue strayed out to moisten his lips. "I'm not doing this just for your benefit, Ray," he said as he pulled on his pipe stem hat. "I'm doing it because it's beyond my control."

Still committed to the unquestioning exploration of Milton's danger zone, I drove him to the outskirts of Crystal City and we stopped in front of the Don't Die Wondering, a totally non-descript store front with no identifying sign at all, which was situated next to an abandoned Loyal Order of Moose hall.

"You wait here," he said officially, then added with a touch of respectful kinship in his voice. "They need this as much as I do."

Before going in Milton pinned to his coat a large button that said Smart Ass Bitch. I watched from outside. He was the only guy in the place. Butting his way between two women who were fondling each other, he slapped a quarter on the pool table and strode to the bar. I heard him whistle for the bartender. An argument ensued. She threatened him with a billyclub. Several patrons brandished pool sticks. They surrounded him and got in his face. As they tribally crowded him towards the exit he jerked and twisted like a hanged man. He was pushed out, accompanied by a chorus of hisses, and crumpled to the ground at my feet.

"I wasn't going to pay for the drink, even if she would have brought me one," he gasped triumphantly at the slamming door.

I helped him to his feet, and brushed at his coat as we walked quietly to my car, his eyes fixed on some indefinite distance in the darkness. Like Ahab, he had the look of someone who had been cut away from the stake, burned but not consumed.

The night's final stop was the Convenient Mart right around the corner from Milton's house. He took a map from his pocket and explained to me that it contained a blueprint of his house, an X marked where his bed was located, indicating that that was where the treasure could be found.

"The woman who works in there is an old friend of Rachel," he said, his eyes growing wide and childlike. "Maybe she'll send it to her." Milton entered the store with a sulky backward glance and came out in less than a minute.

"I left the map on the counter," he said, stooped at my rolled-down window. "You go in there and tell me what her reaction is. I'll walk home." He went a few steps and turned quickly back to me. "What's her name, Ray?"

"Judy," I answered, knowing full well who he was asking about.

"That's got a nice old-fashioned ring to it," he whispered whimsically.

In the eerie glow of the moon, I watched him shuffle away and thought, just for an instant before discounting it as nonsense, that I might indeed be gazing into a mirror. I waited a few minutes before entering the store. The short, plump checkout woman was holding the map and shaking her head.

"He left it in here again," she said in a flat, slightly hostile voice. "Take it to him, will ya?"

I took the map from her and drove to his house. The door was open and I could hear "The Dating Game" theme that began his "Face of Fire" tape. Not wanting to disturb him I tucked the folder into a kitchen drawer. Exiting the house I could hear his voice – echoing like a beaten, dying seal on some wasted, frozen expanse – sobbing, "Rachel."

The Connections Diner

"It's coming Ray, maybe not this decade, but we're moving past the Dawn into the Rising Sun of the Age of Enlightenment. I've been getting goose pimples ever since the vision came to me."

Scott had called to invite me to Columbus to celebrate his 31st birthday and yet another breakthrough in his work. I needed the change of scenery and gladly accepted.

It had been nearly a month since the Lost Weekend that began with me waddling around Arnie's like a shooting gallery duck and ended with my head stuck squarely in the lion's mouth at Milton's. I felt as if my personality had been wrenched a notch or two. I was quieter, a lump never far from my throat. I moved slowly, like someone on Quaaludes. Sometimes it took me several seconds to respond if a student asked a question in class. It was like my life had taken on a momentum of its own while I, Ray Powell, had been relegated to the role of a tag-along, bewildered spectator.

I had no desire for any contact with Judy, the night with Milton having altered my perspective on the potential long-term effects of 17-year-olds. During school hours we would exchange cordial nods but it was evident she, too, had no desire for interaction. At the end of the day, I would slink out the side door and sometimes spot her getting into her Gremlin. I always waited for her to leave. I didn't want her to have to not look at me through her rear view mirror.

I couldn't blame her for avoiding me. For one thing Reagan had been shot at the end of March and the news was filtering in that his would-be assassin had an obsession with Jodie Foster, writing her letters, etc. I had told Judy in February that I had written a fan letter to Goldie Hawn. I told her, kiddingly, that I was known as a "lunar prophet" in Crystal City. She probably thought I was going to jump out at her with a gun or the sweat-stained contents of my diary. I could have told her, however, that I, feeling more and more like a floppy, straw man with a fragile stick for a backbone, was a threat to no one but myself.

I arrived at Scott's house after school on Friday. He was packed and ready to go but had a few phone calls to make. First, he attempted to make a person-to-person call to the Maharishi in Switzerland. Earlier in the week he had awakened in the middle of the night at 4:17 – on his Vishnu digital – and sensed that the Maharishi was finally sending a message. Scott's birthday, 4/17, would be pivotal and he sensed the Great Man wanted to hear from him. The call was not put through.

"I heard someone holler 'It's Scott again'," he said indignantly after hanging up. "Well, someday they'll know. I'm sure the Maharishi knows."

Then he phoned IBM. The secretary wouldn't put him through and finally admitted, after Scott persisted, that she had been instructed, at a specially called staff meeting, not to transfer any of his calls. Scott wasn't surprised.

"I showed up at one of their 'Occult and Mystic' Tuesday afternoon meetings in Columbus. They looked at me like I was a ghost. In a matter of moments I had broken down the head man and he began confessing certain, uh, lustful transgressions with a data base. They asked me to leave."

He had a few other calls to make. First, he tried to contact a Mr. Helmut, someone "way up" in the development of the Cruise Missile. "I know I'd never pass the security check," he whispered, holding his hand over the receiver. "But I need to begin the legitimization process." Helmut was off work that day.

Scott gently quit the phone, pretending to dust it for prints and began whistling an Indian raga. He was a chipper Birthday Boy. There remained a possibility for an August graduation, and he already had interviews lined up for the spring.

"So things are going good in Crystal City," I said. Scott nodded as he deftly deposited some papers in his briefcase.

"I did have a scary experience down there last week, though." He gripped his briefcase's handle tightly and swayed. "I was sitting in the

Union and overheard a girl talking to some friends. She had on bright red high heels and lifted up her legs and said, 'These are my knock me down and fuck me shoes.' I almost fainted but recovered quickly enough to get her number. I called her yesterday but it was no go." He breathed a sigh of relief and loosened his hold on his briefcase. "She could have hurt me, Ray. I have to be careful with these women. I can't afford to let my imagination take my heart too far."

Just as we were about to leave he snapped his fingers and asked me to wait for one more phone call. He dialed up an accountant and made a luncheon date with her for the next week.

"I met her while I was auditing a computer class last quarter," he said as we gathered up his luggage. "I felt she was getting the wrong impression of me so on the last day of class I told her that I didn't want to anesthetize the relationship or send out faulty messages. That the preciseness of her profession excited me and that I was basically just a dirty little guy, kinky, sexy – philosophical, even – and that I had had enough of sterile mathematics. I guess she got the idea." Scott nibbled on his finger like a grammar school kid. "It's just that when she speaks with that executive simplicity all I want to do is come in my pants."

After we got out the door the phone rang. Scott dropped his briefcase and suitcase, unlocked the door and raced inside. When he reappeared on the porch he wasn't smiling.

"That was her secretary calling back to cancel the date. She said she had an appointment with the foot doctor." He yanked his briefcase and suitcase off the ground. "The foot doctor! She just said that to get me." Scott seemed to have shrunk a foot as we walked to my car. "If they just didn't know they had crotches it would be all right." He got in and angrily strapped on his seat belt. "It's not the crotches so much but the fact that they know they have them. That's the problem."

Pulling onto I-75 South brightened Scott a bit and he dipped into his briefcase and gingerly extracted part of his thesis. "I need a new quote that can lead into Chapter One which is entitled 'Kashatriya's Handbook'." He flashed a shield-like diagram at me. "It's like something you'd see Darth Vader wearing. Remember, a decision support system is an aggressive executive with creative intelligence. It's an attitude, not an artifact. A strategy, not a technology." On his diagram an arrow pointed downward. "Fulfillment, Achievement, Action, Knowledge, Consciousness" pointed to "Coming Home."

"I know I've got a nuclear bomb here, but I also realize the necessity to come more from the heart." He bowed his head and tapped his chest. "I'll never be a philosopher king if I neglect the heart. Stafford Beir would never hire me."

Beir was Scott's idol. He worked with Allende in Chile to set up a Marxist government under a cybernetic model. He was the author of "Heart of Enterprise" and Brain of the Firm." Scott had recently written him a letter inquiring about a possible internship in London and was always quoting him both to potential employers and women he would meet at bars.

"Stafford's got the right idea about how societal structure commingles with personal passion," he proclaimed as we pulled off I-75 at the Crystal City exit. "Where are you going?"

"Frank's gonna ride to Columbus with us. One of his ex-wives is down there and I guess he wants to see her and get some things straightened out."

Scott wasn't thrilled by the idea. He and Frank continued at odds and Scott was particularly miffed at Frank's behavior on Valentine's Day, which he felt had ruined his relationship with Mary. She asked him to leave the next day.

"He was out to sabotage me that night, plain and simple," Scott charged in a low, quiet voice. "That 'clitoral concerto' comment he made really upset Mary, but maybe it was for the best. She wasn't really what I was looking for."

Frank was hunched on the porch of his rooming house when we pulled up. It was the same house Scott had moved out of in the fall. Frank picked up the shopping bag that contained his overnight necessities, said goodbye to his 85-year-old landlady and came towards the car. Scott said he needed to glance over his thesis, got out, nodded a quick greeting at Frank and sat in the back seat, head-phoned into a

Maharishi tape.

"How's things going with that young female?" Frank asked, planting himself in the seat and uncharacteristically disdaining the safety belt.

"That got a little out of hand. I ended up laying this romantic quote on her, she freaked and now she won't even look at me."

Frank nodded quickly. "Yeah, you've got to watch that heavy duty romantic angle. It's a genuine quagmire."

"I'm starting to wonder what's behind all of it. Why do I need to discharge all this yearning in the direction of someone I hardly even know. Someone almost totally inaccessible. I think I need to just sit back by myself and figure out what the hell's going on."

"We're all doomed."

"Besides, when I go out, even though I'm way too big to miss, I can't get a woman to look at me. Not that I even want most of them to. It's like I'm spending my time chasing someone I can't get and getting frustrated because women I'm not interested in are ignoring me."

"You've hit on it," Frank moved forward in his seat, elbows on knees. "They won't look at you. I fully understand the anthropological precedent for the indirectness of females, but it's gone way too far. If they want the dynamics to change they ought to work on their own tendencies to turn away and wait, then expect you to somehow find a way to sexually fulfill them." He leaned back, sighed and turned his gaze out the passenger's window. "Every time I fucked my first wife I wanted to keep it in her forever. Just be there. From her it was always 'yes, no, yes, no, yes, no. I don't want to get pregnant.' Hell, I used to put my cock in her face and she would close her eyes and not look at it. It reminded me of when I was six and this eight-year-old enticed me to come out to the garage with her. She grabbed my hand and stuck it down her pants. She said 'feel me.' Hell, I was grabbing her and sticking sticks in the cheeks of her ass. But every time I would unzip my pants and try to show her what I had to offer, she would close her eyes and never look – she'd just giggle." Frank paused for a minute and when he began speaking it was with a sharply constricted voice. "I often wonder what effect that had on me, to have been refused to be acknowledged. It really influenced my thinking about my sexuality. I wonder if I ever got over it."

Frank darted a glance over his shoulder to make sure that Scott wasn't listening. "After similar encounters like that I got into shooting BB guns. It's not surprising that the Hebrew word for penis and weapon is the same. Anyway, that's the direction my libido took. Later I incorporated that aggressiveness into my introverted artsiness and did all right. But I don't need any of it now." He crossed his hands in a once-and-for-all-that's-it gesture. "The problem is that the same nonsense is going on still. It never stops. It makes me sick to my stomach to think of the complexity and severity of the whole sexual trip."

We were about an hour down I-75. The day was one of those technicolor 70mm-screen days you see in the springtime. The fields were green with the fuzz of new crops. Farms stood on gentle hillsides like they do in the gauzy photos that come in cheap picture frames. I glanced back at Scott, who was busy communicating with The Absolute. "Surrealistic Pillow" was on my tapedeck. The strains of "Plastic Fantastic Lover" prompted me to turn to my restless passenger.

"Didn't you tell me something over the phone about you and Patty?"

"Well, it's nothing I'm very proud of," Frank confessed, biting hard at his fingernail, then launching into the story of the ugly termination of his nine-month celibacy.

It had happened on that same first day of spring that found me Romeo and Julieting with Judy. Frank had gone to dinner that evening with Patty, a 24-year-old he had been pursuing for just about the entire length of his celibacy. They had double-dated with his ex/current wife and her 20-year-old boyfriend. The foursome had dined at the Parrot&Peacock then headed to the Club. On the way Frank stopped to give some lengthy directions to a lost driver and when he finally arrived at the Club, Patty was sidling up to Biffie, one of the town's "green knights" who always showed up around unattended maidens.

"Biffie was into his 'Frisbee is the jazz of meta-silence' rap. Patty was telling him how she dropped a previous boyfriend for talking to her on the phone while he sat on the toilet. Biffie said he didn't blame her. I stepped between them and started licking her neck and grinding into her ass. I told Biffie to go take a tinkle. Patty said she thought he'd never leave."

As Frank continued to recount his night of love there was an odd tenderness in his voice. "We went to her house. She had a canopied bed. After we made out for awhile she said, 'I guess I'll have to put this diaphragm in.' We did it. She kept it until morning, then she took it out. I told her I wanted her again. She said she wasn't into it because she had to put that thing in again. I told her I had condoms. She said, 'And you made me put that thing in?' and asked me to leave." Frank shrugged and broke off the filter from one of his Kools. "Boy, I really laid out the cash for that one. I must have wined and dined for two solid months before she decided to come across." I could hear him gulp before continuing in a strained voice. "And you know when I was finished I felt as if my male psyche had been once again lost in the feminine sea. All those couple seconds of ecstasy accomplished was to to make me acutely aware of my spiritual erosion. It's insane."

He took a long measured draw on his cigarette, leaned his head forward and very carefully deposited the ashes into the car's tray. His voice was still slightly choked. "And I'll tell you exactly how she got me on her scent. Everytime I saw her in the bar she'd press her tits up against me. It was one of those 'all-present-and-accounted-for-sir' routines. She was into a total body thing. Heavy infighting. I'll admit that under my guise of cordiality, even celibate, I was still somewhat interested in a tactile encounter. There are civilized ways to approach that, however. But for her it was always, first one tit against me then the other." Frank belatedly buckled his safety belt and his voice took on more assurance. "I've learned my lesson, though. I know how to handle it. The next time I get tits pressed up against me, I'll nip it in the bud." He then came up with a new resolve following the renouncement of his celibacy. "For a woman to relate to me she's going to have to come and get me clean, and leave a little distance in between us. No more of this 50/50 business. I'll be waiting in my own territory around the 45 yard line."

Frank's last few sentences, uttered as we passed the Neil Armstrong Lunar Museum, seemed to snap Scott out of his back seat entrancement. "I was at the Toledo University library just this morning and a female employee got smart with me because I didn't have an ID." He leaned forward and groped at the front seat. "She actually questioned my legitimacy. I told her I'd slap her face. Somebody's got to start calling these women's bluffs."

"Well, I'm glad to finally hear that out of you." Frank turned and applauded in Scott's face. "It's about time you stopped catering to these women with all that philosophical soft presence horseshit. This is no time for reclining detachment. Dammit, we gotta fight. Patton ended up firing at bombers with his .45 pistol. We all could use a little more of that spirit."

Scott rifled through his briefcase as Frank continued, charging Scott with being in love with the "snake charmer's tune" and never being willing to stay in the "foxhole" for very long. "Plus you're always begging women to dominate you."

"Well, I'd kind of like them to at least try," Scott meekly replied.

Frank's wince shriveled his face. "If all you want to do is set up a quick verbal contract and sign on the imaginary dotted line, just so you can get your pants off, fine. Just go right ahead and establish permanent residence in a constantly compromising position. I'll tell you right now, though, it's a sure-fire formula for ultimate failure."

Scott didn't honor these charges with a response. He had heard them before and had answered them countless times. Maybe he was enamored of the snake charmer's tune, as was Marcus Aurelius. Maybe some of his behaviors could be characterized as involving rather delicate negotiations of a primarily sexual nature. The Maharishi himself was a man. And maybe Scott did exhibit some tendencies that could be considered self-defeating. That was a problem as old as civilization itself and he could not concern himself with worrying about it. He had work to do.

"I do agree with you on one point you made earlier," Scott conceded. "These women aren't fighting fair. With this spermicide and those prickly IUDs they're turning it into a combat zone."

An uneasy truce silenced the car for a long flat stretch of road near

Granville, Ohio, before I brought up my experience with Milton and his frightening involvement with video voyeurism.

"It's not just videos," Frank said, "he also has prostitutes wrestle for him from time to time. He's obsessed with watching them giving each other stepover toe-holds."

"Just thinking of that obsession of his with Rachel got me looking at this thing with Judy a lot differently." I forced a laugh and glanced in the sideview mirror." I certainly don't want to walk too many miles in his shoes."

"No one is immune, let's face it." Frank interjected. "Especially when you get near that pornographic edge. I had the misfortune of finding a Penthouse magazine in the trash a few weeks ago and ended up leafing through it. There was one pictorial about a guy and a woman in an elevator. Pretty soon she was down dogstyle and they used the words, 'She lifted up her haunches'." Scott discarded his theoretical text and leaned his head between the seats as Frank continued. "I myself never really got into that hardcore pornographic aspect of sex any more than 3% of the time. Some guys, like Milton, have their lights put out by that stuff and don't even recognize it. I always did the Princess from the Far East with jewels in her hair. That's a bad enough scene. It's all flesh mongering when you get right down to it." Frank cupped his hand to the side of his mouth and whispered. "But if I had gotten into that 'She lifted up her haunches' stuff regularly, I'd be in the state mental hospital now." He turned to an obviously delighted Scott and raised his voice. "This just proves that the fuckfest has gone too far, and if we don't do something about it real soon we might as well just plunge ourselves right into a Dante's Inferno with a bunch of lions and tigers and forget about our souls."

Scott smacked his lips loudly in retaliation. "Don't take it so seriously, Frank. It's all just gristle for masturbation." He smiled wickedly as he leaned over Frank's shoulder. "It's a dirty job but thank heaven someone has got to do it." He paused and seemed to be savoring a thought or two. "Since we're talking about fucking, let's all give our favorite position and analyze what they mean. C'mon. C'mon." Scott was a little kid on a trip, playing license plate games.

I informed him that I wasn't interested in such an analysis since I thought it was, like rating women by numbers, demeaning to everyone involved. "It's not exactly the path to enlightenment, Scott."

After he and Frank confessed their preferences – one for the top, one for the bottom – Scott was ready with his analysis. "It's really quite simple. Ray, you don't want to get involved. Frank, you want to screw one of the faithful, and I want to have a half-trained panther unleashed on top of me."

Frank buried his face into his hands "You're beyond hope, Scott. But as for me I simply enjoy the face-to-face contact, the opportunity for dialogue. Plus it's like having the earth below you."

In defense of his own charge Scott replied, "I just want to be pinned down so I won't fly away."

"You can talk all you want about this madness," Frank said as we pulled up to his ex-wife's residence at the outskirts of Columbus, "but my favorite position from now on is safely in my own territory, waiting."

A blond woman leaned out of a second story window and yelled for Frank to come on up. He grabbed his shopping bag with two hands, looked both ways several times before crossing the street, and smoothly ascended the outside stairs a pair at a time.

***

Scott's house was near the Ohio State campus. In elementary school, he had walked through the famous Oval to get to school. Eisenhower was president and Sputnik was on everyone's mind.

His mother was napping in the front room when we came through the door. She was in her 60s and hardly resembled the lusty woman Scott had talked so much about. The one who had told him, while he was in high school, that if she were a girl his age she wouldn't mind him parking his shoes under her bed; the one who had, when he first went away to college, bought him the tiniest bikini briefs with a lion or tiger knitted on the crotch; the one who had always taught him that it doesn't matter where you get your appetite as long as you eat at home; and the one who had always encouraged him to marry a German girl because they were "always either at your feet or at your throat."

I flashed on seeing the parents of my friends when I was in high school or just starting college. They were middle-aged people. Now Scott and I were not far from middle-aged, I guess, and meeting someone's parents was a rare occurrence, especially after living so long in Crystal City where there were very few parents of any kind to be found.

The house was dimly lit. Scott's father, who was sitting in the living room near the huge piano and cushioned chairs, was a frail, bald, reticent man. He looked like Judge Hardy's older brother. He used to be an engineer, but was now watercoloring his way through retirement.

"You know," the old man yawned and creaked his fingers, "they wanted to kill Jerzy Kozinski in New York. I wonder why."

"Maybe it's because he's a Jew," I offered.

He sighed as he got up to head to his work in the master bedroom. "In the Greek City State the messenger who brought the news of war was killed."

"Dad likes you," Scott said ushering me to my quarters. "He hardly speaks to anyone. I'm kind of getting worried about him since he retired." His voice trailed into a my-father-isn't-proud-of-me-and-time-is-running out tone.

From across the hall Scott's sister popped her head out of the door and said a quick "hi." She was thin, wore glasses and had on a Ohio State Buckeye sweatshirt. Scott informed me that she had recently converted to Judaism and was a social worker but was trying to get a job in a travel agency. That night she was going to a performance of Jacques Brel's music with some members of the Unitarian Date Night Group and had to leave in a hurry.

"You'll stay here in my room," Scott said. "I'll be sleeping on the couch in the den." He supplied me with some towels and left.

I looked around the room that Scott had slept in all his life. There was a double rubber-banded wad of Monopoly money, circa 1955, at the bedside. The little bunk bed seemed like a tomb. I laid down in it to see if I would fit. "Scotty Nelson" was etched in black crayon on the board above the lower bunk. A stick man with huge muscles was drawn on the footboard. The room, like the rest of the house, was dim. There was an Athens, Greece travel poster on the wall and flying saucer lamps from the '50s at opposite ends of the room. The windows were tall and narrow with long beige shades and crocheted, life-saver strings. The house next door was only a few feet away and had been multi-plexed for students. One of the neighbors, an Oriental co-ed, walked down her steps to a sun-roofed Rabbit below. It started to rain.

Through the walls I heard Scott's dad hacking loudly while stroking away at his easel. I laid back in the bunk, wedging myself into this temporary resting place, and tried to drift into a pleasant dreamland. It didn't work. It hadn't worked since that weekend when I ricocheted from Judy to Emma to the streets, and ended up shambling around for three nights like Mr. Hyde. With Milton I had seen how far the murkiness of obsession could go. But where was I in that picture? Ever since I had been outside myself watching, like a member of a Greek chorus, trying to put the play into perspective.

I had been having a recurrent dream the past few weeks about a childhood incident. My dad had taken me to a Knights of Columbus track meet and we were eating at a diner, Connections, across the street from the Cleveland Arena. I was about 12 and beginning to somehow sense I was ready to start locking myself away from my dad, from everyone. That for some reason, perhaps a combination of acute, piercing Catholic guilt and vague, unspoken family secrets, I was about to go to my room and stay there. And that he, further and further withdrawing from an empty marriage into alcohol and 12 hour work days, would be powerless to draw me out.

I was unaware at the time, but I'm sure he saw me – and himself – slipping away. His ulcers and his nervous breakdown, as it was called then, directly tied to the dalliances of a woman who had found out in the newspaper that the love of her life was getting married and reluctantly settled for him. Somehow they stuck together and raised me on a street ironically named Hope Avenue. Neither of them, as the Tennessee Williams line goes, went to the moon, they went much farther. They taught me how to do the same.

In the dream, across the room from my dad and me at the Connections Diner, there was a disheveled guy slurping soup in a booth by the window. No teeth, brown wrinkled suit, slicked back hair like Shemp of the Three Stooges. His eyes stayed down while he talked to himself. My dad nudged me and nodded in the solitary gent's direction. "He has the worst disease in the world." My father leaned close to me and wrung a napkin in his hands. "Loneliness." It was as near to giving me a lecture that he ever came. It was also fair warning. He knew loneliness would be the battle of my life, just like it was his.

Connections. For as long as I could remember, through my isolated teenage years right up to this moment, when it came to women my connections always seemed like the first time I tried to play with one of those balls attached by an elasticized string to a small wooden paddle – a rare hit then all kinds of wild loops and misses. Nowadays I found myself zombied in front of the television; sucking on the moist mucousy ganja and musing about the magic of romance; analyzing into paralysis the whole quirky sexual battleground with Frank and Scott; and convincing myself that only the right woman, not just anyone, could save me. It had to be Lana or Judy or maybe Shirley Jones from "Carousel," that I searched the landscape for behind an invisible shield, like the one in the old toothpaste ads. Retreating, then grasping, then reaching out with eyes closed and head turned away. Living in isolation, longing for connection. The Brass Ring. The Life Raft. Where's the bridge? Where's the harbor?

"C'mon over to the den." Scott yelled cheerily. I snapped up from my reverie and banged my head on the top bunk. Well at least that bump on the coconut, instead of the growing fear that continuation of my present reality would yield the worst kind of nightmare, could serve as an explanation for my tears.

The fireplace was functional. There were upside down crystal glasses and painted butterflies. An old collie named Joe languished on the floor. "Reason and Revolution," "Joy of Sex" and "Concordance for the Bhagavad Ghita" were on the bookshelf. Scott showed me another thesis revision. "It's based on the concept of 'guide, philosopher, friend' which is a much better term than 'technocrat.' I'm getting close." He patted his breast.

The Nelsons and I ate in dimly animated conversation. Mr. Nelson said he couldn't understand how Scott could get so many girls to fall for him, saying, "I don't know what they all see in him." We talked about the mayor of Columbus who had been arrested a couple nights earlier in a notorious red light area at three in the morning. He was a Moral Majority type and claimed he was doing a spot check. The consensus at the table was that the incident would probably help him in the upcoming election. After dinner there was a birthday cake for Scott. Eighteen candles. His mom said 31 were too many and talked about how she felt when he went away to college in 1968. "It was like saying goodbye to my life," she sniffed while Scott gently stroked her head.

By midnight everyone had gone to bed.

***

"What I do is not to be confused with the schmaltzy psychocybernetics of Maxwell Maltz," Scott thundered. "I'd hate to count the number of women who ruled me out as a lover because of that guy. He discredits me."

After touring the campus the whole day, we had gone to a party at one of his friend's houses the next night. Scott had had a few beers and appeared to be having a good time until a woman, upon hearing he was into cybernetics, made the mistake of mentioning Maltz. Scott hit the ceiling and insisted we leave.

"We'll go see Paula," he said, sharply plucking at a wayward eyelash as we exited. "You'll like her. She stopped by to see me on her lunch break when I was down here last month. She had her hair cut in slutlocks, that's what she called them. She said they allowed her to get on top and do all kinds of slutty things."

We eased into my car and began driving the mile or so to her house as Scott continued the story. "She said she wanted to fuck and insisted we keep the blinds open. You know how close the houses are next to mine. I told her my mother would be home at any minute but she said she didn't care. Ray, she unleashed herself on me." There was a vague look of terror, the kind that accompanies the getting of what one wants, in Scott's eyes as we drove through the ebbing and flowing waves of college kids along High Street. "I would have been happy to just go to lunch and talk about my thesis. Plus I sensed she would be using that spermicide, those killer chemicals. Still, I let her drag me into the trenches. Predictably my cock developed a rash and I ended up having to take pills for 20 days."

"If that's so, why are we going to see her?"

A nasty smile rippled across his face and he said cryptically, "It's time she gets a little bit of her own medicine."

We pulled up in front of the apartment. Scott noticed that the light was on and that both Paula's and her roommate Stephanie's cars were there. "One time they both fucked me," he whispered as we inched up the stairs. "Paula was sitting with her skirt hiked up and I had my finger in her and my head in Stephanie's lap. I took my finger out and slowly brought it up and stuck it in Stephanie's mouth. They both got off on that. Women are naturally attracted to each other." Stephanie half-opened the door and said Paula was attending a private party for the mayor. No, she definitely didn't want any company.

"We could go over to Anna's apartment," Scott said anxiously, like a junkie needing to score, as we retraced our steps. "She's a dancer, a Leo and a Jew. She's been putting on a little weight lately and is extremely dangerous. She'd go right for the jugular." He bared his teeth.

I exercised my veto power on that. Instead we grabbed a bite to eat at Burger Chef. It was nearly one in the morning. College kids walked by and pressed their faces against Burger Chef's huge windows. Some pretended to throw up. Others turned and gave passing cars the finger.

***

The next day, around noon, we went to Scott's brother's house. David was a stubby, pork-cheeked fellow who worked as a Columbus city bill collector. He and Scott were both Aries, born 11 1/2 months apart and, since Scott had skipped the second grade, they had gone through school side by side. David was living with a pale, pencil-thin woman who wrote porno material for one of the raunchier men's magazines. She had an eight-year-old son by a previous marriage.

"She's a real hellcat," David murmured as we sat in the kitchen, "but sometimes I wonder what she's thinking, especially in bed."

David asked me to walk to a carryout with him. Right behind us a hippie girl was calling for her cat.

"Did either of you see an orange and white calico?"

"I found a cat last night and ate it." David held his sides, almost bursting as he kept his laughter in.

"Real nice. What if I were talking about a child?"

"Sorry lady, I was only joking," he nudged me then raised his voice. "I was in 'Nam and had a great time."

A car screeched by. "Jockstrap," David howled and shook his fist. Another car roared down the street. "That's it, hilljack, burn rubber and give money to the fuckin' A-rabs."

Returning from the carryout, David gave me a serious look. "Ray, how's Scott doing? He doesn't have any trouble getting laid. He just can't get anybody to love him, the poor guy. I always said that at age 40 he would either commit suicide or really take off. What do you think?" David gave an Italian salute to some kids in a souped-up Camaro before turning back for my reply.

I took his question seriously, having asked it of myself quite often recently, and discovered, to my surprise, that I had a lot more confidence in Scott's future than I had in mine. "There are always perils in being alone too much and you have to be very careful not to get yourself into a dangerous frame of mind but, ultimately, Scott's sense of devotion to his work will pull him through. Scott's gonna take off. Mark my words."

When we arrived at David's house, Scott was on the phone with an Ohio State prof whom he smilingly kept referring to as "The Force." After he hung up we bid David and his preoccupied girlfriend adieu. At the house next door a little girl in a Future Fox t-shirt was jumping off the porch and flapping her arms.

"Farrah Fawcett Jablonski!" a mommy's voice bellowed from inside. "Be careful, you don't have wings."

Scott looked at me sadly. "You don't have wings. That's what they always told me. That's why I'm still here."

We rounded up Frank at his second wife's apartment. He came down the steps a lot slower than he had gone up.

"How'd it go?"

"Okay," Frank stared glumly at the rear view mirror. "Until she pressed her tits against me."

The School Year Ends

By early May, Judy had begun to look at me again. Sometimes she would give me a waist-high wave or a semi-warm smile. I was seeing her more and more in the halls, but was playing it cool. And no, it wasn't a matter of playing. I really was smooth, satisfied at being torchless and remote, the way I'd been most of my life. Now, admittedly, I couldn't say for certain that I would never again be a slave of passion or that compulsion and obsession would be forever strangers. But one truth seemed evident: I was no longer constantly on the lookout. And on a bright mid-May morning I was wearing my detachment very much like an old pair of shoes as I stood in the hallway and spotted Judy approaching, waving her finger.

"I had a dream about you last night. You and someone else I hadn't seen in quite awhile."

"You'll have to tell me about it sometime, unless it's too hot to handle."

"I'll never tell," she teased over her shoulder, clicking her way towards the office.

"Judy," I called just as she was turning the corner. She stopped as if lassoed.

"Did you do any poems for that poetry contest a while ago?" I had been one of the judges. Around 50 poems were anonymously submitted. I had been in my delusional stage about her and tried to find a way to rig the contest for her benefit. I hadn't wanted to hear the results since I was sure that no good could have come from my deviousness, but now I felt I needed to face the music.

"Yeah, I turned four of 'em in."

"Which ones."

"The one about the deer getting shot in the forest."

"Oh, 'Echo of Fear.' I thought that was real good." Mentally I was telling the firing squad to put me out of my misery because, in truth, I felt "Echo of Fear" was equal to "How Do You See The Rain?" which I rated number one because I thought I had recognized Judy's handwriting. I figured if she would have won the contest I might get a chance to present her with the Burger King Certificate for first prize. Death where was thy sting? I do the conniving loverboy trip and Judy gets shafted. There was no forgiving myself on this one. She deserved to win the contest and I deserved to be tossed to the hounds.

"What were some of your others?" I asked absently, still reeling from this most recent of example of deception's tangled web and silently vowing to find a way to make it up to her if it took me several lifetimes.

"'Hopeless Dreams' was the only other good one."

Craving not justice or even mercy but some kind of forgiveness for something, anything, I blurted out, "Look about that 'Romeo and Juliet' quote. There was a full moon and all that but still it was a bit much. I should have known better."

Judy stared at me and slowly nodded. I debated whether or not to stand there for the next 20 minutes in order for the bell to save me or try to say something.

She bailed me out. "Everybody's human, I guess."

"That's what I hear." I smiled and shook my head slowly. "Did you know that I won't be coming back next year? Technically I got laid off but I was going to leave anyway. Does that surprise you?"

"No," she said in a low, soft voice, "I figured you wouldn't be." For an instant she seemed sad, then brightened and finally breathed freely, as if a load had been lifted. "Boy this has been some week."

"What happened?"

"Yesterday I got elected president of student council."

"Congratulations." I shook her hand formally. "Are you happy?"

"Yeah, but it will be a lot of work, although now it looks like I'll have lots of time on my hands around here, compared to earlier this year, anyway." She eyed me with mischief and my gears suddenly shifted.

"It's great to talk to you again. I really missed our conversations. You look like a breath of spring today." She was wearing a ruffled white shirt, purple vest and pale lavender corduroys.

"More like out-of-breath from partying," she laughed shyly and wedged her hands into her back pockets.

"Now you know why I act so strange sometimes." I over-furrowed my brow. "I'll tell you Judy, it's taken its toll on me over the years, and I'm not getting any younger." She had a look on her face that said maybe she was beginning to get the idea.

"Age is just a number, Mr. Powell."

"That's easy for you to say."

"It should be just as easy for you," she said with just a touch of annoyance.

That was fair enough but there was no way I was about to climb back on the merry-go-round for a verbal twirl or play a game of Go Fish for romantic hints between her lines. That was the old Ray Powell, this new guy steered clear of such silliness and deftly re-routed the conversation.

"What did you think of the Freedom Jam?" I asked in reference to a semi-Christian rock group that had played during an assembly earlier in the week. They dressed like Paul Revere and the Raiders and had begun their set with AC/DC's "Back in Black" and ended it with the "Battle Hymn of the Republic." In the middle of the performance the blond lead singer had plucked Judy out of the first row and sang "Every Woman in the World" to her while the crowd shrieked.

"They were all right but that lead singer was a real winner. He wanted me to come on the bus with him to Ann Arbor and do some coke." She rolled her eyes to indicate that she was not born yesterday. "I told him thanks but no thanks."

"His first big mistake was that he should have sung something that fit you, like 'Bette Davis Eyes'." Had I not been in the midst of a personal transformation a comment such as that may have been construed as indication that I was not quite out of the woods yet. But I was content to allow history to be the judge of that.

"Oh, I hate that song," she shivered as the bell rang.

"We'll have to get together and chat some more," I matter-of-facted.

"Okay, just grab me when I'm making one of my cruises down the hall."

I watched her walk away. May and 17. Newly elected president of student council; battling the school secretary, whose daughter also ran for student council president; dreaming about me; arguing in favor of women's lib with the skeptical cheerleading squad; bursting into corridor tears over a mix-up in passing out senior pictures; acting sometimes like a frightened little girl but clearly just around the corner from becoming a possible Earth Mother of the Century candidate. And me standing in the hallway, calling it progress that my eyes were no longer riveted to her and that my heart, mercifully, was no longer beating like a drum.

But, as Caine would say, "The soul doesn't measure time, it merely records growth."

***

"It's right." Scott bowed his head ever so slightly. "I know the Maharishi wants me there."

He had stopped for a visit on the evening I was released from the Crystal City Hospital, where I had gone over the Memorial Day weekend for some minor shoulder surgery, to inform me that he had gotten the California internship with Honeywell and would be leaving in a few days.

"I'll have the perverse pleasure of wearing those three-piece pinstripe suits every day." Scott's teeth glistened through his thin lips. "I don't know if perverse is the proper word but I do get a certain base delight out of wearing them and, more importantly, watching women looking at me while I'm wearing them." Before allowing his gaze to linger too long on the extremely tall nurse who was preparing my release forms, Scott snapped his attention back to the ostensible purpose of his California journey and said he was certain that great wisdom would spring from it.

"Well I don't know how much wisdom I've gotten during this Judy journey I've been on over the past few months, but it's definitely taken its toll on me," I said. "I think part of the reason I came into the hospital was to go under the knife for a little reconstruction."

"Uh, speaking of Judy," Scott began cautiously after the nurse had left the room, "I wonder if you could show her my thesis."

"I think she'd have a hard time understanding it, Scott."

"Oh, she doesn't have to involve herself with it, or read it, or even handle it in any way," he said with a wicked smile. "I just want her to look at it."

"So Swami Scott's looking for a little second hand transcendental voyeurism." Frank's voice pierced the room's quietness. "Well, I've seen this sorry show too many times before and I know how it ends, not with a bang but a whimper."

Scott quickly grabbed his briefcase and, attempting to glide over his injured dignity as best he could, headed swiftly for the door. "I will see both of you gentlemen in the fall."

"Don't take any wooden Maharishi nickels," Frank yelled as Scott disappeared into the hallway. "I'm sorry, but that guy's nuts. I'm just glad I got here in time to nail him. He gives all of us a bad name with those wishy-washy wish lists of his."

We left the hospital and Frank insisted that we drive to Crystal City Park and smoke pot. We parked right next to the softball field where I had first made a move on Lana. It was no longer being used for organized games and the once perfectly manicured dirt infield had blotches of unruly weeds all over it. I told Frank I'd decided to give up marijuana in hopes that abstinence would help me look at things in a more natural, clearheaded light, and also prevent me from sinking into the kind of female-related madness I'd experienced with Lana and had begun to fall into with Judy.

"You're right, he nodded quickly. "It's all tied into that moist, magical pussy-juice frame of mind you can get yourself entwined in if you're not careful." He scraped at his hand, still trying to remove the Stigmata. "The more you suck on this stuff, the more you want to go out and find some cosmic Gypsy fuck queen like that Lana. I think that was half the problem you had with her. She sort of hemp-roped you in. It's happened to me on more than one occasion, too." He carefully sprinkled the pot into his pipe. "Another eight to 10 days with this stuff and I'm through with it forever. That's it." He took a long hit, holding it in until he broke into a coughing fit.

Between inhales and the resultant wheezes and hacks, Frank recounted his week, beginning with a poetry reading he had given at the nursing home. He read "Milking the Dairy Queen," "Potential Wife Number Four Is Still Asleep," and several others, all rife with crazed sexual imagery that utilized reptiles as a central metaphor.

"The crowd was quiet," he reported in a constricted dope voice. "I think about half of them had nodded off. Actually, the only reaction I got was from this one woman who's always kissing the guys at the home. She pinched me on the ass the next day and said 'you little devil'."

The annual Anarchist's Day Parade had also provided Frank the forum for yet another reading, which he delivered in front of the Club amidst hoots from members of Women Now. He had come as a representative of the G.L.O., Guys Liberation Organization, or simply Guise.

"I formed the group, disbanded it, then reorganized it as the only member," he said, citing Thoreau's quote about a majority of one. "I'm a little worried about the FBI investigating me about what I said at the rally. It was definitely borderline psychotic stuff, but if they question me, I could just tell them I was representing a men's group protesting all this women's lib stuff. Even those assholes could probably relate to that."

He had also recently met a woman, Goldy. She was a 19-year-old student who lived on a farm outside town with her parents. "On our first date she complained that her previous boyfriend's mouth was too big." Frank lit up a Camel, having temporarily quit Kools as part of a nationwide boycott. "So when the moment of parting expression came, I made sure I checked out her mouth, parted my lips closely, got that matchup going, then zeroed in." Frank digressed into a social behavior tip, the kind I'd never received from my parents, the nuns or any of the Pat Boone dating books. "You never want to exhibit the same shortcomings that doomed your predecessor. If he was aggressive, that's the last thing you are. If he was too laid-back, you believe that sometimes a swift kick in the butt is good for people. If he was too much into sex, you'd be the first to admit that there was more to a relationship than screwing. If he was wasn't into sex enough, you would be the very last person to minimize physical needs. You have problems, admittedly, but not that particular one, whatever it might be."

Finished with his tip from the top, he smoothly shifted to a summary of the air-tight case for his latest paramour. "Goldy's different, she's not into games at all. She doesn't wear her vagina on her face. It's right there in her pants where it belongs. The whole thing with her is positive. All the others in my life were negative, catastrophic." He reloaded the pipe with craftsman-like care and began his conclusion. "She's totally removed from that Women Now nonsense. She doesn't even know that group exists. She even admitted a real aversion to homosexuality. She kind of said it in an apologetic way, like it would offend my liberalism. I assured her that her views were in conjunction with mine."

A teenage girl exited a propped-up Barracuda about 20 feet from where we were parked. She had on pink shorts and a Lady Doctor tank top and came walking towards our car.

"We'd like to borrow you pipe." She leaned over the window and exposed her breasts. She had freckles and a slight case of acne around her mouth. Although she couldn't have been more than 16, her body could have run for Congress.

"You can come in and smoke with me." Frank offered. She said she couldn't, straightened up to button her shorts, then leaned back down.

I asked her what year she was in school.

"I'll be a sophomore."

"Do you know Jim Hines?" I asked in reference to an English teacher at her school.

"Yeah, he gets high." She nodded her head knowingly while staring at the matchbook Frank had given her. It said, "Eat Out Often." She flashed it towards me and giggled that she could dig that.

I told her to watch herself because I was a high school teacher.

"Are you dating any of your students?"

"No, but there's one I've gotten to know pretty well. We're just friends, though. I'm no dirty old man."

"All men are kinda dirty, but that's okay. You just got to be careful and have a good time."

Frank murmured, "Sometimes life answers questions for you."

She stretched and scratched her belly button. Her shorts popped. Frank mewled. She leaned over again. "If you're raised with love, you love. My parents are always making out. They're real horny. Could I please have that pipe?"

Frank gave it to her and she walked back to her car. Before hopping into the passenger's seat, she bent over to adjust her sandals, straightened up and tugged at her crack to loosen her shorts.

"A lot of women don't want to acknowledge their sexuality." Frank lectured in a monotone. "That's a drag. You can't get around it. Just as long as they don't abuse it. I could see no problems on a desert island with her." He pointed towards the Barracuda. "It would be just me and her and the social mores would simply have to be adjusted. There'd be no bullshit with her. She'd be as receptive to my sexual imagery as Goldy, maybe even more so. I just can't deal with these women who chant. I'm sick of all their lopsided Daoism. You need that divine tension. I'm simply acknowledging the Yin."

She soon returned with the pipe. A pick-up roared by with "Aqualung" blasting on its stereo. "Now don't get too high," she wagged her finger at Frank, then looked at me. "And you, don't you dare leave that girl alone."

Obviously weighing the words of either callowness or wisdom that had just come from the mouth of this particular babe, neither Frank nor I said a word as we drove to his residence and sat silently on his porch, watching the students carting out their belongings as Crystal City began to empty for the summer.

"I'll admit that it was Goldy's young flesh that did it to me," Frank confessed after shutting the porch door so that his landlady couldn't hear. "I brought her back here just last night and we turned out the lights. We moved the mattress on the floor so it wouldn't squeak. She told me she was embarrassed because she was a virgin. I comforted her by saying that experience was overrated and that whether or not her hymen was intact had nothing to do with her being loved." Frank got up and checked the door twice before sitting back down, cupping his hand to his mouth and leaning close to me. "I ate her out for an hour. After we got done she said she never dreamed sex could be like that. I concurred."

Two of his arch-enemies from Women Now walked by and simultaneously shot a look at Frank that would have blown many a man to smithereens. "It's funny, but I used to actively pursue older women," he said, appearing to be checking himself for flesh wounds, as the Birkenstocked pair walked briskly towards the Bonded gas station on the corner. "I figured they could understand me better, but they all ended up getting cynical or burnt out or dykey or else they got into these momism relationships with young guys." He glanced at his watch and remembered he was supposed to meet Goldy just after dark on the edge of town. "I guess I just backlashed back to the basics and I suggest you consider doing the same."

Driving back to Toledo I decided to take a nostalgic ride along the same route I had taken so many times to visit Lana – this time, however, with Judy on my mind and thoughts of how I should deal with her during the upcoming last week of school. Here I was again still dreamily rolling down that same, dark, heart-pounding path past the Crystal City water treatment plant, the Luckey ballfield and the Mail Pouch Saloon, still looking for signs.

On the radio was the voice of the female host for a local show called "Problems Between Men and Women." She was talking about the need for less talk and more action when it came to romance. Her advice to men, "Don't think about it, just do it."

So I continued onto Devil's Hole Road and peered through the slight haze of fog and my own resin-tinted windows. I stopped at the intersection of Devil's Hole and Sugar Ridge but couldn't see Lana's driveway. I twisted and turned the car, flashed my brights and looked closer. Bushes and bent trees had devoured the pathway. It looked like an abandoned Gothic castleway where once wondrous romance flourished; now out of use, out of date, no longer cared for, neglected potholes in the narrowed passageways. Nobody lives there anymore. I surprised her once. She was naked. "Don't freak out," she smiled and raked her silver nails over my jeans. We made love next to the lagoon then paddled down the river, I rowing she navigating, to pick up the twins at Luckey Amusement Park. Standing on the steps in the fall of '76, instantly, hopelessly in love. Coming by to see her so many times when she wasn't there, but never mentioning that I had stopped by. I came too often, anyway. Her kneeling, jeans pulled down, boots still on. Me never saying a word, silently partnering in life's business. Arriving there while she slept or showered or talked on the phone and that last desperate day with the Lennon music on the radio and me pressing against the windows of the boxed-up house – lost again in the midst of the holiday season. And here I am once more, having learned in my six-month journey since then that, as incredibly complex as I used to think things were, they aren't nearly as simple to solve as I thought.

Backing my car out of the driveway I started down Sugar Ridge when I spotted a black-clad figure frantically waving me over. It was Milton standing near his pick-up truck, which was slightly off the road, stuck in the mud.

I stopped and rolled down the window. "What happened?"

"Hi Ray. I was just getting some dirt and got stuck," he muttered. "I'm in a hurry. Help me."

It didn't take long for he and I to rock his vehicle free.

"What's all this about?" I asked.

Milton shoveled in a few more loads of muck and explained he was on his way to the Bargain Barn in Waterville. He had called and told them his brother was a shoplifter and was on his way to the store. He then described himself.

"There's a female security guard there who looks like Rachel." He cleared his throat violently. "I'll act suspicious. She'll apprehend me and search me, but she won't find anything. I'll be polite and forgiving."

Unable to muster an appropriate response I asked, "Why did you stop for the dirt?"

His bleary eyes narrowed. "I'm going to get some prostitutes to stop by and do some mud wrestling," he said with dark excitement. "They're coming over after I get back from Bargain Barn." He harpooned the shovel into the mud and climbed aboard his truck.

Before driving off for his appointment to be arrested and set free, Milton leaned out of the window, cleared his throat and looked me straight in the eye. "You know Ray, I wouldn't be doing anything like this if Rachel would have married me. Everything's different because I let her slip through my fingers."

His pickup sputtered away and finally disappeared into the night. I started my car while tallying the collective guidance I had received concerning Judy. Frank said to go back to basics; Scott, despite initial concern, admitted that in Europe her age would not even be an issue; Bert encouraged me, in a recent phone call, to wait until I was no longer teaching, then jump her bones; Milton clearly indicated I'd be better off if she didn't slip away; the young girl in the park told me not to leave Judy alone; and, if nothing else, this trip down Lana-memory lane has shown me that the whole whimsically romantic scene I had with her was now abandoned territory.

"Anyone else have an opinion," I shouted as I continued on the dark, winding road.

"Remember," the radio talk show hostess said as she was signing off, "it only takes one."

***

On the first day of June, I was at school standing in the doorway alone. Based on what Caine had said on "Kung Fu" last night, that change takes place when you become who you always were, I had decided not to force or contrive anything with Judy, but instead allow things to come to me, thereby learning about who I was from how I responded. She came peeking around the corner.

"Hi Judy." An absence of eagerness was in my voice.

"Hi. How was the operation?"

"No problem."

"Well it's good to have you back. Boy you got a nice tan."

"So do you." A down-to-earth cordiality had become my calling card. She shook her head "not really." She had on those super tight Chic jeans and a white blouse.

"I read the last school paper this morning. Your article on REO was a little rough, but I liked the piece you did in support of the ERA. You made your point well on that one." I was totally issue-oriented and no longer gushy or gawky.

"Thanks, but I'm glad we don't have to write anything for that dumb paper anymore."

"I looked at all your pictures in the yearbook. Some are better than others. I really liked that one with the Powder Puff football team." She gave me an ugh look.

"I guess it's okay but I don't like any of my pictures. That's why I'm on the other side of the camera."

"I'm not photogenic, either," I said with self-effacing charm.

"You took a real good picture, though."

"No, you took the picture." We both laughed easily.

It looked like a day at the Rancho Smootho for me. No more of the looking down and shuffling my feet like Alfalfa.

"Uh, I've got to move my car, " she slung her purse over her shoulder.

"How's that Duster, I mean Gremlin, running?"

"Loud as usual. Bye."

I had never noticed Gremlins until I saw her driving hers. And, true enough, now I never missed one. Yet, I still asked her about her Duster. At this point an old false self would have been cursing me for blowing it. But recognizing an honest mistake for what it was, I felt no need for self-forgiveness. If that wasn't proof positive that I was now a straight-up, self-assured guy, I don't know what was.

***

The last week of school blurred past and there was just one day left.

Instructive though it was, my frozen reactor routine was producing about the same results as my previous daydream believer/homecoming queen motif. All in all, like the song said, it was just another brick in the wall, which I decided to try to break down by writing her a short letter:

Dear Judy,

This past year has been a difficult one for me. Despite my age and the fact that I probably should know have known better, I found myself mixed up about a lot of things – especially you. My reaction to you hit me like a lightning bolt and threw me off balance. I didn't handle the situation very maturely and I'm still trying to figure out why. As you might imagine I have a million theories about what happened and I won't bore you with them. But I want you to know that I was very honest in my feelings about you and that, most importantly, I want our friendship to be preserved. Friends are tough to come by in life and we should always treat them with as much care as we can. I've been really happy that we started talking again and, believe it or not, I think I even learned something about myself during all this. But I still have a long way to go. Life is a journey, Judy, but you already know that since you're a fan of "Kung Fu." Seriously, never, never, ever forget that I think you are a wonderful, beautiful and talented person and that when I look back on my year at Temperance, I will think of you.

Your Friend,
Ray

I gave her the envelope at the water fountain, down the hall from my room, near the library—where she hung out.

***

On the last full day of school, Judy clicked down the corridor and pulled a letter from her copy of "Great Expectations" and handed it to me. The assistant principal was leaning against the water fountain, pretending not to notice the delivery. The letter was on filmy blue stationery, dated incorrectly. It was a month ahead.

Dear Ray,

You're letter really blew my mind. I had no idea our friendship meant so much to you. If I would have known that I wouldn't have done anything to hurt you, because I've never hurt anyone on purpose in my life. I think I'm a whole lot older and wiser than just 17 but I backed off from you because I was real busy and I can't let anyone stand in the way of me accomplishing my goals. Plus, some people at school were getting the wrong idea and I didn't want to lead you on anymore than I already had.

This year is definitely one I'll never forget and I'll never, ever forget you. I'm sorry you're leaving but maybe it's for the best. I need to explore my inner self and find out who I really am. And even though you're old (that's a joke) it sounds like you need to do the same thing. Please forgive me if I hurt you and if you write me I promise I'll always write back.

Your friend,
Judy

P.S. After you told me I had Bette Davis eyes that song came on every morning when I was driving to school. I'm starting to like it.

***

"The more you impose order the more chaos results." I said, imparting some Eastern wisdom to principal Nott at our checkout meeting the next day. He had asked me what suggestions I could give him about how the school could be better run the next year. I was spelling "chaos" for him when I noticed Judy flash by and excused myself. I caught up with her near the water fountain. She was wearing a pale lavender dress with hose and white heels and was on her way to a meeting with the superintendent about student council business.

"I'm glad I saw you today. Thanks for the letter."

"You're welcome." She had a small white purse in her hand and was standing very straight. "I'm late for my meeting."

"Yeah. I gotta get back and finish up checking out."

Several seconds of frozen silence was broken by the ambling appearance of the cafeteria matron on a clean up mission. I turned to her and nodded towards Judy.

"Doesn't she look terrific today?"

The cook heartily agreed. Judy's tan was getting deeper and her hair blonder. She looked like a lavender dream, impossibly young, totally irresistible. She was all business that day, though. I took a lifetime exposure, gently squeezed her shoulder, told her I'd stay in touch and walked away, secure in the knowledge that I hadn't tried to force anything, nor had I ruled out the possibility of getting together. And neither had she.

Before I went back into the principal's office I turned around to see if I could catch another glimpse of her. Judy was gone. I was still looking.

Part Three Re-Incorporation

> Like an echo down a canyon,
> Never coming back as clear.
> Lately I just judge the distance,
> Not the words I hear.
> — *Bob Seger*

The Men's Group

"I found this stuck to the door when I got here tonight." I held up a letter addressed to "The Men." It was from Gary and Dale, our group's non-leaders, whose empty chairs bore mute testimony to their absence for the telling of the final stage of my primal story.

"Read it Ray," said Elvin, a bear-like, recently retired cop and one of the original founders of the group. "I think we all know what's coming." He shifted his weight and scratched at his grey-streaked beard. "When my old man split he didn't even bother to leave a note, the gutless bastard. I can handle this and I think the rest of us can, too."

There were only six of us remaining in the group but everyone quickly nodded agreement with Elvin. After a moment of silence to allow each of us to reflect on our personal abandonment issues, I opened the letter and began to read aloud.

>Fellow Journeyers:
>
>This is perhaps the most difficult thing we've ever done, but we can't pretend anymore that it's not time for us to leave. Tonight as Ray concludes his primal story by re-experiencing the re-incorporation stage, we must ourselves – knowing all journeys are forever beginning and never ending-start anew by separating from this group that we have learned to love almost as much as life itself.
>
>We came to this painful conclusion individually this past week when each of us rea lized he had callously broken the rules of the group by seeking Ray out during the break last week to force totally unsolicited advice on him. We both understood we had gone too far and that we were trying to become, in a sense, the group's shadow

fathers – more concerned with passing on psychic semen than allowing you to experience your own journeys. Steadfastly refusing to wallow in shame about that, however, we have instead chosen to take manly responsibility for our lives and move on.

But before we do that we need to say – among oh so many things that must sadly be left unsaid – a quick word about the struggle we are all experiencing. While listening to Ray's initiation phase last week both of our hearts went out to him and to all of us for what we must go through to be men nowadays. It's been said that in tribes surrounded by the constant threat of war, the initiation rite for young men was the most brutal – often consisting of lip piercing, testicle removing, scarring and the killing of wild animals- because the dangers of living in the midst of constant warfare were so great. So it is with us as we attempt to survive as men and keep the species going in the face of so much societal confusion about what it means to be both a woman and a man. I know sometimes it seems we overly dwell on this reality but we cannot – nor should not – underestimate the kind of psychological battle we must fight in order to set up just the most basic relationship, the kind our ancestors barely thought twice about. We are truly pioneers and, like all genuine pathfinders, have suffered numerous casualties. It's really not a surprise that Ray's friend couldn't take it anymore and chose to end the earth-bound phase of his journey. In many ways it's surprising that more of us don't do the same. But as warriors we know that death is always around us and only by acknowledging it we can free ourselves from the numb existence of shallow self-protection.

And that brings us to why we are doing what we are doing. Sadly, we both realized that our beloved group had become a shelter to protect ourselves, avoid our journey and, in essence, give up living. We also concluded there is a danger that men's groups, in general, foment a kind of masculine nationalism that reinforces separatism-when what we truly need is to move beyond that to true gender transcendence. We cannot allow ourselves to become preening middle class white men sitting around moaning about how we've become victims. That's one drum we must never beat.

So, you may be asking, what's next for Gary and Dale? Well, in a month we will be opening a combination coffee house/video arcade. It will be called Ashes, Descent and Grief – a name taken from the Robert Bly concept of the road we all must travel. But ours will be a fun place, too. Tuesday will be Ladies Night and we will honor all men's movement coupons. Oh yes, it will be located in the room your meeting is taking place, which we have leased and will begin remodeling next week. So if you choose not to disband your group you must find another place to meet. Nobody ever said the road was easy. Here's to a truly enchanted life where all wounds can be dipped in healing water.

With fierce love,
Gary and Dale

For a moment we were silent, then Elvin spoke, "I"m sorry but that Dale always got under my skin, sitting there grinning like a sissy in Boys Town, oops I didn't mean that like it sounded." He rose from his chair and gave a quick hug to Jon, the group's only gay member, who said he forgave him and playfully pushed him back to his seat where Elvin rephrased his observation. "I mean he always struck me as a soft male who had no interior warrior and was completely unable to show his sword."

"Yeah," chimed in Mark, a skinny certified Rolfer with a handlebar mustache, "and Gary was like a aggressive fly-boy male who tried to ascend over his wounds and pretend he had no pain. Actually they were both assholes. I'll never patronize their business."

Everyone in the group nodded defiantly in agreement, simultaneously leaned forward and looked towards Elvin, who turned in my direction. "We really don't know how our group is going to end up, Ray, and we can't worry about that now. All I'm sure of is that everything happens for a reason. Maybe there's no place to go after your story." He looked at me like an exhausted third man on a long distance relay team, reaching out to hand over the baton to the anchor man. "So just carry on, Ray."

"Well it took me a while to get the chance to use the tools I had acquired during the initiation stage," I said as the empty chairs of Dale and Gary were removed from the circle and the remaining members closed in on me. "Then suddenly, just as summer was fading, the women all sort of hit me at once."

Labor Day Rolls Around

It was the first Friday in September and I was sitting in my roll-back chair, gazing out the window at the dreariness outside. A distinct chill accompanied the summer of 1981's final vacation weekend. Record lows were being predicted. An early fall was a certainty. Growing up, Labor Day had always been the most melancholy of holidays for me; sandlot ball winding down, school starting and darkness creeping closer to just after dinner and seclusion time in my room; a billowy black curtain enveloping me, at least until spring arrived and I could get outside to lose myself again in baseball. That annual born-again-through-summer pattern had always saved me – until this year when I had spent the previous three months in a stale retreat mode around my apartment, moping and reading and remote controlling while I tried to figure out what my next move would be once the unemployment checks ran out. Whenever I would go somewhere I was always ready to leave shortly after arriving, while home had become little more than a coldly comfortable place to linger. Actively pursuing a social life had become a daunting concept, but one I had not totally given up on yet. Some other time, though.

The phone rang. It was a kid nervously asking, "Is my Mom there?" I was getting as many wrong numbers as actual telephone calls, though Scott had phoned me earlier in the day and we made plans to go to the Lucas County Fair on Sunday. I hadn't seen him since before he left for California, but I had received a letter from him, in early August from Columbus, in which he claimed the California experience had been a "humbling one" and he had emerged from it a "changed man." He had returned from San Diego in late July, blaming "philosophical differences" for his early departure but hinting there was more to the story, before concluding his letter with a polite and non-suggestive inquiry about Judy.

Judy and I had exchanged letters in early August. Mine had been a mechanical, postcard-length letter provoked by seeing the "Bette Davis Eyes" video on television and being seized with a pang of guilt for not writing her as I had half-promised to do. Even in the stifling lethargy of my secluded summer, I cringed at my behavior towards her during the school year, though the letter she had sent back to me, one that I had read at least a dozen times, underscored her gentle sweetness and hinted that she might have been a more of a kindred spirit than I had imagined.

> Dear Ray:
>
> Thanks for the note. It sounds like you're having about the same kind of summer as I am – boring. I'm working as a Pepsi Challenge girl at outdoor events and getting a lot of sun, which is making me kind of absent-minded, I think, but in my absent-mindedness I haven't stopped thinking about you.
>
> One thing I am getting used to is this full moon stuff you always talked about. I got a book about the lunar cycle and I'm learning about it. Some of the ideas you have are pretty off-beat but I always liked listening to them. I have a hard time believing in things because my life has been filled with negativism from all sides and that makes me want to just work all the time so I can succeed at the goals I set and come out on top and show everyone who I really am. If you knew me better you'd understand just what I was talking about. Maybe someday I'll have time to explain it to you.
>
> When I'm not working I just spend a lot of time in my bedroom, thinking, reading and conjuring up dreams. That reminds me, you should see my beautiful bedroom. I just painted the walls sunflower yellow, put up my canopy bed and bought some beautiful white lace curtains. Those babies cost 70 bucks just for

two windows! My desk is next to my bed and in the middle is a white throw rug. Next to my window I have a table and my rocking chair. That's where I'm sitting now. I have my windows open now because it's raining. I love listening to the rain. Someday you'll have to come over so you can see my room. When I'm in here it's like being in a dream. I just shut the door and that shuts out the world—at least for a little while. Bye.

Your friend,
Judy

Though it was somewhat comforting to realize that I didn't have a corner on loneliness, I simply couldn't afford to romantically meander in the direction of a 17-year-old, as tempting as that might be and as socially-bankrupt as I was becoming.

Right after I put Judy's letter back in my table's drawer the phone rang. It was Bert.

"What are you doing tomorrow night?" he asked.

"Nothing."

"Why don't you grab a date and drive here for the Lakewood Community Talent Show?"

Each year on the Saturday before Labor Day the Lakewood Little Theater would get community leaders together to put on a talent show for charity. Bert had started this tradition five years ago but this year he had to fight for his old position.

"I had to practically beg for the emcee job this year," he said. Apparently some of the younger members of the theater staff thought Bert's humor and musical tastes were a bit passe' and attempted to overthrow him, forcing him to call in some markers. "I know where the bodies are buried around here and even though they eased me out of a few things I'm still going to sing 'Country Roads' and 'Puff the Magic Dragon.' Do you think you can find a lady and come?"

"Actually, I've been out of circulation all summer."

"So I leave for awhile and you end up spending time with Rosie Palm. I thought I taught you better than that. What about Jenny?"

"That's a possibility, I guess. I heard that stevedore she was dating went back to his wife and kids. I could give her a call."

"That's the spirit," Bert said with assurance before his voice took on its familiar calculating tone. "Even though she's not your dream girl, if you show up here with her nobody will know the difference. Plus she's good looking enough you're bound to score points with women around here and, although none of them are perfect, maybe they'll know somebody who might be just what the doctor ordered for you and maybe she'll have a friend for me."

"Sounds like a plan to me," I said laughing. "By the way, anything new on the social front?"

"Well, the girl I had designs on is going with someone else so I guess I won't be able to nail her kundingi, but I met a girl on jury duty last week and we've got a possible golf rendezvous next month." He paused for a moment. "The only thing about her was that during the deliberations she kept saying she'd like to see all men who've been charged with sex offenses burned to a crisp after their penises were cut off in public. This was while we were deciding financial cases. She wanted to go to a firing range with me, but I put the kibosh on that. "

"This is costing you money, Bert."

"Ah don't worry. I'll have a couple tickets waiting for you at the door. Six o'clock sharp."

I'll be damned, the weekend was starting to shape up. Maybe laying low for the summer had simply gotten me ready to roar back into the swing of things. I was starting to get those old Kismet feelings again but because I was clearly dealing from strength and independence, it didn't even cross my mind to concern myself with actively stifling them. Nor did I feel the need to reinforce my position by looking for verification from a Caine quote. I simply called Jenny and asked her. She wasn't doing anything and said she'd love to see Bert.

"Oh, by the way," she said. "I've got two tickets to a play tonight. It's called 'Magic.' I don't know what it's about but it sounds like something you'd like."

I told her I'd be there with bells on.

"Magic" took place in the Continuing Education Auditorium at Toledo University. It was written by G.K. Chesterton and had been used as the model for Ingmar Bergman's movie "The Magician." It was about a conjurer and a young girl. She would go out in the woods to meet him. Her parents disapproved. Finally, the conjurer came into the household and taught everyone about "real" magic. In the final scene he tells the young girl he had been in love with her from the first time he saw her; that he had been a lonely man wandering around the woods when she found him; that he had tricked her by claiming to be a conjurer; and that he was "just a man."

"I knew you were a man all the time," the young girl said as it appeared they were going to live happily ever after.

"I'll bet you were thinking of that Judy chick all the time," Jenny smiled knowingly and fiddled with her braid as we left the auditorium.

"Not really," I shrugged, holding the door open for her. "I think the motif of the young girl as a means of regeneration and ultimately salvation has obvious anthropological validity and certainly works well for the theater but in everyday life you're probably a lot better off if you can find a way to generate your own redemption." Silk should be so smooth.

"Oh, I don't know, those high school guys behind me did the trick for me, especially the one on crutches."

We went to her house afterwards. It was spotless. "I'm no slob," Jenny said proudly. We sat and sipped wine while a Moody Blues album played.

"You know, I'm open to just about anything." She flapped her knees. "Sometimes it's good to have friends that you just have a casual sexual relationship with. Do you have anyone like that?"

"No."

"Well, it's neat. No big deal, but it helps."

"I don't know. I've never been able to do something like that, not more than once or twice, then it gets weird." I leaned away from Jenny and propped my elbow on the back of her couch and rested my head on my palm. "I can't afford to blur the lines of distinction between friends and lovers, there's too much at stake, too much to be lost. I don't need the grief."

"It's funny Ray." Jenny moved a little forward and looked uncharacteristically perturbed. "You're always so heavy about getting together with someone but then you act like you don't need it or something, or you find some excuse why things won't happen. You're almost as bad as Bert." She cupped her mouth and chin into the wine glass for a second. "I'm just telling you, I'm open to just about anything, but don't mind me or nothin'." She leaned back, stretched and yawned herself to her feet.

I sheepishly told her I'd pick her up around four o'clock the next afternoon and made sure I didn't let the door hit me on the way out.

***

A downpour accompanied Jenny and me as we drove the two hours to Cleveland without mentioning the previous evening's conversation. I had taken note of both the validity and oversimplification of what she had said and had concluded that in no way would I spend time defending myself or justifying my position. I only hoped that my silence spoke volumes.

There was a slight drizzle outside of the Lakewood High School Auditorium. The huge hall was packed with over 1000 people. Lots of kids in the rear rows. For a supposedly civic show I sensed a decidedly rowdy atmosphere. I could have sworn I smelled both booze and marijuana in the air as the house lights dimmed and "This Could Be the Start of Something Big," came over the PA.

In an instant Bert popped out of the curtain with a hand mike. He was wearing a red blazer and grey pants. "Thank you very much, ladies and germs," he began, whipping the mike cord behind him. There was silence. "What is this an audience or an oil painting?" A few laughs. "You know normally I would say ladies and Geritol but this is a pretty young crowd."

"Nice hair," a voice boomed from the back.

Bert laughed off the taunt, walked down to the front of the stage, sat on the ledge and began telling the history of the talent show.

"Stick it up your heinie," someone yelled and the crowd tittered nervously.

"Be cool fellas." Bert held up his hands. "This is a family show."

I looked at Jenny and slunk down in my chair. This could be a long night.

Bert had a few jokes. "What's green and flies over Germany? – Snazis."

"Get off the stage," a multitude of voices echoed in obviously orchestrated unison.

"Hey turkeys," Bert yelled. A chorus of gobbles went up. Stoned tenth graders are a tough crowd.

"Nice jacket. Who's your tailor, Bill of Budapest?"

Feigning obliviousness to the audience's rudeness, Bert introduced the first act, a comedy skit starring the Lakewood sanitation director, playing Mr. Whipple, the bumbling spokesman for Charmin tissues, and consisting of lots of toilet paper jokes and a mystery box that everyone would reach into and say things like, "It feels so good." The kids howled.

Bert returned between acts and someone lobbed something on stage. The security guards were called in to apprehend the guilty party before the featured act, the Lakewood Rockers, took the stage. The lead guitarist was a young city recreation employee who also played in one of the top rock bands in Cleveland. The Rockers kicked into "You Really Got Me." The kids went apeshit and screamed for more. The band played "Johnny B. Goode," after which Bert appeared announcing they couldn't play anymore because the lead guitarist had to leave. The crowd loudly voiced its displeasure.

There were some more toilet skits, a Mr. Rogers' take-off with jokes about lisping fairy princes, and a lengthy Dear Abby advice to teens skit with local firemen singing out things like "Don't pick your nose,"

"Never wet your pants," and "Don't do anything I wouldn't do and if you do name it after me." The mayor, noting the rowdiness of the crowd and not wanting the unruly horde roaming the building, canceled the intermission, leaving Bert with more time to kill. He told some new jokes. "What's green and skates? – Peggy Flem. What's green and Italian? – Frank Snotra."

At this point many in the crowd, including Jenny and me, had lost the capacity to cringe as Bert desperately repeated some jokes, did a finger coin magic trick that no one could see and began telling a story in Russian before begin saved by The Girls From Lakewood, a group of secretaries in cheerleaders' outfits who were indelicately characterized by a kid behind us as looking like the losers in a Polish beauty pageant. Four rows left as one before the cheerleaders' gruesome kicking Rockette finale.

One more act remained. It was Bert's specialty, the Hootenanny skit, the one he had gone to the mat for. He re-entered wearing a vest and a strapped-on guitar and began telling how John Denver and Barry McGuire had gotten their start in the Chad Mitchell Trio. The crowd was stunned to silence as Bert continued giving a short history of Hootenannies, beginning by tracing the origin of the term.

"What do you get when you cross an owl with a billygoat?"

"A hootin-nanny," some girls yelled out. They were from one of Bert's acting classes and had been trying to save him without much success the whole evening.

Following an abbreviated version of his pet story, Bert was joined by three other members of the folk group. "We're going to sing 'Puff the Magic Dragon'," he announced as he began strolling and strumming.

"Puff you," several voices barked.

A frail woman who was playing the tambourine summoned Bert and began whispering in his ear even as he tried to pull away. He had mentioned her to me a few times as someone who was constantly vying with him for control of the theater's agenda. Apparently she had been "gonged out" of the previous year's show before she could finish her performance as Joan of Arc. She had refused any assistance to free her from the stake and had remained in the background during the rest of the acts, sometimes shouting religious invective while a little kid sang "Let's Twist Again Like We Did Last Summer," or an old guy accordioned "Lady of Spain." Bert finally yanked himself away from her and began telling the story of Puff.

"It's about growing up."

"It's about dope," someone countered from what remained of the audience. A chorus of "right ons" rose from his seat mates. The security guards stood with their hands behind their backs near the exits, looking at each other, frequently checking their watches.

An interminable version of "Puff" ensued with Joan of Arc stage whispering to Bert between verses. He would then attempt to explain more to the increasingly unruly crowd. At one point the vice mayor, still in his fairy prince costume, came out to attempt to silence the throng.

"Show us your prick," a voice ordered. He retreated. Bert strummed vigorously in conclusion then bowed deeply, graciously acknowledging the contribution of his back-up group. When the curtain mercifully came down, there were about 200 people left.

Jenny and I were among the handful of well-wishers who stayed to pay their respects. Lightly-rouged 15-year-olds stood in the wings glancing down at their breasts. Bert sat alone, guitar in hand, feebly thanking those who acknowledged the difficulty of his task. I told him I thought it was his finest hour and Jenny have him a big smooch. She had on a short white flowered vest, Jordache jeans, and black spiked heels, by far the most stunning woman there. Bert's stock with the remaining group went up just from Jenny's attention. Someone announced that a post-show party would take place at Lakewood's White Door Saloon. Bert gave us directions and said he would change clothes and join us then.

"I'm glad my parents didn't make it to this one." He put his guitar in its case. "That rock group really brought in a bad element."

***

"You sure left in one hell of a hurry yesterday, Casanova." An Eastern European woman with a beehive hairdo, corncob pipe mouth and tiger leotards said as she glared at me when I entered the White Door, somehow having mistaken me for a party animal.

"Sentimental Journey" was on the box. This was a shot-and-a-beer place, second-generation white people, that appeared to be undergoing a decor change. In between old-time ad placards for Fels Naptha, Ovaltine, Viceroy and Lucky Strike were framed prints of paintings by Rubens. The atmosphere, aside from the naked Rubens women, reminded me of the bars I would go to with my dad in the '50s, waiting while he had one more and played the bowling machine with women who looked like those in the cigarette posters. Just like then, the Cleveland Indians were now on the tube and the Saturday night crowd was in a festive mood, rounds of boilermakers circulating.

Bert appeared in brown slacks, one of his white golf shirts and a brown sweater vest. He was toting his guitar case. A few people from the show spotted it and groaned. Bert smiled good-naturedly and ordered a rum and Tab. Before long he gingerly removed the guitar from the case and began tuning. Esther, the woman with the floating knee cap whom Bert said he would marry if he hadn't found anyone by age 35, joined Jenny and me at a corner booth. Esther was a chubby-cheeked, dark-haired woman in a jeans jump-suit and Pluto long-sleeved t-shirt. None of us were drinking. I ordered three root beers at the bar. The bee-hived bartender looked at me like I had just confessed to some war crimes and mumbled, "This ain't no ice cream shop, loverboy," and slammed down the drinks. For some reason I didn't feel the need to address this case of mistaken identity, choosing instead to remain as reluctant to speak up as I had been when waiting for my dad.

Bert was in the corner strumming away, backed by the same group that had been on stage with him for the bitter finale, all except the religious woman, who refused to walk into gin mills and instead was celebrating at the Pop-n-Fresh donut shop. Bert warbled "If I Had a Hammer," "This Land," and a repeat version of "Country Roads." Someone in the back requested "Mama Don't Let Your Babies Grow Up To Be

Cowboys," but Bert leaned to the side and yelled out of the side of his mouth, as if it were coming from someone in the crowd, "'Leaving on a Jet Plane'," and sang with a lump in his throat. After finishing with a flourish he ducked out from under his guitar and strode to our booth. The patrons' response was mostly a strong, borderline-hostile silence. Bert seemed puzzled at his inability to stir the after show crowd.

"What's wrong with these people, nobody's singing," he slumped next to Esther. "I guess we'll just have to wait until the piano player gets here."

He motioned me towards the outer edge of the booth and made a discreet eye flicker towards Esther. "She's adopted. She found out who her mother was by sneaking a look into her doctor's files. It turned out to be a woman she had as a theater director. I told her you were into the cosmos, Ray. Esther's into some spiritual stuff, too."

It turned out that Esther, who was a volunteer at the Lakewood Little Theater, had allegedly talked to Ben Franklin's image at age 11, when knocked unconscious by a basketball, and had been into spiritualism ever since. "I guess I'm a descendant of some witch that Elizabeth Montgomery played in a TV movie," she confided as Bert nervously nodded and looked for the piano player.

I caught Bert's eye and motioned him towards the aisle. "Esther is really nice, you ought to make your move."

"What about you and Jenny?"

I shrugged.

"Yeah, I know," he sighed. "I still want an athletic girl, still preferably Slovenian. Besides it's not good to be involved with someone at work. If you can't get it up you've got to face her everyday, but if I don't meet anybody by the time I'm 35..." His voice trailed off.

"She really likes you Bert and 35 is getting closer."

"Mebbeso," he cupped his hand on the side of his mouth, "but her thighs and that darn kneecap. We'll see."

Bert eased back low into the booth but was up like a yo-yo when the piano man arrived. Everyone was singing. The mayor bought pizzas. Bert threatened, and then produced his guitar. He threw his voice and it requested "Solitary Man." In the midst of his lengthy interpretation, someone kicked on the jukebox and "Dirty White Boy" surfaced. Bert joined us again, his guitar stowed for the time being.

Jenny and Esther were locked in close, giggling conversation. "Say ladies," Bert began tentatively, "if you don't mind I've got a few things I'd like to talk to Ray about. Man talk." He heh-heh'd. "Maybe we'll go outside for a little stroll. Be back in half an hour or so. Okay?"

They simultaneously flicked their wrists.

As we maneuvered out the door, Miss Parsons and Mrs. Grimes, the two women who had vied with Bert for control of the show, walked by and offered Bert perfunctory congratulations. Miss Parsons' smile seemed especially phony.

"I had a date with her sister for racquetball." Bert swallowed hard. "She called me up two hours beforehand and canceled. I got stuck with the court time. Then I asked Miss Parsons to play." His voice lowered. "She hid from me. I mean, it wasn't like I asked her out for moonlight dancing. The next time I saw her she was at the driving range hitting with some fraternity schmuck. I felt like jamming the driver down her throat. I don't usually feel like that and I'd never do it, but she hid from me." His eyes watered and his voice cracked.

"How do you get along with the other one?"

"Not too bad. After she got married I got to know her a little bit during rehearsals for 'The Glass Menagerie.' I probably could've married her while she was single, but she wouldn't talk to me. This year they both tried to take the show away from me, but they couldn't do it." His voice dripped with pride, before hardening. "You really liked that rock number, didn't you?" I nodded. "So did the kids," he sighed, then brightened. "But never mind that shit," Bert rubbed his hands together briskly. "We've got places to go, things to do. Let's roll." He quickened his pace towards his car.

"Where are we going?"

"I figure we got about 50 minutes max." Bert hustled behind the wheel and warned me not to slam the door or else the rust would shake down. "We can take a quick spin over to the Marriott on 150th. It's about 10 minutes away. There's this chick I want to check out." When his Pinto started on the first try, Bert was certain that was a sign of good things to come.

On our way to the Marriott I told him how Jenny had come on to me the night before. He screeched to a halt at a stop sign. "Ray, this is no time to be Platonic."

"I know, but I kind of made a move way back when I first met her and she told me that she didn't want to have a physical relationship with me. She said she had ruled it out. That bothered me a little but we were still friends, then she got this silly-ass boyfriend, then she breaks up with him, takes up with a married stevedore who dumps her and now she lays this on me. But she never acts like she's attracted to me or nothing. She's always talking about how cute other guys are or what nice little butts they have, but she never seems to notice me. I'm always complimenting her and saying how nice she looks, but from her? Nothing. Then all of a sudden she lays this on me. It's like a barrier has already been built up and it would be just too awkward to break it down. Maybe I'm only interested in women who click with me right off the bat. Or maybe I'm not interested in someone's who's interested in me, like that Groucho joke about not wanting to join a club that would take him as a member. Anyway, it's not just something I can turn on and off. I've never been into winning over reluctant maidens or grudgingly getting their favors. And as far as just sex goes, obviously I can take it or leave it."

Once again the rationale for my behavior had been wonderfully articulated. Once again I remained on the far side of the invisible barrier.

"Talk all you want but this is no time to be Platonic."

We eased into the parking lot near Shenanigan's, the lounge at the Marriott. Bert hurried to the door then stopped to finger brush his hair in the mirrored entrance. The pregnant ID checker waved us past.

"I knew it, there she is." Bert snapped his fingers, then made a triumphant fist. He pointed to a perky blond in the coat check room. "Don't look, don't look." He led me around a corner into the hallway by the men's room. Bert appeared on the verge of pinching himself at his good fortune.

"Her name is Mia. I talked to her last week. She was winking at me the whole time. She's 21 and just about to move out of house and home into a place of her own. But that's not the best part." Bert gazed at the ceiling and silently thanked his lucky stars. "She was an usher at the theater about six years ago. She reminded me of that last week, then I remembered who she was." Bert heaved a huge sigh, almost as if he were debating whether or not to complete the story for fear that he might endanger his streak of good fortune. "She would always carry around this funny-looking pen and giggle a lot. Well one day I asked to see it. She gave it right to me. It had a guy with a swimsuit on and when you pressed the pin the guy's trunks came down and he had a hard-on." I looked back at the girl and noticed her eye twitching wildly. Bert went on gleefully. "I finally forgot about that and – wham – I run into her here. I can get her to put on her old usher's outfit and fulfill one of my fantasies, possibly buy her a pizza afterwards. I already told her to call me be my first name. I mean, she winked at me."

Due to my recent experience with a certain 17-year-old I was in no position to wax judgmental, plus I was starting to develop an appreciation for anyone even half-willing to take a shot at making a connection, no matter how seemingly futile it might be. I had enough caution for everyone in the Marriott and then some, so I wasn't about to discourage Bert. "Sounds promising. At least you know where she works."

"Yeah, it's just like you and that Judy."

"No, Bert. She's really a little too young. I'm leaving well enough alone for now."

"Good plan. You'll catch her after her first great love falls apart. It'll be perfect."

"Whatever happens, happens. I'm not forcing anything."

"Don't worry, you can't miss." Bert dug hands into his pockets and produced a small flashlight pen and note pad.

"What are those for?"

"Getting numbers and info, buddy," he said, flicking the flashlight. "Actually, I just want Mia to notice me taking down numbers, maybe get her a little jealous." Walking past the coat check room Bert suavely saluted Mia with his pen and notebook. Her eye twitched. "What did I tell you?" he said, his lips barely moving.

We sashayed into the elegantly furnished main room. The waitresses wore Danskin tops and flowered slit skirts and walked softly over the thick carpets. The place was jammed. Raisin Cain was the name of the band doing a Blood, Sweat and Tears medley. The lead female singer had on a tight Barbarella suit and was banging on a tambourine. She rarely smiled and during instrumentals she would go to a glass-topped table and sit with a woman who looked like a head nurse in a German mental hospital. Their conversation seemed intense. Bert positioned us against the brass rail, in full view of the coat-check room.

"By the way, Bert, have you been hitting any parlors lately?"

"No, I'm giving them up. They're degrading. I'd been thinking about it for awhile, then I went to a place downtown last month and that convinced me. I picked this Amazon and got her to sit on my face. I almost suffocated. Then she stuck her finger up my ass and it hurt so bad I couldn't get hard. I had already negotiated with her so I had to fork over 80 bucks for nothing. She wouldn't even give me a smile." He winced at the memory. "Another thing," he gulped and darted a quick look behind him. "No more lifeguard technique. I don't want to get into any details but let's just say that I learned my lesson the hard way with a waitress who turned out to be a waiter."

"So it's no more parlors and no more lifeguard technique." I shook Bert's hand. "Good, you don't need that stuff."

"Anyway, I've got a better idea to get women." He reached into his back pocket and pulled out a Smuggler's Inn napkin. "I've decided to put an ad in the personal section of Cleveland Magazine. It'll only cost me 50 bucks."

He showed me the napkin. On it he had written a list of 12 qualities he was looking for in a woman: Blond; Slovenian; likes foreign languages; five-five or under; loves to travel; non-smoker or narcotics user; bubbly; 31 or under; attractive or cute; never married and non-bisexual; athletic, with body intact; citizen of any country except those in Africa, the Middle East and the Orient.

"Then I'm gonna write, 'Any woman fitting five or more of these categories, please call me'."

"This is a great ad, Bert, I'm sure it will be the only one like it. There ought to be lots of women who can fit five of those categories."

"I hope so. I want them to get the idea of what I'm looking for, but I don't want to rule too many women out." He neatly tucked the napkin back in his pocket. "And speaking of women," he grandly gestured in the direction of the main seating area. "I think I just spotted someone to get Mia's attention."

He wasted no time heading towards a table where two women were sitting with four guys who looked like the group therapy patients from the old "Bob Newhart Show." Bert kneeled and rapped to one of the women. He was mapping things on his hand like a playground quarterback. In a moment he was her escort to the dance floor. Vested, he twirled then was solidly close as the band answered his request for "Silhouettes." The song's end found the lady safely bowed and bent in Bert's embrace. A kiss on the hand cavalierly sealed their parting. It was apparent even to the casual observer that she had been spoiled.

I "Bravoed" his return. He wasn't surprised by the performance. "She really lit up when I started to talk to her, didn't she?"

"Mesmerized. What's the story?"

Bert had met her a month earlier at the Harley Hotel Lounge. Her name was Zaritsa. She turned out to be the younger sister of a guy he had gone to grade school with.

"She's blond, loves golf, is 26, Slovenian, doesn't smoke and we get along great. She even called me up last week. She's a solid B-, but there's one problem." He laughed and shook his head slowly. "She looks exactly like her brother. I hadn't seen him in a long time, but I ran into him two weeks ago. We're going to be partners in the Union of Poles Over 30 Golf Tournament next week. He's a nice guy but if I ever tried to make it with her I couldn't get him out of my mind. I don't think I could do it."

"I think you're jinxed."

"Not really. I just hope Mia saw me with her." He checked his watch. "We better get rolling, can't keep those ladies waiting."

Walking past the coat check room, Bert saluted again. Mia's eye twitched again. When we hit the door he conked his forehead with the heel of his hand. "I knew it. I blew it. I forgot to pretend to write Zaritsa's number down. Ah, no big deal."

With the Marriott's neon beacon guiding us to his chariot, Bert talked excitedly about the future. He was going to move out of his parents' home and get a pad on the other side of Lakewood. He was due for a promotion in October and would use the extra cash to take his parents to Europe in the summer. "My dad's retiring this year and I want to show him and my mother the time of their life." He would put himself and Esther on the Beverly Hills diet and go to a family wedding in July. "Just to prove to the relatives I'm not gay. Even the kids at the theater think I am. They write things like 'Mr Stykes is gay' on the play programs. I pretend I don't see it but it hurts." He found a watered down Masters program that could grant him his seventh degree. "Someday I'll be in the 'Guinness Book of Records'." He was positive the '80s would be great.

"I'm this far from being self-actualized." He held two fingers an inch apart. "I've got a list of 10 women, 11 if you count yet-to-be-met. I'll be putting my ad in next month. I can stop back here and visit Mia anytime I want. Plus, there's a 27-year old just dying to go out with me. Unfortunately, she's Ukrainian and Hungarian but maybe we can be buddies. The future looks great. I'm just kinda stuck in the present."

For the trip back to the White Door he needed to start his Pinto with a screwdriver. "Hey I know what I wanted to tell you." He pounded his hands together and rubbed me on the shoulders. "I saw this show on 'Good Morning America.' It was about how we're going to live to 120 in good health. So look at it this way, instead of our lives being half over, we're really just teenagers."

"Maybe that will give me enough time to get it together, too, but never mind the future," I said as we took shortcut back. "You ought to take advantage of the here and now with Esther."

"I had my chance once." Real regret marked his tone. "We went to a car rally in Rocky River and I saw her take a piss. We were in a big field. First, I went, then she went. Old Esther Mills squatting there. I saw her profile. I should have said, 'Let's do it back to back, the one who finishes first gets to look at the other.' I should have told her 'Lets go' – but I didn't." The Pinto coughed to a halt just outside the tavern.

"And you," Bert pointed a trigger finger at me as we approached the entrance. "This is no time to be Platonic."

Jenny was ready to go. We all shook hands. The piano player started tickling the ivories. Bert was up again, unpacking his guitar to good-natured groans. In the parking lot Jenny and I could hear his voice above the others crooning "Heart of my Heart."

***

"Boy, did he have a nice little butt." Jenny regaled me with a tale of Dynamite George, one of her lovers, on the way back to Toledo. "He was real effeminate. We were like twins. He made his money in insurance before he got into explosives. He's in a Mexican prison or loony bin someplace. He was about 15 years older than me and could fix watches. We made love in my Toyota on the rollback seats. He spoke French to me and could roll joints while he drove."

We made great time and Jenny insisted on catching a brew before the bars closed. We went to the Sawmill Lounge. Half Nelson was playing. I ordered a couple Mooseheads and we sat at a side table.

"What did you think of our conversation last night," she asked, bobbing her crossed leg and shifting her braid from one shoulder to the other.

"I don't know. I'm pretty confused by the whole situation."

"So what else is new? Hey, there's Duke." She yelped and jumped up to greet a lumbering guy in a Timbers' Lanes softball jacket and white cowboy boots. They hugged and rocked. Duke lifted her up off the floor and spun her around. Her legs jostled a guy wearing a t-shirt that said Liquor in the Front, Poker in the Rear. No one gave a shit. Duke put Jenny down and went across the bar to get his drink.

"Duke's an old friend," Jenny said excitedly. "He's in insurance. He's a lot different from you. In fact, everyone I know is a lot different than you. I haven't seen him in a couple months. I don't know what it is with these insurance guys, but I've always dug 'em."

Duke returned. The band broke into "Somebody Help Me."

"Mind if I dance with the lady?" Duke baritoned. He peeled off his softball jacket revealing a black silk shirt with the number 21 on each upper sleeve.

After the dance Jenny bounced back to me while Duke mingled with the band. "Do you mind if I leave with Duke?" she asked, grabbing her purse. "I mean, I'm not the answer to your problems. I don't care what you say, all you think about is that Judy chick, if anybody. Besides, Duke invited me to the Prudential Million Dollar Round Table Party next week. It's the second year in a row he's made it."

I didn't mind at all and furthermore didn't even bother to muster an internal rebuttal to her analysis. Duke was standing on the bandstand talking double indemnity to a member of Half Nelson's backup quartet. He saw me leaving and stuck out his paw.

"Hey, no hard feelings, bucko," he grinned, cupping my back with his left hand.

"No feelings, hard or otherwise, there big shooter."

Lana Returns

The dapper and eternally youthful Scott Nelson appeared in my doorway, having arrived later than expected for our county fair trip, and found it necessary to explain the huge Cordoba he had parked in my driveway. "It belongs to Stella. She's this 62-year-old woman I met at McDonald's. I've been spending some time with her recently. But I won't get into that. How are things going for you?"

I motioned for him to come in. "Not bad, I've been laying low this summer as far as women go, but yesterday I went to Cleveland with Jenny to see Bert.

"Ah, Ms. Jenny, the masseuse," Scott said with a slight bow of his head. "I trust she's as healthy as always."

Scott had an uncharacteristic coyness written all over him and while I told him about Jenny's advances towards me he said nothing but simply strolled slowly around my living room examining the few posters on my wall as if he were killing time in an art gallery, occasionally punctuating my words with an "uh-huh." After I stopped talking he waited a few moments, seemingly absorbed in the intricacy of a Cleveland Cavaliers pennant, before clearing his throat and asking with studied dispassion, "And Ms. Judy, have you heard from her?"

I knew how to put an end to this performance. "Yeah, I got a letter from her. Most of it was a description of her bedroom. She suggested I come over and see it for myself."

Scott stood frozen, expressionless. He started to fall forward ever-so-slowly, like a collapsing corpse, but revived himself with a head-shake. "She should be 18 soon and that might put you on better ground. Nevertheless, Ray, for God's sakes be careful." Though a trace of panic remained in his eyes he found composure quick enough to deliver his standard line, "In Europe, however, this would not be an issue," in near-record time.

"I know Scott, but I'm worried about getting mentally strung out over something that obviously can't go anywhere."

"You're doing it again." he said, wagging his finger at me. "Don't turn her into some cold object of obsession. She's a young, warm, moist, burgeoning female soul. And body." He halted his drift into Teenage Delight Land with a hastily furrowed brow. "Beware of that clinical distance, that analysis. If there's any way to put up a barrier you'll do it. You've turned it into an art form." His brow eased into a slight arch. "Don't allow barriers to inhibit you – as it appears you recently did with Jenny – just follow the truth of your own spirit. Then you'll be suitably prepared to crash through the barriers, climb over them or," a tiny smile curled the corner of his lips, "slither underneath."

He sat down carefully on my couch, leaned back and examined his meticulously manicured fingers. The still chilly air had required a filmy scarf which was draped over his shoulders. He crossed his legs and placed his feathered chapeau on the precisely folded London Fog rain-slicker at his side. His briefcase rested at his feet. I lowered the TV volume. "The Picture of Dorian Gray" lost its voice.

"Speaking of slithering, what happened out there at Honeywell this summer?"

Scott flushed. "I'll get into that a little later, maybe when we go to the fair this evening. I need a wholesome environment to relate that story."

Since I had never known Scott to delay the telling of one of his tales for any reason, I honored his reluctance with a change of subject.

"What happened to Karrie? The last time I saw you two, you looked like the model couple. Frank even said he could sense wedding bells, which is what I thought you were looking for."

"That's what I am looking for, but she wanted something more conventional than I could supply. She gave me this clinging, intertwined Norwich Vine plant." He folded his hands together and winced. "Very symbolic. She said she couldn't spend any more time with me."

"Well, I'm sorry it didn't work out Scott, but it seemed like a pretty good relationship, and you needed one."

"You're right." He wrinkled that weathered brow a little and sighed.

"She helped me relax and concentrate on my work, but she wanted more than I could give and I couldn't lead her on. She's a fine woman, one who truly understands that the brain is the sexiest organ. She was willing to go to rather extreme lengths to fathom precisely how to get involved in her own pleasure." Scott paused and a sparkle came to his eyes as he savored a very private thought. "She was also gracious enough to overlook, certain – uh – peccadilloes on my part, but it just wasn't right. I think she needs someone who's a little more traditionally oriented than I am. Plus, I'm really looking for a taller woman."

"So you're out on the streets again."

"I am at-large," he bowed his head and nodded while deliberately leafing through a copy of Mother Jones.

I noticed that he was wearing a belt with an alligator on the buckle and kidded him about his trendiness. He explained that it was a gift from his brother.

"I like the preppie look," he candidly admitted. "It's very efficient. I like the square-shouldered look and the short hair on women. It's very boyish. I'm discovering my attraction to women is somewhat androgynous and I'm enjoying that discovery." He smiled distantly. "But enough of that, I've got some news about my thesis."

Scott explained that numerous revisions had been made since we last spoke. "I've cut back drastically on much of the braggadocio." He folded his hands on his taut stomach, Buddha-like, and gazed lovingly at his briefcase. "My new title is 'The Knowledge Business: The Phone Company at the Dawn of the Age of Enlightenment.' It's about old Ma and Baby Bell – they're up to something. The phone company is at the fundament of the central network of the world that I've been talking about all along."

"That makes sense, but is that going to change the sentiment of the work?"

"Not at all." He closed his eyes momentarily and slowly shook his head with resolve. "It's all still based on the fact that the absolute is eternally at rest and the relative is ever changing. Plus, the prospectus of content remains the same as does the last chapter, 'Vision of Possibilities,' which contains several, uh, seminal concepts." He tapped his chest. "And, of course, throughout the work I stress that at the fundament this must all come from the heart."

"So are you finally going to graduate?"

"It looks good for next June. I'm just going to take one of my chapters out and submit it." He help up one finger and began dipping into his briefcase. "I've decided to take on the empiricists. It's about time someone gave them a little of their own medicine."

Before he got cranking, I reminded him that if we were going to make it to the fair we should be leaving soon. He told me to give him a little head start then swing by his place and pick him up. He wanted to change clothes.

"There is one thing I wanted to tell you, Ray. I was riding the bus last week and I met this Chinese woman who's a grad student in computer science. I gave her all of it." He stroked his briefcase. "Everything."

"You didn't."

"I did. She understood every word. She has that holistic background." He folded his hands together and his eyes glistened. "Spiritual, you know. As she left she mentioned how amazing our conversation was. How everything fit together. I told her 'Infinity is structured in each moment,' that's Hegel. I'll definitely follow up on her."

"That brings us back to 62-year-old Stella," I said as Scott checked his watch and readied himself for departure. "You're not intending any friskiness are you?"

"Absolutely not!" Indignity elevated his voice. "I just enjoy her company, although I did confess to her that I've been having fantasies about her daughter. She's my age. I may be sleeping in her room sometime. Stella has this huge house in Crystal City on Gypsy Lane." He smiled at the symbolism. "I'm even considering moving down there for the winter. We'll just sit around and stoke the fireplace. She's a very attractive woman and I know she could be regally imperious if she so desired, but mostly we just talk." He adjusted his hat in the hallway mirror. "She loves it when I touch on my thesis."

***

When I came by to pick him up, Scott was sitting on his porch chatting with some black kids. He was ready to go with nary a last minute note to be added to his thesis. He was wearing a windbreaker, a grey Ohio State t-shirt and loose-fitting jeans. There was no sign of the briefcase or even a notebook. He did, however, have a copy of his resume in his back pocket which he took out and held up over his head as the youngsters tried to jump up and grab it. He handed the resume to me and I began reading it as a few of the kids mouthed some of the terms written on the single sheet of paper. It was short and to the point, billing him as a "Child of the Cybernetic Revolution," stressing his "Planetary Consciousness" and listing his chief work reference as "Accounts Payable Bookkeeper, Maharishi International University."

"Never mind the camouflage," I said. "Tell me what happened at Honeywell?"

"I don't think it would be wise to mention that just yet. I'll tell you what happened when we get to the car."

On the way to the fair he grudgingly related his tale of woe. He had been working long days and had turned out a technical manual the first month he was there. They loved his work but had deleted several Maharishi quotes from the forward.

"Are those the philosophical differences you talked about?"

"Those were enough to tell me I didn't want to do that kind of work," he sighed. "But I still would have stayed until the end of September except, well, I was asked to leave." He wrinkled his nose like a bad little boy. "I had just completed the manual when I met this woman in a bar. She had her jeans tucked into her boots. She looked like she was in heat." Scott was speaking in an uncharacteristic monotone, usually he told his dirty stories with animated delight. "I had a book with me, 'Morality and Foreign Policy.' She asked me what it was about. I told her it was the kind of volume my mind could linger on. The music was quite loud so I stood real close to her and talked in her ear. Pretty soon I was licking inside her ear. She asked me to describe myself. I told her to think of me as a 'conflict in search of denouement, or – better yet – a dialectic nearing rapprochement'."

She asked him if he wanted to go over to her place but informed him she was living with a man. Scott deftly passed on that but found out she worked at Metron, a "spy place," and stopped by late the next afternoon. "I told her I was having fantasies about her and that the reason I licked her ear was that I wanted to find out what she tasted, and smelled like all over. She shut the door. We just got off looking at each other and talking filthy. Ray, I outdid myself. I went too far." He buried his head in his hands. "I was using my imagination so much I felt like I was on LSD. As I was leaving she pulled her panties back up and said that at long last she finally understood the meaning of the term 'provocateur'."

Scott took a deep breath and gazed out the window. "Three days later I got called into the office by my supervisor. He turned on a recorder and I heard a tape of the conversation I had with the woman at Metron. He was the man she was living with. Apparently they got off on things like that, but he couldn't handle how far I had taken it. I had to sit there and listen to the grunts and sighs and gurgles, everything. Ray, the tape even sounded wet. And the way we talked about keyboards was, frankly, nothing more than out-and-out smut. I wrote up my resignation letter there in his office and was on a plane the next day." He blew his nose into a tissue. "I think I finally realized the error of my ways. I've got to stop entertaining these prurient thoughts about women. It's not so much the thoughts, it's the degree of entertainment that needs to be curbed." He reached in his back pocket for the security of his resume. "Dammit, why mince words. I've got to get this masturbation under control. Eventually that is. I mean, after all, the impossible does take a little longer."

Passing through the gate I mentioned to Scott that this was the first county fair I had attended in nearly 20 years. Walking along I found myself gaping at the young girls from a distance, just like the last time I went, while other guys were sledge-hammering, throwing baseballs, tossing rings and winning stuffed animal trophies. There was a freak show. The PA system, which had replaced the old barkers, said over and over, "Fat Albert, world's biggest man. At his present rate of growth he'll weigh over 1000 pounds. Unbelievable size, unbelievable man." Scott remained outside while I went into see Albert. He was a jovial fellow, a nice guy who gently said things like, "Don't talk to me while I'm eating or I'll sit on you." Another bachelor, I guessed.

"This is more like it," Scott said breezily as we strolled the midway. "I need to do more wholesome things like this." He was smiling and talking with kids he seemed to know when a tall, braless teenaged girl in tight jeans and spiked heels passed near us with an "I've Got It" sticker stuck on her ass. Visibly shaken, Scott ordered a beer.

"I knew I'd be tested," he whispered after slowly regaining his color.

I felt as if I were being tested, too, and I was passing. Here I was spending the day before Labor Day casually drifting through a county fair atmosphere, just like millions of folks all over the country, seemingly unaffected by yesterday's letting Jenny go her own way, seemingly immune to obsessing about Judy, seemingly unable to even recall when the last time I had even thought about Lana, and seemingly content to kick back and not worry about anything. I felt a genuine kinship with the lanky, gaunt hillbilly guys with slicked down hair who were walking around looking like made-over-by-Montgomery-Ward mountain men. Like them, I was just takin' in the sights.

There was "Little Jimmy. It will be a long time before you forget this tiny fellow." Also, "The World Smallest Horse. If you can sit on him he'll run right out from under you. You'll think you're in a vest pocket rodeo." As the crowd thinned and the sun was on the verge of vanishing, an Elvis impersonator barked in the direction of a group of preteens who were teasing, hiding and playing tag. Convinced that nothing but good news awaited me I was waiting to have my fortune told by an orange-haired Gypsy, her arms a rainbow of ruptured capillaries, while Scott had maneuvered himself in line for the ring toss, but the "I've Got It" girl walked by again, this time clutching a three-foot banana. When she put it between her legs and started riding it, Scott woozily extracted himself from the line and announced he had to leave.

"It was a good decent attempt," he proclaimed in the parking lot. "But wherever you go they still know they have those crotches."

As I was about to drop him off in front of the Skyrocket Lounge, across from his ghetto home, he turned to me and his eyes were watering from the draft beer, the wisdom gleaned from his humbling California experience, but most of all from the breadth and vision of his work.

"You know what I'm doing Ray," he said softly, proudly. "I'm validating the work of those great Romantics, from Plato to Shakespeare to El Greco and Galileo to the God-intoxicated Spinoza. Ray, they called him an atheist, the man we now refer to as God-intoxicated, the man in my heart-of-hearts late at night I believe." Tears of joy streamed down his cheeks. "To the grand Immanuel Kant and all the rest from that flourishing Renaissance time that sanctified the human spirit. My work is simply saying that we now have the technology to unequivocally prove that, not only were they right, they were Absolutely Right."

He teetered slightly as he got out, then leaned back into the car for one last point. "Don't be reluctant to sit down at the negotiating table with any woman, even Judy. Remember, you've got to be willing to get your hands a little dirty, Ray." He rolled up his sleeves on his windbreaker. "While I've got to refrain from getting in up over my elbows."

***

"Guess who's in town?" Ritchie, my ad salesman friend and singles' bar denizen, asked me over the phone just as I was about to hit the hay after my homespun evening at the county fair. Of course I knew who he was talking about, but I couldn't say the name.

"Lana. I just saw her at the Thunderthigh Lounge. Her mother's getting a divorce and she's in town to help. She's staying at Cindylu and Pete's. Her mother's husband won't let her stay in the house. She's living in West Virginia with this Steve guy and his grandmother. She's married again but was talking about getting it annulled. I guess she went out to Kansas for awhile but some kind of farm deal fell through. She looks different but, trust me pal, she's still as hot as a god damn firecracker. She'd like you to call her."

"Why the hell can't she call me? Doesn't that bitch know how to dial a phone?"

"Whoa, I thought you'd be happy to get some quick in and out action because if you don't I..."

"Give me that phone number. I've got a few things to tell her."

Dialing her number I felt as if the nine months since she left hadn't even happened; the serenity of the summer and my recent-as-today brave claims about detachment had disintegrated, in a matter of seconds, with the rumbling force of an underground nuclear explosion.

"Hi," she cheerily answered.

"What the fuck is it with you anyway? What's the game now? How's your unicorn-dicked third husband doing?"

"I'll talk to you later. I'm going to hang up."

"So what else is new." I steamed in my chair for awhile but I knew I had to see her. I knew from my educational psychology courses that I needed to work through my anger towards her. I also was beginning to sense that if I ever was going to get any better at these relationships I ought to start approaching women a little more constructively than by my usual avoidance/explosion pattern. So I called her back and we both agreed that we had to talk and made a tentative date for the next day. I'd call her in the morning at Cindylu and Pete's to set up a specific time.

That night I slept fitfully and dreamed about walking up the creaky steps of my childhood home on Hope Avenue and hearing my mom listening to "The Guiding Light" on the radio. Or was she talking to someone on the phone? Or was that Lana I overheard talking to another guy on the phone? Or was that me she was talking to? Or was that Lana talking to my dad and when on earth was he going to get home from work and do something about my mother's staying out to all hours. And why didn't I just fall down those steps and make it easier on myself. And why, from the time I was a kid to right this second, did I feel just as alone and frightened when I woke up from a scary dream as I did during the nightmare.

***

When I called the next day she wasn't there. My heart sank. In three minutes the phone rang.

"I was here all along but told Peter I didn't want any calls. Why don't you come over around five. I've got to spend the afternoon with mom. Ciao."

I arrived at five, inhaled deeply and rang the bell. She answered the door. Her hair was buzzed short and her face was fuller. She had on a bulky salt and pepper turtleneck and loose grey corduroys. She looked far from frumpy but definitely a little frayed around the edges.

"Don't say it. You hate my hair." She cringed slightly before settling into an exaggerated pout. "So do I but I'm going for a new look. Maybe it will cut down on my lust."

"Oh brother." I wanted to turn around and run like hell.

"Only kidding," she sang off key. "I had to have something to say to you. You look beautiful." She squeezed my arm and sighed.

Pete and Cindylu were watching "Starting Over" on cable and Cindylu was thinking aloud about what to do for dinner. She just couldn't make up her little mind and finally said, "Oh, I'll just let my husband decide."

"That's the spirit," Lana laughed and made a power-to-the-people-fist.

I didn't think the Revolution would have ever come to this but diplomatically chose not to comment.

Lana and I decided to go out and grab a bite to eat. When we got into my car she gave me a big hug for "all we've been through." We went to the Hungry I, our one time special place. I ordered some wine.

"That's a change," she noted. I rarely drank and had always lectured to her that alcohol was a death drug. Once she blamed my lecturing for her alcohol dependency. I wasn't interested in talking about my sipping a glass of wine. I did, however, want to show her how I was developing a new understanding, forged by an emerging awareness that little could be gained by retreating into a "you bitch, you bastard" motif. That in order to truly understand a relationship as severely intense as ours we needed to painstakingly and sensitively explore our history of specific, learned inappropriate behavior patterns that more than likely funnelled back to the womb. Only then could we make any mutual or individual progress.

"So you actually married this chucklehead," I loudly began.

"If you want to talk about it calmly I will." She fingered her wedding ring which looked like it might have belonged to Steffin's grandmother.

"You're a two time loser, plus. Why on earth did you actually marry this joker?"

"I'm not going to sit her and...."

"Well stand up them," I shouted. She smiled uneasily and flipped her short hair. I calmed down a little and we engaged in some small talk about politics and sports during which she was her usual irresistible self – smiling with her eyes, accidentally-on-purpose playing footsies, breaking into laughter in mid-sip, then stopping that laughter with a sigh when I told her I had played in an end-of-summer volleyball tournament and was named to the all-tourney team.

"A cosmic jock," she whispered, "no wonder I can't stop thinking about you."

"Well you didn't seem to be thinking about me the last time I saw you."

"That day on the balcony was awful." She stroked the stem of her glass. "Everything was hitting me. The girls were inside laying on a guilt trip, Lennon getting shot was horrible and I didn't know Steffin. . ."

I rolled my eyes at the image of him goofily bounding up the stairs with his pizza change purse in his hand.

"Steffin," she tried to continue, but I laughed again.

"I'm sorry." I wasn't. "But in a way that guy saved me. I was hurt, angry, lost in love and all that but when I saw him it helped me pull the mask off of you, and the blinders off myself. What was it that you always used to say, 'By the hand of the thief we are delivered'." I straightened in my seat and lowered my voice as the waitress kept her distance. "You knew exactly how I felt about you and no one can deny the special bond there was between us, yet you chose to mislead me about your bisexuality and lots of other less important things, always being careful, though, that you never really directly said anything specific – as if life were split hairs and technicalities. You of all people should know better than that."

Her face twitched with suppressed emotion.

"Lana," I reached out for her hand. "You know so much, feel so deeply, have such incredible wisdom. Why were you so just plain insensitive, so inconsiderate?" I paused and gulped, hoping for an explanation that I knew wasn't coming. I felt myself turning up the volume again, my voice somewhere between a scream and a moan. "I can't believe that you were so mixed up but I guess you were. And I'll admit that I probably, more often that not, just heard what I wanted to hear." I cleared my throat but my voice still broke. "But if you could have just approached me honestly maybe we could have resolved this thing somehow, at least before it turned into a runaway train."

She was biting at her lip as I went on. "It breaks my heart to think of some of the things you've been through and obviously I'm not blameless in this mess. I should have acted more like a man, whatever that means, and just boldly swept you away or something, but for God-only-knows-why I didn't. I know now it's kind of a bullshit rationalization but at the time I thought I wasn't supposed to be as crass as all that. I had to be cooler, more sensitive, hipper."

She looked at me and smiled as if to say that everything I had just said was what she liked about me. "Well if you really want to know it was the twins, I just didn't think. . ."

"Wait a minute," I snapped. "When are you going to stop hiding behind your kids. For Christ sake, you don't have to do that."

Suddenly she was crying hard. "I never meant to hurt you. This thing with Steffin. . ."

I stifled a giggle. She stared a don't-you-dare stare. It didn't work. I settled for a condescending smile as she continued. "I didn't plan it all along. It just sort of happened. I hope you don't think I deliberately misled you."

"I know exactly what happened," I snarled. "You were looking for a way out and baited the hook for this fishy character and he finally bit and probably hasn't stopped grinning since the first time you grabbed his rod."

She looked like she was going to leave, but suddenly remembered that I was driving.

"One day I talked to you on the phone and you said you didn't know how you'd get along without me. Two days later I had become 'one of the people in town I certainly plan to keep in touch with.' I figure Steffin snaked himself in between those two calls. Is the honeymoon over yet?"

"What do you mean?" She managed to look in my eyes.

"I mean living in the backwoods of West Virginia with Steffin's grandma doesn't exactly sound like your style."

"Who knows, maybe the honeymoon's just beginning." She jutted her jaw.

"Right," I said, having retrieved my low, quiet voice. "In a few months, if not sooner, this guy's gonna be sitting around trying to figure out whether or not he should try to figure out what hit him and you're gonna be looking elsewhere. Don't you see how you're heading down that path?"

My prediction was not honored with a response as I prepared to deliver, movingly I hoped, the conclusion of my prepared script.

"You can write this whole thing off to just another adolescent male's wounded ego, but that's not the issue. The real issue is just plain old-fashioned insincerity and half-truths and confusion, denials, and manipulation and expediency and how they literally chip away, speck by speck, at a person's soul. I should have known what was going on when you refused to give me a birthday present. Refused. Adamantly. Saying I was expecting too much, as if I were infringing on your precious feminine space with some kind of totally unjustified patriarchal ownership number. But the first time I was with you, lest we forget, you had my cock in your mouth before I could step out of my pants. On your knees and in control, and me just standing there, getting sucked in. What a way to go through life."

"What about the magic?" She searched my face.

"In the end it was magic all right." I quoted Caine. "Yours of deception, mine of illusion."

We left our untouched reubens on their plates. Walking to my car, I gently squeezed her neck and she buried her face in my shoulder. We went back to my place. I flicked on the tube. The holiday fare featured "Picnic" with William Holden sweeping Kim Novak off her feet and the whole town living happily ever after, all during a whimsical, beautifully-scored 1950s Labor Day weekend. That wasn't quite how I remembered our family's holiday get-togethers, which would invariably touch off two or three weeks of silence between my parents. Lana, who once told me about visiting her first step-dad in the Toledo Mental Hospital on Thanksgiving, laughed cruelly at the romantic tone of the movie classic and talked about her afternoon with her mother, making divorce plans.

"Every time she got married she was always so certain," she said, her face half-frozen into a grimace. "But each marriage turned out to be so. . . . . fragile."

She kicked off her shoes, laid back on my couch and patted for me to sit near her. She unbuttoned her pants. "Whoops, sorry," she apologized, "but I need to breathe." I kissed her. She told me how her work had been accepted into an art show in Wheeling.

"It's a good one. You don't have to be as hip as Ann Arbor."

She suggested a trip to the bedroom because my couch wasn't comfortable, but I wanted to talk. I told her I felt battered and punch drunk, sometimes, and that I needed strokes. We hugged. I told her how deep down inside I knew that what we once had was real and undeniably wondrous. She sighed agreement and admitted she should never have gotten married.

"I carry your last letter with me all the time. It was beautiful."

I told her that if I ever got married, I'd want it to be in the spring, then I'd honeymoon in Paris.

"I'd say something but I better not." She licked her lips shut, then burst through. "Just don't marry some dumb woman. They're all over the place."

I got up to go to the bathroom. Her "Can I watch?" was not totally unexpected or unappreciated. I gave her a mock frown. She countered with, "Oh well, sometimes it's a hell of a lot easier to say stuff like that than to really think about things."

When I came back she was lying there like a baby doll. I kissed her passionately. She grabbed my dick and said she wished there could have been another blizzard or two for us to get stranded during, or perhaps a desert island might have done the trick. I told her how sad it was that we had grown so far apart as we talked on the telephone and looked at each other across crowded bars, each conjuring that very real person we had fallen in love with into a barely recognizable stranger. We held each other like preteens.

"You know Lana," I whispered, "I'd always feel so empty after we had sex and you'd leave. Post-coital depression." I said it like I was calling down a canyon.

"I didn't. I always felt really good."

Driving back to Cindylu and Pete's through a nearly empty Toledo we held hands. Mick Jagger wailed about "Wild Horses" on the tapedeck.

"I felt lust for you tonight," she confessed. "I like the way you're just a little rough." She shivered. I had a potshot for Steffin but bit my tongue, clearing the way for her, "I'll miss you even more now."

I stopped in front of the house. "Will I be hearing from you?" she asked, fiddling with one of my buttons.

"I don't think so, Lana, but if you're ever back in town, call."

She looked like the moon might if it were being swallowed up by the sea it used to rule. We kissed. I went home. It was drizzling. Soft rolling thunder rumbled and I was quietly certain that some kind of major resolution had taken place in my life.

That night I slept a deep, peaceful, dreamless sleep.

Distant Love

"You wouldn't even want to know some of the insane things that have been happening since I moved into Sally's place. I think she put a curse on it."

I had called Frank for some advice but he seemed to be enmeshed in a new set of problems since he had picked up an apartment lease from his ex/current wife. Having a fairly pressing issue of my own, however, I refused to indulge him like I usually did.

"Never mind that Frank, what I wanted to talk to you about is this letter I received today from Judy, which has come right on the heels of some other distressing female-related things. Just three days ago I basically said goodbye to Lana forever after she stopped back in town and really left the door open for me. Two days before that Jenny practically did the same thing and I blew her off. And now Judy sends me this. I'm wondering what the hell's going on and what am I expected to do?"

"In Eastern mythology the female is often shown as being active and initiatory, so that aggressiveness has always been there." Frank's voice settled into an almost professorial tone, quite different from the panicked strains that accompanied his claim that his apartment was cursed. "As men we have to be able to respond to the call of the age. In King Arthur's time the knights would begin their journey by entering the forest at the darkest point. Well, now the forest is coming to us, but things are still just as dark. But before I can make a specific recommendation I need to hear that letter."

"I've got it right here. It came with a little black Scorpio seal on the back. What do you think of that?"

"She's got you zeroed in, that's obvious, but let's hear the whole thing."

Dear Ray,

I'm sorry for not writing sooner but I've been real busy. I must have started to write you a dozen nights but when I did I usually was so tired that I just got undressed and plopped into bed instead. I also went white water rafting in West Virginia two weeks ago and last week I entered the Monroe County Fair Queen's contest, but finished second. (I did win the swimsuit competition though.) This guy I was kind of seeing never even bothered to show up. I found out from his brother that he started driving south and just kept going. I did get some other news this week though. My old boyfriend called from Ft. Lauderdale and said he might come up and visit me. He's that unfinished business I told you about. I was 13 when we met. Everybody was after him. He picked us up in his car one night. My cousin asked me if I wanted to go up and talk to him. I said sure and when I got up front he just laid one on me. Right on the lips and that was that. It was just like that magic you're always talking about. He doesn't want to let go completely but he doesn't want to have a serious relationship either. I've kinda been holding onto my dreams for the two of us, but I'm starting to think that it might not work – that maybe it's time to start something new. Anyway, I just finished a song that somebody might be able to put to music. I thought of you a little when I wrote it. It's called "Distant Love," so if you hear it on the radio someday you know where it came from.

It bobs
In and out of sight,
Never revealing its true identity.

Years have passed now,
And still I know not what the object is.
My eyes are seeing a sailboat,
But my heart sees a lost soul.

    Your friend forever,
    Judy

"What do you think Frank?. . . Frank. . .Frank."

When he finally retrieved his voice, panic had returned to it. "That's one of the most frightening things I've ever heard, but she obviously understands you better than you've ever dreamed possible."

"That's like it is with you and that 19-year-old, isn't it?"

"Let's put it this way, distant love about sums it up for Goldy and me. It's all over between us, although I did make an indirect proposal to her on my 30th birthday. Hold on a second." I heard him slam a door or window shut in the background and when he retrieved the phone he began speaking in a much lower voice. "I guess I was feeling old. Another angle is that I thought she might be pregnant, but she wasn't. I called off the relationship in the middle of August when I realized the whole thing got down to me driving the nursing home truck out to her farm and chasing her around the house after her parents left to watch her brother play Pony League baseball."

"How did you handle the fact that you proposed to her."

"It didn't mean anything to either one of us. She didn't even bother mentioning it. Hell, I've proposed to nine women and told 24 of them I was in love with them. I was sincere 19 times." His voice elevated back to normal. "C'mon down tomorrow night and I'll tell you more about what's been going on. It's all been pretty wicked. But watch out for Judy, that young flesh can really do it to you. Bye."

In a moment the phone rang. I figured it was Frank with a clarification, but it wasn't.

"Ray, it's Judy."

"Oh my God. I was just talking to a friend about that letter you just sent me. Thanks, it was really sweet and I love that poem." My heart was pounding through my temples. "I'll be damned, Judy, I knew you were psychic the first time I saw you. How are you doing?"

"Not so good. I was going to this big costume party with my supposed friend Trudy, but at the last minute she got a date with the guy who's the father of Barbi Mason's kid. He doesn't even have a driver's license yet, so they're just going to hang out at the pool hall. I've got my costume on and everything but now I can't go because Trudy's the one who knows the people at the party."

"That was terrible of her to do that. What's your costume?"

"I'm dressed as Marilyn Monroe. My dad always liked her. My middle name is even Marilyn. I guess she died about a year before I was born. I've got on this white sleeveless dress. It's pretty low cut. I was gonna curl my hair and dress as Shirley Temple but I decided not to."

"Are you all alone?"

"Yeah. My mom and dad are at a party, of course, so's my sister. Hold on. I thought I heard someone coming up the driveway but no dice. I may go out and cruise around Luna Pier or go over to Lost Peninsula."

"You're all dressed up with no place to go. I feel like that a lot of time." Astonishingly I had relaxed to the point of being just plain thrilled to hear her voice. "Say, when's that guy coming up from Florida?"

"Probably never. Anyway, I've had it with him. I'm getting a farewell portrait for him this week. Ft. Lauderdale isn't in my plans anymore. I guess I'm a freebird."

After a few seconds of silence I heard a lip-smacking sound over the phone. "What are you doing?" I asked.

"Mmm. I'm just kinda tossing these grapes in my mouth and looking out at the lake. I do that a lot. I really love it when there are storms. It's really eerie. I've seen lights out there plenty of time. UFO's or something. I spend so much time by myself that I see things and think sometimes I'm nuts because there's nobody around to see them with."

"I can identify with that, but I'm starting to do a little better and now I don't worry so much about whether or not somebody's around to validate what I see. So take heart, the older you get the less you care."

"I'm more worried about what's going on tomorrow night. Me and Terri were supposed to go to the Southside Roxy but she got invited to a wedding by the guy who's the groom. He told her she's the kind of girl who makes him not want to get married, if you can believe that. So she decides to break the date she had with me for tomorrow. She said a wedding only happens once."

"That was rotten of her."

"Yeah, I'm thinking about going out with this Brett guy. He's in love with Terri and she thinks he'll show up anytime she wants."

"Don't get involved in pettiness. Don't use this guy to get back at Terri. You might hurt his feelings."

"Yeah. I guess you're right. Anyway, I met this other guy at the bowling alley. He said he'd take me to the Dixie Electric. If he backs out, I'll go by myself."

I told her to be careful in bars, watch out for weirdos and don't go to any parties with strangers.

"You sound like my dad. Me and Terri figured out that you've got some kind of father figure thing with me."

"That's part of it, maybe, but certainly not all of it, that's for sure."

"That's okay. I guess I need advice sometimes, but I think you think you know everything about me."

"No, I don't. I know you're full of surprises."

"Listen. Do you hear them?"

"What?"

"The waves. I'm holding the phone out the window."

"Slightly." I momentarily flashed on Lana sighing at the moon over the lagoon while we talked on the phone for hours.

"Do you think you're going to be staying around here for awhile?"

I told her I was and there was a pause. "Are you still there?"

"Yes, of course. I was just thinking of this weird guy who keeps bugging me while I'm babysitting. He comes over and wants to have pillow-fights all the time. All these immature guys are driving me crazy."

Before her last statement I was about ready to ask her what was so bad about pillow-fights but amended that to career concerns. "Aside from babysitting, are you working anywhere else?"

"Well, I just got a job at Claire's Boutique in the mall. I'm a clerk and I pierce ears. I'm also still ushering at the Sports Arena every now and then." There was another pause and I could hear her breath quicken. "Oh, I've been reading this sun sign book. That Scorpio stuff is just like you say. I also bought some Moon Boots. I thought about you a little bit when I did. By the way, I finally found out where that street that you live on is at. I made Terri drive by it yesterday. It looks real busy." Her voice softened into something that sounded a million miles away from the one she had been speaking in, "I'm changing my mind about you."

"What was that?" I stood up, my ears ringing.

She repeated her words slowly, clearly. "I said I'm changing my mind about you."

I reached desperately for something to say. "Yeah, I'm a pretty nice guy." The game had gone smoothly up until then, I had even had my feet propped up like the cool guys in high school or college would do and was deftly fielding her dual-meaning flirtation with no problem, and some clever repartee of my own, but the right-down-the-middle-ness of that last pitch caught me looking. "Uh, you sound pretty happy, now. Maybe talking to me helped you forget that party."

"I almost did."

I apologized for mentioning it.

"That's okay. I better let you go."

"Maybe we could get together next week. Do you work every night?"

"Almost."

"Well, I'll stop by Tuesday or Wednesday. I might even have a surprise for you, kind of a pre-18th birthday gift."

"Great."

"Judy, you made my night by calling. You could knock me over with a pillow."

"Oh you. Bye."

I was on the verge of hyperventilating. She caught me way off guard.

I wasn't prepared at all. Anyone could tell she wanted to get together, just like Jenny had and Lana, too. I was starting to see a familiar song and dance unfolding here. Were my latest movements still nothing more than my typical two-step out the door – my most recent, noble-sounding justifications merely different terminology for my ever-evolving lexicon of aloneness? A face on the turned-down tube caught my eye. Doing the local weather was a woman who, in 1970, had promised to perform live sex with one of the members of the MC5 rock group at a benefit in Crystal City for the White Panther Party. I had pulled a similar retreating act from her in the Club 10 years ago as I pulled with Judy tonight. Maybe these grooves run deeper that I thought. If that's true where do I go from here?

I headed for the phone, called information for Judy's number and dialed it crisply. The night was still young. After 20 rings I hung up. She'd obviously taken off.

I turned up the television and sunk back in my chair, bowed but not beaten. I'd be seeing her next week.

***

Frank peeked out the door, heaved a breath of relief, invited me in, then peered outside before pulling the door shut and bolting it. Southern Comfort bottles and cigarette butts were strewn around his tiny efficiency.

"I have just had a profoundly sobering experience," he announced, slinging himself on the floor and leaning back against his mattress. "I think I've finally learned once and for all the dangers of promiscuity."

"You and Scott both," I said. "He just got burned in California."

"It's in the air," Frank sighed fatalistically. "We all get nailed sooner or later. Scott has had a pretty free reign for along time. I'll admit I thought I could get away with walking the same psycho-sexual tightrope." He rubbed his hand almost maniacally over his face. "I should have known I'd get tripped up."

In hushed tones Frank explained that an hour or so before I arrived he had been napping when someone rattled at his door. "I was barely awake. It was this Alice woman dressed like Helen of Troy. She scared me to death. I met her a few weeks ago at Varsity Lanes. She picked me up. She's 45 and is the food stamps checkout person. Her husband's been gone about 15 years. I slept with her two weekends in a row. Since then she's been bombarding me with this pornography." He rose, waited briefly on one side of his window then darted past it, fished into the top drawer of his small dresser and carefully extracted an old-fashioned postcard. "Here's the evidence, it's dated Vienna, 1948, and has a picture of some black GI's drinking with half-naked white girls. She also sent me this short story called 'An Insignificant Climax'."

Frank thought he heard a sound outside, stuffed the postcard back into his drawer and put his ear to the floor like Tonto, listening for about a minute before determining the ground was free of hostile hoofbeats. "I glanced through the story. It's about a woman who intercepts a note from her best friend to her husband. The note talks about how much her friend longs for her husband's cock. The rest of the story is about how the wronged wife churns over the times the three of them had been together, remembering conversations in a different light. Alice attached a note to the story saying, 'I make sure I read this every other day whether I need to or not.' It's totally sick. She addresses this pornography, and that's exactly what it is, to 'Frank, my laugher, I mean my lover.' She even sends it in the food stamps envelope. I don't think she'll ever stop."

Lacing his shoes as if they were combat boots, Frank went on to say that before his nap his 19-year-old cousin had visited him. "He's from my mother's side of the family, of course. He just joined the Army. He's got a tank tattoo on his arm. He told me he's getting married to a girl back home that he hasn't slept with yet, but her mother has jacked him off twice while the older sister watched, plus, he's already screwed the youngest sister. The whole thing smacks of incest. I'm from such a long line of God damn white trash hillbillies I may be totally beyond hope." Frank got to his feet, then bent way over to examine closely the contents of his room's lone ashtray. "I got to get out of this apartment.

Let's go downtown. This is about the last time for me, though."

After painstakingly scrutinizing the stove, the lights, the toilet and the outside through the curtains to make sure everything was safe and secure for departure, Frank intimated that the day's activities – especially coming out of his nap to see a grotesque Helen of Troy at his door – had taught him once and for all the folly of his ways.

"Maybe it's exactly what you needed, Frank."

"I think it may have been." He double-checked the lock on his door and felt for the Camels in his shirt pocket. "Plus, it's right on top of about six or seven psychodramas in the past two months. It's been said that clarity comes at the conclusion, not the beginning, of a journey and I've definitely reached the end of my rope." He scratched at his five-o'clock shadow and allowed his hand to slip down around his throat. "I'll never again be foolish enough to believe I've transcended the madness. I now realize what I've suspected all along, that the fire's pursuit extinguishes it. From now on I'm going to stay out of harm's way. I'm going to quit cigarettes, pot and alcohol, concentrate on my yoga and writing, and just work at my job and keep my house clean. No more mad ravings. I'm just going to simply imitate what's out there enough to get by."

As we walked towards the Club, I noted that the streets had been widened over the summer. The thoroughfares of Crystal City had been made more travel-able for the '80s. The small town really wasn't built to handle all the students and cars that had arrived in the past 10 to 15 years. When I had first attended classes there, not many students had cars. Now the entire town was locked in a near traffic jam as the semester geared up.

"I graduated 10 years ago, that's hard to believe." I said as we passed the recently gutted Bonded station, now the future site of the Zeta Beta Tau fraternity.

"In some ways there's not a whole lot of difference," Frank intoned, looking every which way then proceeding across the street in double quick time. "I was just reading this book on Kerouac. They had an interview with him in the mid-'60s. He was talking about how modern man's problem was rootlessness and emotional homelessness. It's even worse now. The late '70s really blew everybody apart."

I thought of Lana and I and glimpsed an unflattering picture of myself, wishing and hoping and dreaming about her, frozen still and peeking through my fingers, as she drifted further and further away while I settled into a kind of second-hand existence; a half-life of internal conversations and interminable analysis where no one is ever at home. Thankfully that fate no longer awaited me, for I had at last opened my eyes. Hadn't I?

"Moving to Toledo and seeing all those people hanging out and hoping to find somebody was really depressing." I said as we walked past a Church Street house that had been decorated with signs like "Don't Change Dicks in Mid-Screw" when Nixon resigned but was now festooned with a National Tractor Pull banner. "It's even more so when you find yourself right there in lockstep with them. I'm just happy I met Judy. In a lot of ways she kept me from bottoming out after Lana split. It's funny but whenever I mention her to guys they always give it a 'Va-va-va-voom, girls never looked like that when I went to school,' but it's really not the flesh, it's always the spirit."

Frank nodded slightly, stopped, then looked behind him. "Yeah, but sooner or later you get into that tactile aspect with the flesh and it all turns into a deadly morass. It's a one-way ticket to a personal Holocaust no matter how you look at it."

"It doesn't have to end up that way Frank, " I said as we walked past a duplex I was evicted from in 1972. "Ah, I wanted to tell you, Judy called me Saturday right after I talked to you. We're going to meet this week. She's going to be 18 next month. It may be a little risky but I'm considering giving it a shot."

Frank halted, stood very erect and rubbed his hands together. "That sounds like a wise move actually. You can probably operate on fairly solid ground with her. She's not like the banshees that inhabit this town."

The familiar sounds of Man Overboard greeted our arrival at the Club. They played a lot of '60s music. Frank spotted his ex/current wife (the divorce was still 80 bucks away) stopped in his tracks and announced he was going across the street to space out in the library courtyard.

"I may swing by here in a while," he said, backing out the door. "It all depends if I can regenerate myself."

There was a good crowd on hand. The college students were back to town. Several freshmen girls were huddled around a Ms. Pac Man game right next to a huge mural that had been painted by one of my old roommates. It was a take-off on the "Last Supper" with frogs and dogs and assorted reptiles replacing the disciples. There was no sign of the Savior. The band played "For What It's Worth." At the corner of the bar I spotted Tim, one of the town's leading "Deadheads." His eyes looked like fried eggs.

"That Asian chick just dumped me, Ray." he grimaced as I pulled up a stool next to him. "I also got canned from my job."

Tim explained that a Japanese woman he'd been seeing for almost a year had broken off with him because she had sent her parents a picture of Tim wearing a tie-dye shirt and a Jerry Garcia wig, and they had threatened to pull her out of school if she didn't split up with him. He had also just lost his job at the university cemetery, having been warned during the summer about showing up late for work but figuring he had solved that problem by getting loaded, passing out in the graveyard and waking up on time at the job. Nonetheless he was given the bum's rush at the end of August. He reminded me a lot of myself a decade or so earlier. I was his age then, tall and gaunt, sitting alone in the Club as the fall approached, not really knowing whether I was coming or going.

"My Japanese girl came out to see me at the boneyard once," he groaned. "Everyone out there asked me if her pussy was horizontal, those assholes."

I told him about how out-of-place he seemed and how he would have fared a lot better back in the '60s.

"That's what this dude told me the other day," he said as Man Overboard finished a Velvet Underground medley. "He was just drifting through town. He was part of the Rainbow People in 'Frisco when he was 12. He was actually near the bus with Kesey and knew the guys who were the models for the Furry Freak Brothers. They were from Detroit and really weren't roommates."

The band began playing its break music. Tim yawned and shook his head. " I better go home and saw some logs. It would sure be nice to get some lady to come home with me and spend the night, but I'm beginning to think that if I'd get laid it'd be some Moral Majority chick trying to convert me." He got up and put on his Army jacket. "I'll bet it was different 10 years ago."

After Tim left a young woman with a tiny head and braces on her teeth tapped me on the shoulder. "I was listening to you guys. I'm from a long line of kids in my family who came to the Club. It's my watering hole. It used to be in the early '70s if you weren't a hippie you just didn't come in here. Things really have gone downhill."

I told her that I had seen a change in the high schools in the last few years, that the kids were getting it together politically and that a growing number loved the music and the concepts of the '60s.

"This is how it was up here in '67, right before everything hit," I said as she listened intently. "You'd be surprised how many similar kids there are to you. Not a whole lot, but even back then it was a pretty small percentage, really. But remember, ideals are more important than numbers. It may take a while for things to turn around, especially with Reagan in office, but they will. Just don't give up hope."

Before she went to the other side she told me I ought to come back to campus and be a guru or something. Nearby a woman I had known for years was celebrating her birthday. She was beyond drunk and told me that I had always reminded her of Michael Rennie in "The Day The Earth Stood Still." "I always thought you were kinda neat and mysterious," she said, reeling backward and bumping into a real short guy walking by with an even shorter woman. They were both dressed as rabbits. "He's teaching a self-help class this quarter," the birthday gal whispered admiringly after righting herself. "He's been through a lot. Women Now sometimes publishes his poems." She hiccupped.

"They're shaped like frisbees."

"Oh brother," Frank moaned as he sat down next to me. "I didn't need to hear that, especially after what just happened across the street." He ordered a cup of coffee and told me he had just run into his old archenemy, the Mussolini woman, in the library courtyard.

"We were in a poetry workshop at the nursing home this summer. She was the leader of the class." He stared for a long time into his coffee before taking a sip. "During our last session she set up a hypothetical situation for this 91-year-old guy in the class. She said, 'Suppose you see a woman leave a theater and decide to follow her. Tell me what you would do.' He said he'd probably take her purse or whatever. I looked at her and said 'whatever.' She kind of blushed. I think she realized it was over, that you couldn't take this fishing-for-rape nonsense any further than she had taken it with that old guy."

He held his cup to the light and examined the bottom. "At the time I had an inkling that I had glimpsed the initial death throes of this feminism battleground madness, and I think I may have been right. We just had a nice conversation across the street and she didn't even have on her Don't Die Wondering button. I took that as a healthy sign." He savored a deep gulp of coffee. "You know something. I really respect her. She's a fighter and she knows I don't want any rapists walking around. I've always been opposed to that." He looked out of the corner of his eye and cupped his hand to his mouth. "I'll admit I spent most of those poetry classes staring at her breasts. She can be a damned attractive woman if she wants to."

Near us Frank's ex-current was moving to the music, bending at the waist and shaking her ass like a chicken. She was surrounded by three or four wooly-haired young guys. Frank leaned close to me. "I ought to say to those guys, 'Hey fellas, that's my wife – bug out'." He laughed demonically then quieted himself. "To tell you the truth, the best I ever had it was when I used to pretend she just stepped out of 1100 B.C. to fuck me."

Frank finished his coffee and announced he was heading home. "I intend to write an unedited letter to an ex-fiancee," he proclaimed while gazing into the coffee grounds. "Simple and honest. No nuclear warheads aimed between the eyes. We may be able to work something out." He took a few steps towards the door but came back to check the coffee cup one more time. "I've got some work to do around the apartment. I think I'm also about ready to start flossing my teeth." He said a quick goodbye and scurried through the exit.

Man Overboard was on break and "Knockin' on Heaven's Door" was playing on the juke. A beefy bartender was lecturing one of the new crop of freshmen on Crystal City mythology. "There's a saying that you'll never find your true love here at the Club."

He was right. I know. I tried.

***

A few nights later I was stationed back in my living room debating whether to visit Judy when my Quixote print – Don trying to fly with a shattered wing – fell off my wall. Should I pick it up or leave it grounded and, more importantly, what did the falling signify? Were all romantic quests doomed or was the nobility of the effort enough? Perplexed, I opted to let it lay and focused on the tube for some signs of what to do about Judy.

There was a news story about a truck driver and his wife who were trying to trade in their 14-month-old son on a '77 Corvette. Materialism does nothing for me. Click. "PM Magazine" was rating Jerry Lewis' Telethon performance, "A trifle too many tears," was the consensus. Ditto for cynicism. Click. Reagan announced the naming of Wayne Newton to the President's Council on Physical Fitness. Some lean times are ahead. Click. PBS saluted Rodgers and Hammerstein with my all-time favorite song, "If I Loved You." I think were getting warm. Click. A talk show had a segment entitled, "Single Living Not That Easy." They stated that soon 25 percent of the nation's households would be single dwellings, and that there had been a 70 percent increase in men living alone in just 10 years. They claimed single people were lonely and vulnerable and died at an early age. "Dropouts of the

Me Generation." They closed with a song specially written for singles entitled "Still Looking Within." If that doesn't get me out the door, nothing will. Click to dark.

I gathered up Judy's gift, something I had once given to Lana who had ultimately disregarded and diminished it. I was sure Judy would not do the same. As per usual, symbolism and regeneration were on my mind as I headed to the mall.

As I walked through Macy's, past the women who looked like mannequins, I spotted her eyes at 100 feet. She seemed to be looking for me. Her hair was a little longer than when I had last seen her three months earlier. She had on beige dress slacks and a white blouse with a "Miss Judy" nametag. She was boutique official.

"I was just thinking about you," she said, wagging her finger. "What's in the box?"

"It's that surprise I told you about."

She reached for the box. I put it behind me and her breast brushed against my chest, weakening my knees momentarily.

"Don't get grabby," I teased and held it at arm's length away from her. "First tell me how you're doing."

"So, so." She folded her hands behind her and rocked. "But Noah, that guy who drove out of town a few weeks ago, just came back and started bugging me. He left right before you arrived. I had to act rude to get rid of him." She began sorting through children's earrings depicting Disney characters. "I'm just helping out here while Kathy takes a little break. She should be back any minute. There's not enough business for both of us because of the economy. I guess you came at the perfect time."

"It was in the cards." I shrugged. She nodded. "Besides, there's a full moon coming up."

"Yeah, I noticed it going home last night," she said matter-of-factly, an old hand at this lunar stuff.

Kathy came back sucking on a McDonald's Labor Day Coke. "That Centipede really beat me up. Thanks, Judy." She looked at me. "Can I help you, sir?"

"He's with me," Judy said as I smiled and waited while she got her purse from the back room. When she emerged from behind the curtain, we waved good-bye to Kathy and began a leisurely stroll on the mall.

"How's school going?"

"Boring, boring, boring." She gave an indifferent nod to a slick-haired guy in front of the Tuxedo Junction, a formal attire rental shop. "But at least I'm busy. I got student council together and we've already come up with a Homecoming theme, 'Hollywood Nights.' I'm also going to be one of the tri-captains on the Powder Puff squad."

I pointed to an open bench between the Gap and the Bottom Half. "This isn't the most romantic setting for a pre-18th birthday present," I said as we sat down. She laughed and sat very straight. Then I handed her the plain brown box with a gold-embossed "Gulliver's Fine Gifts" sticker. "I'm not one for wrapping presents."

"That's okay." She carefully opened the box and gently pulled apart the soft tissues. Her eyes flared. "Wow."

"It's a real crystal ball – Austrian lead. Guaranteed to have special magical powers."

"It's beautiful," she leaned forward and gazed into it. "I can see over there." She pointed back to Frederick's of Hollywood where an armless, headless figure modeled a peignoir. "This is the best gift I ever got. I have the perfect place for it. In my room, right next to my bed."

I also gave her a card. "I wrote some words of wisdom for you, of course." That piece of news came as no surprise to her. "You can read it later, though. Do you like the front?" There was a picture of a ruby-lipped lady holding up a black mask to her eyes. A red feather brushed her cheek. I inscribed the card, "To Judy, a woman of the '80s."

"It's really pretty," she said, unable to totally remove her gaze from the crystal ball. "I'll read it right when I get home, don't worry."

She waved proudly to a girl passing out sausage samples at Hickory Farms then fished into her purse and produced a small picture. "This is for you. My mom took it this summer."

She looked rosy-gold beautiful, though the photo didn't do her eyes justice. On the back she wrote, "To a very special person, who I have an awkward relationship with."

"Even you have to admit you look great in this picture."

"It's okay."

Judy kept waving and nodding at people. "We're like a big family out here." Two girls behind Camelot Music's counter kept staring at us and giggling. "Don't mind them, they're always like that." She snapped her fingers. "I know what I wanted to tell you. One of the big fights Noah and I had was when he found that 'Romeo and Juliet' quote you gave me. It was in my car. He wanted to throw it out the window, but I grabbed it from him." She furrowed her brow. "It got all wet but I dried it out and stuck it with your letters someplace he could never get at." Her tone of triumph drifted into a few seconds of silence before she added, "I think the only thing I liked about him was that he helped me forget about Rob from Florida a little bit." A tear started in her eye.

"That still hurts, doesn't it?" I brushed at her hand. She sniffed and nodded.

"It's not easy getting over that stuff, Judy." I cleared my throat. "I can certainly feel for you. Last December I had this big split up with that woman, Lana, I mentioned to you. I left school in the morning and we had it out down in Crystal City. She left town with another guy."

"So that's what happened. The rumor around school was that you were really upset about John Lennon. Boy, if they only knew."

"It was a mess. We had been seeing each other off and on for about four years. She was living with one guy then got involved with a lesbian, it was crazy. I called her from school that morning and that's when I found out she was leaving town with the other guy. It was a total surprise and really threw me for a loop."

Judy gulped, looked at me in the eye and sighed. "That really sounds sad. I've had some pretty wild ones in my time, but never anything like a homosexual."

I picked at a small callous on my baby finger. "Sometimes when you think you've found the right person you can become blind to everything and keep holding on, like with you and Rob. Then when it finally ends you think you're going crazy and either you crawl in a hole or you start reaching for anything that comes by." I sat on my hands while Judy looked away. "And I think that's what I tried to do with you. When I met you I was in bad shape, really confused and it was like you represented rebirth or something."

She opened her eyes real wide and drew back.

"That's a heavy way of putting it, but you know how I am." I grabbed her hand firmly. She managed a smile. "But that's the reason I rushed you so quickly. I was hoping you could take Lana's place and save me." My free hand poked at her shoulder and I intoned somewhat dramatically. "But what I'm finding out is that the only person who can save me is myself. More words of wisdom."

After a slight pause she deadpanned, "I wish I would have been taking notes during that."

A voice came over the mall loudspeaker announcing that there were only a few hours left to take advantage of the Lion Store's Moonlight Madness sale.

"Judy, you'll probably never know how much you meant to me during those days. How excited I was to see you. How much fun it was to talk to you. And I still feel the same way. With the help of your friendship, I grew up during the past year and realized a lot of things."

"You meant a lot to me." she said softly. "I was pretty lonely too."

"Never be afraid to take a chance and speak what's in your heart," I paraphrased Caine, "that's how people find each other."

"Is that one of those 'Kung Fu' lines?" she asked, a little disappointed.

"Yeah," I nodded, somewhat embarrassed at my reliance on scripted sentiment. I was about to tell her that, but she spoke first.

"I'm waiting for my sister to finish shopping. It's a pain to take her but my Gremlin is broken again and I'm driving my mom's car so I don't have much choice. I've been running around so much lately that I don't know if my head is still attached to my bod."

I told her I had to get going, too. She carefully put the crystal ball back into its box.

"I wrote a character sketch about you for my composition class the first day," she said as we stood up and smoothed our apparel. "I began it at the donkey basketball game. I only got an A- on it. I must not have buttered up Mrs. Weith enough. She really liked it but said it was more about my feelings than it was about you."

I told her I'd like to read it sometime and that I might be able to learn something from it. "Thanks for the picture and I'm glad you liked the crystal ball. When you look at it I hope you'll think of me."

"I will. I promise."

We hugged and I kissed her on the forehead.

"It was great seeing you, Judy. I'll keep in touch."

She stood very still and looked me clearly in the eye – in the kind of gentle, encouraging way that made it easy for me to do the same.

"You better," she said. "Bye."

Without a hint of wistfulness, I began to move away. But, try as I might, I couldn't help wondering if I was turning from obsession into freedom or just retreating from a possible real connection into the same sad abyss?

I traced my steps back through Macy's, past the mannequins who looked like women, and into the parking lot. I located my car wedged between a Buick Riviera with a Love is the Liberace Museum bumper sticker and a big old orange and white Silverado with a sign that warned, If I Don't Get Laid Pretty Soon, Somebody's Gonna Get Hurt. Undaunted I gazed heavenward and thought about Judy and how she had helped me to move from bitterness to hope and how that would carry me through my aloneness as much as anything. Wouldn't it?

Still, September's fresh, late-evening air once more enveloped me with the promise of romance's timeless possibilities, and the chimney above the Baskin-Robbins struck me with its resemblance to some grand, ancient watchtower. From where I stood on that fine blue night, I could have been looking at the moon in the sky over the Spain of Cervantes.

The Men's Group

"I don't mean to sound crass, Ray, but I'm dying to know which guy committed suicide?"

In his role as temporary non-leader, Elvin led off the post primal-story discussion, which was designed for the group to ask questions, analyze what they'd heard and/or grope for larger truths. And although I had hoped for an accolade or two for the mythic scope and romantic whimsy of my tale, this was a no-nonsense crew that eschewed sentimentality.

"Who do you think?" I used the accepted device of answering his question with a question, not as part of a semantic game but to allow each member of the group to learn something about himself. They all knew the procedure and were more than happy to jump in.

"It had to be Bert," Elvin quickly said, his 30 years of police experience bringing a tone of tired certainty to his voice. "The guy had an M.O. of avoiding women like something out of an abnormal psychology book. Plus, he was living in a total dream world and I'm sure when reality kept hitting him, even he had to snap."

"I'm not so sure," offered Mark, the mustachioed Rolfer. "Since my training is in body work I sensed that Scott, with all that heady meditative stuff, was on his way to trouble because he was ignoring the physical side of his being." Mark stroked at the waxed end of one of his facial handlebars. "And all that business about enjoying being dominated by women while simultaneously having delusions of grandeur about conquering the world is not a prescription for mental health, to say the least." Everyone in the group loudly seconded that one before Mark emphatically concluded, "I'm not a betting man, but if I were I'd say it was Scott."

"As a gay man I know a lot, maybe too much, about anger towards women," Jon chimed in through clenched teeth. "Frank sounded like a closet rageaholic with his sickness directed at women in general and his mother in particular." Jon folded his arms across his chest and his voice relaxed a little. "Frank's anger and paranoia must have done him in. Believe me I can relate."

A quick poll of the remaining members found two votes for each of my three friends and a shared eagerness to find out what had happened to everyone in my story.

"In the two weeks since I started recounting my journey I've done some homework and discovered updated information on the main people. It's been quite an investigative process and I'll fill you in a little later, but first I'd like to hear what you have to say about me and what you learned from my story."

All six heads went down as one and a dozen feet shuffled. Finally after an awkward, pained silence Elvin stuffed his hands into his bib overalls and let out a deep breath. "You know, none of us are currently in relationships, Ray, and I think you hit on some of the reasons why. The truth has no special time, its hour is now and always, and the truth of the matter is that, whether we're willing to admit it or not, we don't have the skills. Just like you, we returned from our journeys intact but not healed and, just like you, what we brought back with us are the tools of avoidance."

Mark's perfectly Rolfed posture sagged noticeably before he spoke. "Yeah, you spent your time on the threshold, rationalizing and romanticizing your reasons for avoiding women and waiting to be transported from isolation to an awareness of loneliness and then to the kind of magical connection that you said you used to fantasize about as a teenager. You never made it." He tried to straighten his body but it remained slightly hunched. "Neither have we."

The group's discomfort lingered like man-made fog and I searched for words to evaporate it. What I wanted to say in my defense was that, at the least, I had nobly sought core truths in hopes they would transform my experience and evolve into profound self-acceptance; that, at the minimum, I tried to live fully in the moment with an appreciation of the cosmic humor of the human condition and that I succeeded, to a certain degree. But that when I tried to rid myself of my patterns of evasion, buried somewhere in childhood and layered over and over and over ever since, it was like attempting to rip out miles and miles of lateral interconnected, multi-rooted morning glories. A guy could break his back trying without making any headway at all, so I simply said to the group, "If given the chance I would never check the yes box for a Would You Like To Spend Your Life Alone question. But here I am."

With each group member's averted glance giving me a silent mandate to move on to another topic, I began telling the guys about the players in my drama. Jenny married Duke, honeymooning at the Prudential Blues Festival in Hartford, Connecticut. They have four children and a few years ago began co-sponsoring massage/insurance retreat weekends in the Marblehead, Ohio, area. Lana divorced Steffin and very early on got in on the ground floor of the Codependency Recovery Movement. She worked for a short time as a guest host on the radio show, 'Problems Between Men and Women' before getting her big break in the early '90s, illustrating the self-help best-seller, "Courage to Squeal," which combined the principles of primal scream therapy with a 12-Step guide to whistleblowing in the workplace. As the inside flap of 'Courage' says, she is currently living in the "loving, nurturing company of myself, somewhere in the Rocky Mountains."

"What about Judy?" three voices simultaneously asked.

"Shortly after graduating from high school she disappeared, even her folks didn't know where she went, or at least they wouldn't tell me. I didn't hear from her for five years before she finally sent me a letter saying she had joined the Navy and was studying to be a nurse." I flashed on the intensely lonely day I had received that letter and how I waited a long time to write her back, content to dream and savor rather than act. And when I did finally write her she had moved without leaving a forwarding address. "When I finally got in touch with her mother a few days ago, she told me Judy was living in landed luxury high upon a hill in Hawaii and was married to a Frenchman who was old enough to be her father. I told her that it heartened me to know that at least someone's life turned out like 'South Pacific.' She said she'd be sure to pass that right along to Judy."

"I know we're not supposed to get into shouldas and couldas," said

Randy, Elvin's recently-divorced son who was the most skeptical member of the group, understandably not having yet worked through his resentment about having been dragged, in hand-cuffs, to his first meeting by his dad. "But you missed the boat on her, pal, by not hopping on her bones or at least pawing her a few times."

"Randy, for Christ sake, grow up," Elvin barked and glared at his offspring before turning to me. "What happened to the guys, Ray?"

"I talked to Scott's sister last week and she said Scott married Kimberly Vishnu, the one he thought was sabotaging him. She said her brother knew that if you couldn't lick 'em, marry 'em. Scott and Kimberly were working as independent TM consultants, having been in the news a few years ago for leading a million meditators — via the Internet, the central nervous system for the world that Scott had always talked about — in a world-wide "Rise Up" meditation designed to restore the near 90-year-old Maharishi's diminished sexual prowess. The way she talked it sounded like Scott's was a real happily-ever-after story."

"So it's down to Bert or Frank," Elvin leaned forward and smiled knowingly. "My money's still on Bert."

"Actually things started out promising for both of them shortly after my story ended. Bert placed that ad in Cleveland Magazine and his old standby Esther was the only one who answered. This discouraged yet, surprisingly, motivated Bert to give her the go ahead to start planning the wedding. Around the same time Frank got married to a woman from Tennessee he had met at the Crystal City bus station while she was waiting for her boyfriend to get out of prison. That marriage lasted about a year, during which time Bert abruptly called off his engagement when he spotted a wart on Esther's toe and decided to give himself until he was at least 50 to find another woman before settling on Esther, removed wart or not. In the meantime, Frank tied the knot for a fifth time with a Puerto Rican woman who one night escorted him out of their apartment – on the business end of a knife – when she discovered that he was still officially married to two of his previous wives. He recuperated from his wounds at his mother's house before heading into total seclusion from which he never returned."

With their averted glances and choked silence the group's members seemed to be saying that they knew how easily it could have been any of my three friends, any of them even – and they all looked as if what they had heard in my story had hit so terribly close to home that they were each considering sleeping over at a friend's house tonight.

Finally, and without a trace of satisfaction for having guessed right, Jon spoke. "Frank, I knew it. Sooner or later that non-stop anger turns inward if you don't let it go." He got to his feet and gave a quick clap-clap-clap of his hands to get the group's attention. "Speaking of letting go of anger, is anybody going to patronize Gary and Dale's Ashes, Descent and Grief when it opens."

Each of us looked at Jon as if he were asking if we were men or mice. All the thumbs around the room turned down, followed by the exchanging of mechanical, white-men high fives. We also quickly and unanimously agreed to disband the group – giving gruff, rocking, teary-eyed hugs to each other – and do what we all did best, which was to go our separate ways.

As I was walking out of the meeting, Elvin called to me from behind. "Ray, I'm sure you know what next Wednesday is?"

Of course I did. "Yeah, it's the 30th anniversary of Lennon getting shot. Every year on that date I think of what happened to him that night and of what happened to me the next morning. It always brings thoughts of Lennon and Lana and loss."

"Think about it though," Elvin said. "With you finishing your story that started way back when and now with the milestone anniversary, is this not some kind of heavy full-circle shit?"

When I started my car in the dark parking lot, a radio talk show blurted on and a woman was bemoaning the fact that men just didn't want to make a commitment. Oh God, if nothing else, please spare me this Cosmopolitan-inspired half-witted drivel about commitment, I thought to myself as I turned onto Detroit Avenue. Most of the time in my life I had no problem absenting myself from just about anyone and everyone. But now and then, with little rhyme or reason, I was eager to turn myself over, lickety-split, to someone lock, stock and barrel – like a scrapman ready to be salvaged.

You call that a fear of commitment? Don't I wish it were that talk-show simple. Don't I wish it were that easy, on some bright commitment-friendly day, to wash away the deep set grooves of isolation forged by lifetime patterns of withdrawal . Wouldn't I be a real sweetheart of a guy if I could, during some candlelit evening – with a card and a promise – undo decades of shy smiles and across-the-room waves and most movement being movement away, heaping layers and layers of time on my already stunted development. Saying a man fails at developing intimacy because he has a fear of commitment is like saying an alcoholic drinks because his throat is dry.

I twisted the radio off. That was better. Driving home that night I passed the all-boys Catholic high school in Lakewood where I had graduated from in the '60s and thought about how little I had changed since then, having gone a kind of – as Elvin would say - full circle and arrived back still alone on a Friday night. I remembered riding the school bus home every day and praying that Kathy McDermott – who lived just down the street from me on Hope Avenue and attended the public high school – would get on the bus, which she sometimes would, and sit next to me, which she never did.

I have been thinking a lot about Kathy McDermott lately – long brown hair, baby-doll pout, short-skirted slinky walk, always riding around in Chevy convertibles with greasers. In fact. I probably think as much about her, whom I never even said a word to, as I do of most women I've ever known. It wasn't that she was my ideal, it was more that she set the standard for so much of my interaction with women.

Interaction that invariably found me looking through, behind, over, and beyond all kinds of women who were too young, too old, had too many kids, were too cynical or too eager or clearly on the rebound; women who were too attractive or not attractive enough or who might give me AIDS or, all else being equal, still would be totally unable to handle a sensitive lifetime bachelor; and women who, just like me, seemed to be intimate only with distance and whose tendency to withdraw had long ago become second nature and for whom prolonged eye-contact was as impossible as staring into the sun and whose conversations about relationships had long ago taken the place of relationships and who, in spite of it all, kept listening – as a safecracker would for tumblers catching – for something that might open up this once-and-forever still-looking cage.

But who knows? Perhaps now, after getting my primal story out, there will be no more of that nonsense for me; maybe now I'll be perfectly content to just head home to my apartment and turn on the tube. And settling into my couch – clicker in hand, remotely controlling my life—I just may be quite satisfied to sit there and sigh or laugh or dream or become moved beyond words by what flickers across the screen in front of me. Especially tonight, because "Kung Fu: The Legend Continues" is on. It's a rerun of the follow-up version of the origianl show, is set in current-day America and features Caine and his policeman son. In tonight's episode Caine instructs his son about how to develop perspective. In a flashback the young boy has been frightened because he stood too close and stared at a temple figure. Caine takes his son to the back of the temple and points out that what had been terrifying up close now appears to be nothing more than a toy.

"Distance," Caine says to the now relieved boy, "is everything."

That's hard to argue, I guess, given that my last couple decades have been defined mostly by gaps and voids, with me frenetically going through the motions of trying to forge a meaningful career – the kind I was brought up to seek - out of a stream of expedient, unrelated teaching jobs; and of trying to develop a meaningful bond – like the kind I still Technicolor dream of—out of a sporadic string of short-lived, relationships that, quite often, have made me feel more alone than when I was by myself.

And at this stage of life, there's certainly no getting around the looming reality that, in the words of Dylan, "It's not dark yet, but it's gettin' there." Still, there's also absolutely no reason to give up hope for something to happen that is, at the very least, minimally magical or quasi-transcendent. After all, optimism is always warranted. That's just common sense.

Made in the USA
Charleston, SC
09 December 2011